WHEN OLD MURDERS RETURN

"Maybe Nina realized she wasn't working out and didn't want to lose the role to you," Mason said with a nudge to Vicki's shoulder. "So, she destroys the stage so no one can have it. Can't get fired if there's no play to be fired from."

"Maybe. But I doubt it. Nina is pretty self-absorbed. I'm not sure she even realizes the rest of us think she's underperforming."

"You said eggnog?" I made it a question. "And it was in a thermos?"

"Yeah."

"And there were smashed pumpkins? And cut sandbags?"

She nodded, and then paled, catching the connection. "Wait. You don't think . . ."

"I'm not sure what I think." But all of those things sounded awfully familiar. If this were an isolated incident, I could play it off as a coincidence. After everything else that had happened, however . . .

A pattern was forming. French roast coffee at the Banyon Tree. Smashed pumpkins. Eggnog in a thermos. The threat of a pen through the eye. The JavaCon mug. The dented teapot. I could go on and on.

Every one of those incidents and threats connected back to murders I'd solved . . .

Books by Alex Erickson

Published by Kensington Publishing Corp.

Death By Spiced Chai

A Bookstore Café Mystery

ALEX ERICKSON

Kensington Publishing Corp.
www.kensingtonbooks.com

KENSINGTON BOOKS are published by

Kensington Publishing Corp.
119 West 40th Street
New York, NY 10018

All Kensington titles, imprints, and distributed lines are available at special quantity discounts for bulk purchases for sales promotion, premiums, fund-raising, educational, or institutional use.

Special book excerpts or customized printings can also be created to fit specific needs. For details, write or phone the office of the Kensington Sales Manager: Attn.: Sales Department. Kensington Publishing Corp., 119 West 40th Street, New York, NY 10018. Phone: 1-800-221-2647.

The K and Teapot logo is a trademark of Kensington Publishing Corp.

First Printing: November 2022
ISBN: 978-1-4967-3665-9

ISBN: 978-1-4967-3666-6 (ebook)

10 9 8 7 6 5 4 3 2

Printed in the United States of America

1

The chalk outline held a still-smoking gun in its hand. There was no blood, no actual body to be seen. Just one of those little yellow triangles with a black "1" resting over the heart. The words, *Victim of the Heart,* were embossed at the top, just above the outline's head. Beneath, was James Hancock's name.

A sense of pride washed through me as I rang up the sale. My dad's latest novel was a hit. I'd sold at least six in the last hour, which, for my bookstore café, Death by Coffee, was a lot. It probably helped that with the recent remodel, I was able to place two bookshelves near the stairs that led up into the bookstore portion of the store. One held only James Hancock novels. The store *was* named after one of his books, so it seemed only right. The other held books by local authors. Admittedly, that one was looking a bit spare at the moment, but I hoped to fill it up soon.

Death by Coffee had been busy for most of the day. I was working upstairs alone, leaving the café portion of the store to our only two employees, Beth Milner and Jeff Braun. Everyone else who worked at the bookstore café was part of the ownership, me included, and couldn't be there all of the time.

"This is a series, right?" The woman took the book and flipped through the pages, pausing to read a passage near the end.

"It will be." *Scars of the Heart* and *Fear of the Heart* were due to be the next two novels. Dad had called me to tell me how excited he was to be writing the new series, and had given me complete plot outlines and titles. "I can give you the names of the next two books, but book two won't be out until next year."

"Thank you." She continued reading what appeared to be the final chapter. Why someone would do that before reading the rest of the book, I'll never know.

I grabbed a pad of paper I kept near the register and scribbled the name of the books with a tentative publishing date for each. I couldn't help but admire the stationery as I handed over the slip of paper. Death by Coffee's stylized logo topped the page. The stationery, like the remodel of the upstairs, was new.

The woman tucked the page into her recently purchased book, thanked me once more, and then made for the door.

"A new series?" A man in corduroy pants and a button-up shirt approached the counter with

Dad's book in hand. "He hasn't finished the last one."

"He will," I promised the man. "He needed a break from Alden Kaine." The Kaine books were popular, but Dad was tired of the detective's surly nature and wanted to do something less dour.

"I see." The man paused at the counter. "It's insulting to the reader."

"Insulting? How?"

"Making us wait. What gives him the right to decide to work on something else when there's a series he has yet to finish. He should be working on unfinished works, not starting something new."

What gave Dad the right? *How about the fact he's the author of said books?* I kept my smile in place, though it was growing strained. "He wants to make sure the books are the best they can be. He needed the break, and this particular series was calling to him. I'm sure you'll love it."

"We'll see about that." He placed the book on the counter. "You don't have a signed copy, do you?"

"Not on hand, no."

"You're his daughter, correct?"

No matter how many times it happened, someone recognizing me as the daughter of author James Hancock always caught me by surprise.

"I am. Krissy Hancock." I held out a hand.

"Hamish Lauder." He shook, and then wiped his hand on his corduroys. "Take the name down. If you would, pass it on to Mr. Hancock. I'll stop by in a week or so and see if you have signed copies, preferably one with my name attached."

The urge to tell him that Dad had more important things to do crossed my mind, but I merely nodded and said, "I'll see what I can do," as I rang up the sale.

"Let me give you my address." Before I could say anything, Hamish grabbed the pad of stationery and scribbled out his home address. "Perhaps you could deliver the book when it comes in."

"We'll see."

Hamish took the book and started to walk away. He paused by the stairs. "I hope your father learns to respect his readers more. No matter how he tries to justify it, his delay is an insult to us all."

Eyes from all over the store locked on Hamish, and then turned to me, as if waiting for a biting response. Instead, I waved. "I'll let him know."

And with that, Hamish Lauder tucked his book under his arm and marched from the store.

I leaned back against the wall with a sigh. That sort of thing happened more often than I cared to admit. Having a famous father was nice and all, but sometimes, people forgot that he's a person with an actual life with wants and needs.

Downstairs, nearly every table had someone sitting at it, but there was currently no one else in line at the drink counter. It appeared as if the busy day was starting to slow, which was a good thing. Beth and Jeff would need breaks, and if we remained hopping, I wasn't sure two of us could handle both the upstairs and downstairs alone.

Mason Lawyer was the only one available to call in if it came to that. My best friend and co-owner of Death by Coffee—and Mason's wife—Vicki

Lawyer, was an actress in a local play, and couldn't come in. And Lena Allison . . .

A wave of melancholy washed through me. Lena had worked for us since we'd opened the place but had recently left Pine Hills for college. I was glad she was chasing her dreams, but I did miss her and her dedication to her work.

I opened my mouth to say something somber, but the cat bed next to me was empty. Vicki had taken Trouble with her when she'd left earlier in the day, meaning there was no store cat to talk to when I got maudlin. I wasn't keen on talking to myself, especially since half the town already believed I was crazy, so I left my thoughts unuttered.

The phone rang. I picked it up before the second ring, thankful to have someone to talk to, even if it might be someone calling to complain.

"Death by Coffee, this is Krissy speaking. How may I—"

"Krissy Hancock?" The man's voice was quiet, as if he were whispering into the receiver.

"Yes?"

There was a pause where all I could hear was the man's breathing. The pause went on. And on. And on.

"Is there something I can help you with?"

The breathing continued. It wasn't heavy breathing, like he was trying to weird me out or anything; just normal, through the nose breathing. I glanced downstairs, but neither Jeff nor Beth was paying me any mind. Neither were any of the customers. The only other person upstairs with me was an elderly gentleman sitting in one of the chairs we kept for people who wanted to read. He had his head back, eyes closed, and a war novel lying open on his chest.

"If there's—"

I was cut off by a click, and the line went dead.

I looked at the receiver as if it were somehow responsible for the strange call. It had come in on the store line, not my personal cell. I didn't know if that meant anything or not.

I hung up the phone and then waited to see if the man would call back. It was entirely possible he'd been trying to speak, but something had gotten messed up and muted him. Of course, since I could still hear him breathing, it wasn't very likely. Maybe he'd forgotten what he'd wanted to say and he'd get back to me later.

The door opened downstairs and a man wearing a police uniform and hat walked through the door. He scanned the store, eyes going first behind the counter where Beth and Jeff worked, before passing over the three steps that led up to the bookstore, and finally, onto me.

A wide smile split his face, which showed off a pair of to-die-for dimples, before he headed my way.

My heart fluttered, but I did my best to keep the pleasure off my face as Paul Dalton ascended the steps to join me at the counter.

"I thought you were supposed to be working," I said, resisting the urge to throw myself at him. I still couldn't believe I'd gotten so lucky, yet here he was, the man of my dreams, standing before me, blue eyes sparkling as he took me in.

"I am," he said, taking off his hat. He ran a hand through his sandy-brown hair, which was just shy of too long. I wondered if it would turn into a sandy blond if we were to run off to a beach somewhere and spend a few weeks under the sun. "But not much is happening that needs my attention at the moment."

"Considering your job, that's a good thing."

He nodded. "It is. Have you been busy?"

"Some, but it's died down. Have you seen Dad's new book?"

Paul glanced over his shoulder, toward the bookshelf with all of Dad's books. "I haven't."

"I think you'll like it. It's about a cop working a small town that is ravaged by a series of murders. He's assisted by a local woman, who can't seem to keep her nose out of his business, and well . . ." I was practically beaming by then. "And then the sparks fly."

Paul chuckled. "Sounds kind of familiar."

I felt a blush coming on, much to my annoyance. "He might have been inspired by my experiences since coming to Pine Hills." Experiences which included far too many murders, but hey, at least something good was coming out of them.

Paul took in the rest of the bookstore, nodding as he did. "You know, I haven't been up here since you remodeled the place. I like the new layout."

"So do I." The bookshelves were taller, and the layout itself was far more customer friendly than the old one. "The top shelf can be a pain to reach when it's busy, but no one's complained as of yet."

"That's good." Paul turned his hat over in his

hand, a nervous gesture I'd seen him make before. "I'd like to stay and chat, but really should
get going. Are we still on for tonight?"

A swell of joy surged from somewhere deep inside me and it took all my self-control not to squeal
when I said, "Of course." Ever since Paul and I had
started dating, I'd felt like a teenager with her first
serious boyfriend.

"Good, good."

"Are you ready to tell me where we're going?"

He plopped his hat back onto his head, tapping
the top of it to secure it into place. "Nope."

"Not even a hint?"

"Not one." He paused. "Well, maybe one."

I leaned against the counter, chin in my hands.
"I'm all ears."

"Dress comfortably. We won't be sitting still."

A dozen ideas shot through my head. *Is he taking
me dancing? For a long, romantic walk?*

And then, a mischievous voice. *Back to his place?*

"I'll pick you up at your house tonight at around
seven," Paul said.

"I'll be waiting."

I watched him head down the stairs and out of
the store, mentally cataloging which parts of him
I'd like to see moving the most.

All of him, I decided.

I went back to work, but my mind wasn't on it. I
had hours yet before our date, and the wait was
going to be hard. Paul and I had been dating for a
few months now, and had known each other for
years longer than that. So far, the shine hadn't
worn off of the relationship. I hoped that it never
would.

There wasn't much to do upstairs, and since Jeff and Beth had it under control downstairs, I began straightening the bookshelves. Most people were considerate when they went through a bookstore. They'd pick up a book, check to see if it might be something they'd enjoy, and then they'd put it back where they'd found it if not.

Others, however, were not so considerate. They'd set books down on their side, put them in backward, or on a completely random shelf. I couldn't count the number of times I'd found a steamy romance shoved in with the latest *Diary of a Wimpy Kid*. I knew that sometimes these misplaced books were left there on purpose. You know, a big joke, adult book in the children's section. Ha-ha.

Kids.

I'd just finished straightening a few shelves of the ever-popular mysteries when a scream ripped through the store. I think my spirit briefly left my body from the shock of it, before I spun to find a woman standing, pointing at her coffee. Nearly everyone was on their feet—the only exception being the sleeping man with the war novel. His snores were interrupted for a heartbeat before he continued his late afternoon nap.

No one was lying on the floor, and no one seemed hurt, so I hurried down the stairs, joining Beth, who'd come running at the same time I had.

"What happened?" I asked. My first thought was that the woman had burned herself on the coffee and we'd be looking at one of those lawsuits that would be splashed all over the news. She appeared unharmed, however.

But she was most definitely not all right.

The woman was pointing toward her coffee cup. Nothing seemed wrong with it from the outside. I wondered if she'd ended up with a café mocha when she'd wanted a French vanilla, but her reaction was far more violent than getting the wrong flavor merited.

"What's wrong?" I approached the table, and her cup. Beth stood nearby, as if uncertain if she should approach too closely.

"I can't believe . . . You . . . This place!" The woman sputtered. She appeared to be in her midthirties, with short cropped, brown hair. Her glasses were frameless, and went well with her features, which were soft and inviting, despite her apparent shock.

I leaned over to get a good look in the coffee cup, which was still half full of coffee that had turned a light brown from what had to be a whole lot of creamer.

Floating inside, was a cockroach.

"There are *roaches* in the coffee!" The woman shouted it loud enough to be heard three blocks away. There were gasps all around and a dozen lids hit the tables as customers checked their own coffees.

"There has to be some mistake," I said, though how, I didn't know. The evidence was floating right there in front of me.

"A mistake?" the woman laughed. It sounded half-crazed, like she might burst into tears at any moment. Honestly, I didn't blame her. To think she'd drunk half of her coffee before realizing what was inside. "That's more than a mistake. What if I get sick?"

"We'll make it up to you. Free coffee. A refund."

My mind raced. I was concerned about the well-being of the customer, of course, but I was also worried about what this meant for Death by Coffee. *What if she does sue?*

"I . . ." The woman spun on her heel and ran to the women's restroom.

"Beth?" I wasn't sure what I was asking. Panic was starting to set in. Nothing like this had ever happened at Death by Coffee before.

"No one else has found bugs in their drinks," Beth said, keeping her voice low. "And I'm positive I haven't seen any all—"

The bathroom door banged open and the woman staggered back out. "There's more in there! What kind of place *is* this?"

"What?" I rushed across the room and entered the women's restroom. Thankfully, no one else was inside because, quite frankly, I needed a few moments alone to gather my thoughts.

At first, I didn't see anything. Someone had left one of the sinks running at a trickle. I turned it off absently as I scanned the floor, but didn't see any bugs—roaches or otherwise—anywhere.

And then, one skittered out from beneath the farthest stall from the door.

"No, no, no." I could feel myself pale as I opened the door to find a half dozen of the critters scurrying around the toilet. The restroom was otherwise clean, which struck me as odd. We took pride in keeping Death by Coffee shipshape, yet, here was evidence we'd failed.

I stood over the bugs, wondering what to do. I wasn't about to pick them up with my bare hands. Even gloves wouldn't help. And what if there were more? What if the entire store were infested? They could close us down!

Calm down, Krissy. I took a deep breath, and then closed the stall door, as if I thought it might keep the roaches contained inside. *I can handle this.*

I left the women's restroom and brought out the big yellow cone that warned the room was being cleaned. Instead of leaving the door open like we normally would, I closed it. From there, I knocked to make sure no one was in the men's room, and then checked for bugs there. Blessedly, there were none.

When I returned to the front, nearly every customer had left, including the woman. Half-drank cups of coffee sat on tables, and in one case, someone had smashed a donut onto a chair. As if that would help us with our roach problem.

"Did you get her name?" I asked Beth. The words came out almost mechanically. I wasn't quite in shock, but I felt a lot like I did any time I came across a body. This sort of thing wasn't something I was used to, or expected to ever find. Not in my place, anyway.

Beth shook her head, and then glanced at Jeff, who did likewise. "She took off as soon as you went in to check. I tried to stop her, but . . ."

"It's all right." One deep breath. Two. "Check the backroom. Look for any signs of an infestation." I glanced at the door. Should I close up Death by Coffee altogether? Or should I keep the women's room closed and set the men's room as unisex until the roaches were under control?

"I haven't seen anything," Jeff said, eyes darting around the store like he was afraid bugs would start seeping from the walls. "But I'll give the back a good look."

"I'll clean up out here." Beth blew out a breath, causing her lower lip to flutter. "I can't believe this."

Neither could I, but it had happened. "All right. I'm going to call an exterminator." And then . . .

My gaze drifted toward the restroom where the roaches waited. My stomach churned at the thought of going back in there, but I had to do something. If we let it get too far out of hand, the bugs, as well as the stigma they brought with them, could spell the end of Death by Coffee.

2

Despite not finding any further infestations, I decided to close Death by Coffee early. It wasn't as if we were getting many customers anyway. Word had already spread, and it was keeping people away. I had a feeling that by tomorrow, everyone in Pine Hills would know about our little roach problem. I hoped that when it was cleaned up, the good news spread just as fast.

"What's this I hear about cockroaches?"

I glanced up from closing out the register to find Vicki coming in through the door. She was dressed casually, yet she looked like a movie star. If she'd wanted to, she could have landed any role in any movie she chose, but had instead taken to the stage, albeit casually. She was happy to be the owner of a bookstore café, though her parents still blamed me for her decision not to become Hollywood's next big star.

"I called an exterminator. Someone is coming

in the morning to check it out," I said. Beth and Jeff were already gone, and the lights were out upstairs. "I'm hoping it's an isolated incident."

"How is it even possible?" Vicki scoured the floor, but there were no bugs. "We're careful."

"These things happen, I guess." I rounded the counter with the money bag in hand. "People were freaked out when it first happened, but they'll be back."

Vicki rubbed at her temples and sighed. "I suppose. Everyone's talking about it."

"Great." Of course, they were. Nothing happened in Pine Hills without the rest of the town knowing about it within minutes.

"Rita caught wind of it and she and her buddies are hitting the phones pretty hard."

Rita Jablonski was the resident gossip of Pine Hills. Between her, Andi Caldwell, and Georgina McCully, nothing escaped notice.

"Once we make sure there are no more bugs, I'll be sure to have a word with her," I said. "Get her to spread some positive rumors."

"Is there such a thing?" A smile found Vicki's face, though I could see the exhaustion behind it. "Seems to me, people only want to talk about something when it's bad."

"It could happen." I paused. "How are you doing? You look tired."

"I am." She leaned against the wall. "We've been pushing pretty hard with the play, and with Death by Coffee, and a kitchen remodel, I feel pulled in a thousand directions."

"You're remodeling your kitchen?"

"Mason's idea." This time, her smile was fond.

"Ever since we remodeled the upstairs here, he's gotten the bug." A pause. "No pun intended. He plans on fixing up the kitchen before moving on to the backyard. He's got all these plans, and I fear he's going to run us both into the ground."

"You could tell him no," I said.

Vicki laughed. "I could. But I kind of like it. He gets so excited, and well . . ." She trailed off, eyes glimmering with thoughts that were most definitely of the private kind. "Anyway, I'm done for the night, and since you obviously are done here, I was wondering if you'd want to go get something to eat. Mason's already eaten, so it won't hurt his feelings if I don't get home until late."

"I wish I could." I glanced at the clock. I still had time, but I wouldn't for long. "Paul and I are going out tonight."

"Oh, really?" She leaned forward. "Anything I might want to hear about?"

"No clue. He's keeping it a secret."

"A secret?" She grinned. "You know you'll have to tell me all the details afterward. Unlike Rita, I'll keep it between us."

I grabbed my things and headed for the door. "If there's anything to tell, I'll be sure to let you know."

"You do that." She followed me outside, and over to my orange Escape. The vehicle stood out among the sea of blue, silver, red, and black cars that dominated the streets. "I suppose I should get home anyway. Mason will likely be elbows deep under the sink with no idea what he's doing."

"Have fun with that."

"Oh, I will. I'll send pics as soon as he inadvertently breaks something."

We parted with a good-natured laugh. Mason wasn't *that* hopeless, but when he did make a mistake, Vicki enjoyed ribbing him about it. He always took it stoically and with a laugh of his own. The two of them were good that way, and I hoped that if and when Paul and I ever got serious enough to want to live together, we'd end up the same way.

I made a pitstop at the bank to drop off the money for the night, and then headed for home. Thoughts of Paul's plans—both immediate and future—kept me from dwelling too much on the bugs at Death by Coffee. I knew that when I went to bed tonight, I'd likely dream of them.

If I went to bed.

And *if* I were alone.

I was grinning by the time I pulled into my driveway. I was about to climb out of my Escape when my cell rang. I answered with a chipper, "Hello?"

"Oh, my Lordy Lou! I heard about what happened with the bugs in the store. Can you believe it?"

It was a testament to how good I was feeling that my smile didn't slip as I got out and headed for the front door. "Rita. It was nothing. They're already gone."

"I wouldn't be too sure about that. Bugs like those have a way of sticking around. Why, I had a friend who had to have her place fumigated a half dozen times over and she *still* has bugs crawling up the walls. She's just about beside herself."

I unlocked the front door and placed my foot in

the way, just in case my fluffy orange cat, Misfit, decided to make a run for it. Tonight, he was nowhere to be seen.

"None of them were crawling up the walls," I said. "They've been removed, but I still have someone coming in to make sure they're truly gone tomorrow. You should let people know that the problem is taken care of, and that it'll be double-checked. No more roaches."

"We'll see," Rita said. There was a pregnant pause before she asked, "Do you think you can get me an autographed copy of *Victim of the Heart?* I'd ask James myself, but I don't want to be a bother."

I dumped my things on the table. Misfit peeked at me from around the corner in the hall, and then he vanished back toward the bedroom. "I'll see what I can do," I said, echoing what I'd told Hamish Lauder. "Just as long as you make sure everyone understands that what happened at Death by Coffee won't happen again."

Rita was silent for a few seconds. I knew she'd do whatever I asked since she thought of herself as my dad's biggest fan. She'd also always had something of a crush on him. She might be dating a guy named Johan Morrison now, but I doubted that dampened her enthusiasm for anything written by James Hancock that she could get her hands on.

"I'll talk to Andi and Georgina," she said, which was agreement enough. "I don't think any of us truly believed you had a problem you couldn't fix."

"Great. I'll have Dad send some books as soon as I talk to him." And then, to sweeten the deal,

"Maybe I can get an early copy of *Scars of the Heart* for you as well."

Her gasp of pleasure came through the phone loud enough to rattle the speaker. "Oh, well, that would be fantastic! I would love to be able to show it off at the writers group. And there's this book club I was thinking of joining. If I could show them an early copy directly from the author, they'll just pop!"

"I can't promise anything, but I'll ask him." I headed down the hall and found Misfit under the bed. His eyes were wide, and he cringed back from me like he thought I was going to give him medicine or take him to the vet. "I've got to go, Rita. I'll let you know what Dad says."

"You do that, dear." And then, faintly, "An early copy! Wait until Andi hears about this."

I clicked off and tossed my phone onto the bed. "Hey, Misfit," I said, crouching down. "How about you come out?" I held out a hand for him. He just stared. I tried to reach for him, but he scooted back, deeper under the bed.

"What's up, buddy?" I asked, nervous. The last time he'd acted this strangely, someone had broken into my house and locked him in the laundry room.

A loud bang caused me to jump, and Misfit to shoot out from under the bed. He was down the hall and gone in seconds.

It took me only a few moments to realize the sounds were coming from outside. More thumps and bangs echoed as I hurried from the bedroom, into to the living room, and peeked out the window, certain something terrible was happening outside.

A moving truck sat in the driveway next door. The bangs I'd heard were coming from there.

"Huh," I said, mentally willing my heart to resume its normal pace. I didn't realize someone had bought my late-neighbor's home. Then again, the Realtor selling the place, Vanna Goff, wasn't exactly a friend of mine. In fact, she would have been happier if I'd up and moved myself, believing that I was somehow responsible for the lukewarm interest in the place.

Curiosity got the better part of me and with a calming word to Misfit, wherever he'd gotten off to, I went outside, and across the yard, to meet my new neighbor.

Clanks from the moving truck told me someone was inside it, so I headed there, instead of for the house.

"Hello?" I called as I rounded to the back.

A short, stocky woman appeared, carrying a box. She had shoulder-length brown hair hanging loose, and her brow was furrowed in concentration. She came up short when she saw me.

"Uh, hi." Cautious.

"I'm Krissy Hancock." I stuck out a hand, and then, realizing there was no way she could shake it while holding the box, stuffed it into my pocket. "I'm your new neighbor."

The moment my name crossed my lips, the woman's face clouded. "Oh. You."

Her tone made it clear she wasn't thrilled about meeting me, but I refused to let it bother me. "I thought I'd stop over and say hi," I said. "I can't stay, or I'd help—"

"That's all right. I have it." She stepped past me and carried the box into the house.

That was odd. I waited by the truck until the woman returned. When she saw me still standing there, she scowled.

"Is there something I can help you with?"

"No." I felt like an intruder, but didn't want to just walk away. I had no idea why the woman disliked me, considering we'd just met. "I'm not sure what Vanna said about me—"

"Nothing." My new neighbor entered the truck, found another box, and carried it out.

I pressed on, determined to play nice. "I figured that since we're going to be neighbors, it would be nice to get to know one another. As I said, I'm Krissy Hancock. You are . . . ?"

"Caitlin." She paused at her front door, mouth opened as if she might say more. And then, with a snap of teeth, she entered the house. This time, she closed the door behind her.

It was clear I wasn't wanted, so I turned and headed for home. Besides, I had a date to get ready for. I couldn't spend all night trying to decipher why Caitlin already disliked me.

I showered and got dressed, and tried my best not to be too offended. Caitlin might have denied it, but I'd put money on Vanna having said something. She might not have realized the impact her comments would make on my new neighbor. Sometimes a careless word is enough to sour perception.

But I could worry about that later. Now, it was time for Paul.

Misfit remained hidden as I finished getting ready, which was a good thing, I supposed. While I wasn't dressing up for tonight's date, I didn't want to be covered in cat hair either. Misfit had a tendency to shed on everything, especially when I was trying to look nice. And while I did as Paul requested and dressed casually, I made sure to dress nicely at the same time.

I filled Misfit's bowl with dry food and got him fresh water, just in case I was out longer than usual—or, if things went well, all night. The thought made my toes tingle.

My phone dinged, telling me I had a text. My heart did a little hiccup. I was worried that something had come up and Paul had to cancel. Since he was a cop, that sort of thing happened all the time. But when I checked, I didn't recognize the number, and I had no contact for whoever had sent it. I clicked the text open.

Your life is a lie.

I blinked. What?

I typed, **Who is this?** and set my phone down on the counter and stared at it like it might leap up and bite me. Something about the text made my skin crawl and my stomach tighten, though there hadn't been much to it.

Thumps came from next door as Caitlin continued to move her boxes inside. Misfit crawled out from behind the couch and slunk his way into the kitchen to eat. Not even the loud sounds could keep him away from food when he was hungry.

"Come on," I muttered. I half expected the text

to be from my ex, Robert Dunhill, or maybe Mason's dad, Raymond Lawyer, though why either of them would text me such a cryptic message, I didn't know. After the day I'd had, I was in no mood to play the mystery game.

A solid minute passed with no answer. Then two. I was just about to give up on it as a prank when a new message popped up.

Look

I looked, but there was only the one word.

"Okay?" After another minute, I moved to my window and looked outside, just in case that was what the mysterious texter had meant.

Caitlin was still hard at work. A car I didn't recognize was sitting in my other neighbor's driveway. Jules and Lance must have company, but that would have nothing to do with the strange texts, would it?

Nothing else moved outside. There were no packages sitting on my stoop, no car with tinted windows sitting on the street. It was just another day in my neighborhood, where the only weirdness was happening on my phone.

And then a car I *did* recognize appeared. It coasted down the road and then pulled into my driveway. Paul. My heart went all pitter-patter, and I decided right then and there that the texter could wait.

Paul saw me at the window and waved me out with a smile and a friendly honk. I returned the wave, and then hurried over to the counter for my phone. I was about to pocket it when a new text arrived. This one had no words, just an image.

I assumed the picture had been taken with a cell

phone camera due to the angle. It looked as if whoever had taken it, had done so covertly, and not very carefully. The angle was wrong, and the image slightly blurry, as if the photo had been taken in a hurry. I *did* recognize the diner it had been taken in; J&E's Banyon Tree. And, despite the blurriness, I also recognized the people in the photo.

The first was a woman. She was dressed casually, hair pulled back into a ponytail. She was pretty, though that was hard to tell from the photograph. Her face was turned toward the camera. I couldn't make out her expression, due to the distance and the blurry image quality.

Shannon. Paul's ex.

Or was she?

Because the man she was with was Paul Dalton. He was wearing his police uniform, though the hat was sitting on the table between them. He was leaning forward, lips practically touching Shannon's cheek. I couldn't tell if he was about to kiss her, or if he'd just done so, but from the way he was leaning, I was positive that was what the image had captured.

My entire body went cold and a pain like a hot poker seared through my chest.

Paul and Shannon? Together? That couldn't be right.

But the proof was right there before me.

Paul honked again.

It was time to go.

I closed the text and stuffed my phone into my pocket. There had to be a reasonable explanation for the photo. I'd just have to ask Paul about it.

Yet when I left the house and climbed into his car, I couldn't bring myself to broach the subject. I managed to smile, managed to nod when he asked if I was ready, but that was all I could do.

Because deep down, I wondered.

Was he truly happy to see me?

Or was Paul Dalton planning on dumping me for a woman I'd assumed he'd left in his past?

3

"Are you all right?"

"Hmm? Yeah, I'm fine." I tried on a smile, but it felt as forced as it truly was. "Just thinking."

"Looks like they're some deep thoughts."

I nodded absently and went back to staring out the car window. I hadn't had the guts to bring up the photo to Paul. A part of me hoped that it was a fake, that whoever had sent it used one of those programs—Photoshop, perhaps—to make the two people in the photograph look like Paul and Shannon, when in fact, it was really just a couple of random lovers.

I glanced over at Paul. He was smiling as he drove, completely oblivious to the torment going on inside me.

Well, considering his question, maybe not so oblivious.

"It's been a long day," I said with a sigh. "Someone found a cockroach in their drink at Death by Coffee, and there were more in the bathroom. We cleaned them up, but someone is coming in tomorrow to make sure there are no more. I'm pretty sure we got them all, yet I'm worried there's going to be an entire nest of them in the walls and we'll need to tear the building down and put it back together again before we'll be allowed to reopen."

Paul glanced at me briefly before returning his eyes to the road. It made me think of all those TV shows where the driver would stare at their passenger while talking, never once looking at the road in front of them. Silly thought, but I think my brain was doing its best to distract me.

"That sounds bad. Do you really think they'll close you down?"

"No." I shrugged. "I don't know. I'm probably just overreacting."

"You'd never do such a thing." The smile in his tone told me he was ribbing me, but I struggled to find the humor.

"I also got a call while I was at work. Some guy just breathed into the phone after asking for me, and then hung up."

"You don't know who it might have been?"

"No clue. I didn't recognize the voice."

Paul grunted and his brow furrowed. "Could it have been Robert?"

"I doubt it. He might be annoying, but Robert would never pull something like that." If Robert wanted to get on my nerves, he'd just show up and start whining about his love life. For some reason, he thought using me, his ex-girlfriend, as a sounding board for his new relationship was perfectly normal.

"If they call again, let me know. Maybe we can figure out who is calling."

"Like, you'd put a trace on the phone?"

He snorted. "We don't have that sort of technology here. But we'd find a way." He took a corner slowly. "Was it just the one call?"

I opened my mouth to mention the text, but snapped it closed without saying anything. The text came complete with a phone number, which might help Paul trace who sent it. But it would also result in him finding out about the picture of him and Shannon. I so wasn't ready to deal with that yet.

"I have a new neighbor," I said instead. "I don't think she likes me."

"Do you know her?"

"Not that I'm aware. She acted like she knew me, though."

"You *do* have a reputation." He was grinning as he said it.

"It felt like there was more to it than that. I got the impression that someone had already talked to her about me. And not in a good way."

"Didn't you say you had problems with the Realtor selling the house?" At my nod, he went on. "That's probably it. She let slip that you were a pain in her butt, rightfully said or not, and the new neighbor remembered the comment."

"Maybe." But I didn't buy it. I mean, who tries to sell a house by telling the prospective buyer bad things about the neighbors?

We fell silent as we weaved through Pine Hills traffic—which was little more than a few cars coasting slowly up and down the road. Pine Hills wasn't a big town. We didn't have a mall or chain restaurants or even a fast-food place. Every business was locally owned and operated, which meant there was a sense of community here that was a far cry from what I'd grown up with in California.

There was a slight bump as Paul turned into a parking lot. As soon as I saw where he was taking me, my heart sank that much further into my stomach.

"Ta-da!" he said, putting the car into park. "I hope you like bowling."

"I do," I said, eyeing the building. "But I'm not very good."

"That's all right; neither am I." Paul got out of the car. I followed him with a decided drag in my step.

McNally's Alleys was the local bowling alley; the only one in town as far as I was aware. I'd been there once before, and had made a complete fool out of myself when it came to the actual game. The place was small, with only eight lanes and a small arcade off to the side where the kids would sometimes hang out. As we entered, memories came flooding back, each a slap across my already psychically bruised face.

Paul led the way to the counter where a teenager sat, looking bored. He didn't bother asking for shoe sizes, just stared until both Paul and I gave him the information he needed. He took Paul's money, nodded toward the first lane, and went back to staring blankly ahead.

We gathered our rental shoes, and carried them over to the lane closest to the entrance. The door opened and a man with curly brown hair that was just this side of too long walked in. He hesitated when he saw us walking toward him, but when we veered off toward the lane, he huffed out a breath and headed for the counter.

"Ever been here before?" Paul asked as he sat down and slipped on his ugly bowling shoes.

"Once."

"I've come a few times, all with colleagues." Meaning other cops. I wondered if that meant my nemesis, John Buchannan, or if he was talking about the chief of police—and his mother—Patricia Dalton. "I figured we could relax and have a little mindless fun. You've seemed tense lately, and with what you told me about your day on the way here, I do think you could use the release."

"Yeah. Maybe." I kicked off my shoes and wedged the rentals on. They were a little too tight at the toes and were loose at the heel. I knew I was going to end up on my butt by night's end.

"Hey, Krissy?" I looked up to find Paul giving me a worried look. "Is something wrong? More than a bad day, I mean."

The image of Paul and Shannon floated through my head. Was it a kiss? Or was it bad timing, where he'd been forming a word that began with a "W" while leaning in close to Shannon.

Really close.

"Nothing's wrong." My gaze traveled across the room, to the far lanes. A family of redheads were laughing and throwing strikes like the pins were rigged to fall. Two lanes down, the guy who'd just come in was pulling on his shoes, watching us like he could hear us and was interested in my answer. "This is where I met Will. He used this lane, in fact."

Paul rocked back like I'd slapped him, and then he went ahead and did it himself. His hand met his forehead with a solid thump. "Why didn't I know that? I'm sorry."

"Don't be." This time, my smile felt a little more natural. "I never told you."

Will was one of my exes. He'd left town for a job in Arizona, and we were still friends, so it wasn't like there were hard feelings.

But being here, where I'd met him and his two friends and colleagues, Darrin and Carl, did bring back old memories. Back then, Shannon and Paul were an item as well. Or maybe they were about to start dating. I wasn't too sure of the timeline, but it was most definitely back when Paul and I were just friends.

"We could go," Paul said. "There's no reason—"

"No, let's bowl." I stood and went over to the electronic score machine and punched in our initials before picking up a ball. Using both hands, I rolled it down the lane, hoping I'd have better luck than the last time I was there. The ball rolled down the polished surface and clipped the last two pins on the left. They went down, taking a friend with them.

"Nice throw," Paul said. "I admire the form."

I stuck my tongue out at him and took my next throw. Another two pins. So far, so good. For me, at least.

Paul was better than he let on, and I think he in-

tentionally threw some bad balls, but overall, I had
fun. Slowly, my concerns over the photo, over the
bugs at Death by Coffee, and the memories that
had flooded me the moment I was through the
door, faded. We were just a couple of people,
throwing balls at pins, without a care in the world.

Until we weren't.

Paul's phone buzzed as he threw what should
have been an easy spare, but turned into a gutter
ball. He pulled his cell out of his pocket, scowled
at it, and then, with an apology, stepped away to
answer it.

My mind went immediately back to my concerns over our relationship. Was Shannon calling
him now? Was she asking him to come over to her
place? Or was she scolding him for going out with
me when he should have stayed tucked away with
her?

*Stop it, Krissy. You're letting your bad day color your
thoughts.*

I hated the doubts that were creeping in with all
my heart. I should trust that Paul wouldn't cheat
on me. He'd tell me if he wanted to break it off.

And yet, the doubts refused to relent.

I glanced over toward the solo bowler. He was
holding his bowling ball in one hand, but was
watching Paul instead of his lane. When he noticed me looking, he winked, and then sent his
ball zipping down the lane for a resounding strike.

Good for him.

Paul barked something angry into the phone,
drawing my attention back to him. He glanced at
me, his scowl deepening, before he said a few
more clipped words. His entire body slumped as

he ended the call and shoved the phone back into his pocket.

"Bad?" I asked, dreading the answer.

"Something's come up. They need me."

My brain was so stuck on Shannon, I completely missed what he was telling me. "They?"

"I've been called on duty," he said. "I'm needed at the Banyon Tree."

It was like another punch to the gut. If it kept up, I was going to be sick. "You have to go to work? I thought you were done for the day."

"So did I." Paul looked like he wanted to punch something, but all he did was yank off his bowling shoes and put on his own. "I'll drive you home before I head over. They can wait for me."

"No one else can take this?" The Pine Hills police station was small, but there were usually enough cops on duty to handle pretty much everything without having to call in the cavalry. It made me wonder if whatever had happened was bad.

Or if it were a cover story.

The photo was taken in the Banyon Tree.

And it was where Shannon worked.

"Apparently, we're shorthanded tonight after a couple of older cops called in sick. And since I'm the son of the police chief . . ."

"You get called in."

"Hazards of the job, I guess." He rose, and waited for me to finish changing my shoes. We were only halfway through our set, but that was all right. I'd lost all enthusiasm for the game. "Ready?"

"Yup."

We deposited our shoes at the counter, and then headed outside. The night was clear, but there was a faint chill on the air that made me shiver.

"Do you know what happened?" I asked as Paul started the car and we headed back toward my place. "At the Banyon Tree, I mean?"

"She didn't say. Just told me to get over there and take care of it."

That could be anything, though if someone were dead, I imagined Chief Dalton would have told him so.

We didn't talk for the rest of the way home. I kept wondering if Paul's surliness had to do with being called in to work in the middle of our date, or if there was more to it. When he pulled up in front of my house, he gave me a quick kiss on the cheek.

"I'm sorry about this, Krissy. I'll make it up to you."

"It's all right. Call me when you know something."

He nodded absently. I got out of the car and watched him drive off. This was definitely not how I saw my night ending, yet here I was.

I went inside, fighting to keep my head up. This wasn't my fault. This wasn't even Paul's fault. Something had happened, and he had to deal with it. Nothing more.

Yet, why did I feel like we were nearing the end of something monumental?

Misfit was snoozing on the couch when I entered. He glanced up at me once, and then went right back to sleep. He didn't question why I was home so early, which, of course, was the cat thing to do.

I started to put on a pot of coffee, but caught myself. Coffee, even decaf, often kept me up all night, and while I wanted to wait for Paul, I didn't want to be sitting up in bed until three in the morning.

Instead, I grabbed a box of spiced chai tea, which I'd taken to lately. Yes, I know it has caffeine, but I'd somehow convinced my body that it didn't. Or maybe I was fooling myself. Either way, when I drank it, I found I could go to sleep easier, so tea it was.

As soon as the water was on, I dug out a word puzzle to keep myself busy. I made it all of two words in before I had my phone out and was looking at the picture that was sent to me. Whoever had taken it had been sitting farther away than I'd realized. I wondered if Shannon was actually looking at the person taking it, or if she'd just happened to glance that way when it was taken.

Maybe it's not Paul.

The clothing was right, and he did enjoy eating at the Banyon Tree, so it would be a surprise if it *weren't* him. And besides, why send a random picture to me if it had nothing to do with anyone in my life?

I used my fingers to increase the size of the photo, zeroing in on the man's face. It turned it grainy, which, combined with the blurriness, made the face an unrecognizable blob. These days, you could take a really nice photo with a phone, so I wondered if the cell used was an old one. Did it make a difference if it was?

I reduced the photo back to its original size. There was no question that it was Paul. I'd recognize him anywhere. I knew the set of his shoulders, the way he held himself when he was tense or tired or excited. No amount of staring at the picture would change who it depicted.

"Why were you with her?" I wondered out loud. And was there really something going on at the Banyon Tree?

It was all I could do to keep from calling the place and asking.

But I didn't. I drank my tea and worked on my puzzle, hoping that Paul would stop by and tell me what was going on. I might not get along with either Eddie or Judith Banyon, but I didn't want anything bad to happen to them either.

Hours passed. Misfit moved from the couch, to the bedroom, and back again. I finished my puzzle book, and was considering another, when I realized it was well past bedtime.

Paul wasn't calling, nor was he coming back.

With a lump in my throat that refused to relent, I headed for bed, eager to put my bad day behind me.

4

Mornings are like new beginnings. A mental re-set that can set previously dire circumstances in a new light and make them seem a whole lot less, well, dire.

I woke up the next morning feeling a million times better. The cockroach problem at Death by Coffee would be taken care of, if it weren't already. I'd win over my neighbor, no matter what she was told about me. Paul and I were, and would remain, on good terms, despite what the person who texted the image might believe. And those calls and texts . . . ?

They meant nothing. It was just someone trying to stir up trouble.

I whistled as I got ready for the day. Misfit didn't seem so sure about my good mood, but he duti-fully followed me to the kitchen, where I fed him and gave him a few comforting pats on the head.

After I downed a bagel and coffee—complete with a chocolate chip cookie floating in it—I headed for Death by Coffee to see how things were going.

By the time I got there, morning rush should have been in full swing, but only a couple of people were inside, sitting close to the door like they might make a run for it at the first sign of a creepy-crawly. I couldn't blame them. I'd probably act the same way if it had happened elsewhere.

"Krissy!" Vicki rounded the counter and gave me a quick hug. "I didn't expect to see you today."

"I thought I'd check on our unwanted visitors." I glanced toward the women's restroom. It looked just like it should, with the door closed, and no sign that it needed to be blown up.

"The pest control guy has already been in and out," Vicki said. She led me back toward the counter, which, due to the shop's dead state, was private. "It appears as if our guests *were* only visiting. There's no sign that they'd taken up residence."

"That's good." I breathed out a sigh of relief. Despite how I'd woken certain that the roaches were a thing of the past, deep down, I was still worried. "Now we need to let everyone know it's safe to come back."

"Word will get around."

"And if it doesn't, I'll call Rita."

Vicki laughed. "You do that."

Movement upstairs caught my eye. Vicki's black-and-white cat—and Misfit's littermate—Trouble, was sauntering through the shelves like he owned the place. In some ways, I suppose he did. Since we'd opened, he'd been the store cat, and outside of a few mishaps early on, he behaved himself and kept away from the dining area.

"Mason is in the back looking over applications," Vicki said, following my gaze. "Jeff came in to open, but since we were dead, I went ahead and sent him home. I hated doing it, but he didn't seem to mind."

"It'll get better." Now that I'd proven to myself that Death by Coffee was up and running as it should be—albeit with fewer customers—I had other business to attend to. "I'm going to get some things done around town. Call me if you need me."

Vicki leaned against the counter and shook her head. "I doubt we will, but if it gets busy, you'll be the first I call."

I left, feeling even better than I had when I'd woken. Yesterday had been a disaster of a day. Already, today was proving to be a good one. I was still worried about whatever had happened at the Banyon Tree that had drawn Paul away from our date, but if it was something really bad, I'm sure I would have heard about it by now.

Then why didn't Paul call last night?

I scrubbed the thought from my mind as I got back into my Escape. He didn't call because he realized I might already be in bed by the time he finished up at the Banyon Tree. It was also very likely he'd had to take care of paperwork afterward. I fully expected to hear from him sometime today.

I did a quick check of my mirrors to make sure no one was coming, and then I was on my way.

The drive was quick and pleasant, and I found myself humming a tune I couldn't quite place. Had I heard it on the radio recently? Something I'd overheard while at the bowling alley? It was still bothering me as I pulled into the lot and parked in one of the numerous empty parking spaces.

The Pine Hills library was in a sad shape. Only two cars were in the parking lot, outside my own, and it was likely they belonged to the people who worked there, rather than anyone browsing the shelves. A blue tarp that was starting to turn gray was strapped to the roof and the brick of the building was marred by old paint from when someone had vandalized the place a few months back.

You'd be forgiven if you thought the library was abandoned.

The inside wasn't much better than the outside. Water damage caused by the hole in the roof made one half of the entrance unusable. The floor was torn up, and the smell was, to be kind, almost unbearable. There was no indication that repairs were going to start anytime this century, which didn't bode well for the future of the library.

I held my breath until I entered the library proper. While I could still smell the heady scent coming from the lobby, here, it was muted. Two levels, complete with books and movies and magazines, made up the library. The place was never busy, but when I walked in and saw not a single person outside the librarians, Cindy and Jimmy Carlton, and the young woman at the kid's desk whose name I couldn't remember, it felt as abandoned as it looked from the outside.

Cindy was pushing a cart down the aisles. Books in need of shelving lay atop it. She moved slowly, as if her joints were bothering her. Either that, or she was trying to make the mindless task take up more of her day, since there wasn't much else she could do without people to help. The woman at the children's desk looked half-asleep as she typed something into the computer.

It was Jimmy who saw me. His entire body tensed, causing his muscles to bulge briefly beneath his sweater vest, before he strode over to where I stood. For a librarian, he was well-built.

"No," he said, crossing his arms and barring my path.

"No, what?"

"You're not welcome here."

I blinked at him. Where was this coming from? "I'm just picking up a new book."

Jimmy shook his head. "After what you've done? I don't think so."

I stared at him. He stared right back. Cindy glanced over at us, and she pressed her lips together so firmly, they turned white, before she turned away.

I was at a loss. I'd worked with the Carltons before, helped them out, even. Death by Coffee had donated quite a few books to the library, and I'd assisted them on various events they'd run. The last time we'd talked, I was pretty sure we'd parted on good terms, so this sudden cold shoulder had me stupefied.

A gnawing feeling began working its way through my gut. "What's going on, Jimmy? I really have no idea why you're upset with me."

He narrowed his eyes.

"Seriously," I said. "I have no clue as to why you're mad!"

He continued to stare. I started to wonder if I'd have to turn around and leave with no explanation

when he made a come-with-me gesture and turned
and walked away.

I glanced over at the children's desk, but the
woman there was staring hard at her computer.
She was no longer typing. It was obvious she was at-
tempting to avoid my gaze.

What is going on here?

I followed after Jimmy, certain my good day was
going to come to a crashing halt right then and
there. He led me to a pair of old computers in the
far corner. He sat down in front of one and
brought up a browser. He typed for a few seconds,
the computer whirred and thought for twice as
long, and then he sat back and crossed his arms
with an expectant look on his face.

I leaned forward and read what was on the
page.

> *The library deserves to be torn down, buried in
> its own rubble. Bad management has led to horrible
> conditions. Just walking inside is like walking into
> a sewer. And don't get me started on the Carltons.
> Old-fashioned to the point of being antiques. They
> are running the library into the ground, and un-
> less someone steps in and removes them, they'll do
> the same to all of Pine Hills.*

I read the paragraph twice with a frown. "Who
wrote this?" My mind went back to old murder
cases where other hateful messages were spewed
online, but this one felt different somehow.

"Like you don't know," Jimmy said.

"I really don't." There was no name at the bottom of the page, so it wasn't signed.

But it *was* a post added to a larger thread, which meant there was likely a username attached.

I scrolled back to the top, and there it was.

K. Hancock.

I felt myself pale. "That's not me."

"That's not your name?"

"It is, but I didn't write it." I reached across Jimmy and used the mouse to close the page. "Someone else did that."

"And used your name?" He sounded skeptical.

"They must have." I couldn't help but remember how my new neighbor had treated me. Could she have read the post and having heard my name from her Realtor, assumed I was an online troll out to badmouth innocent people? "Or perhaps it's a case of mistaken identity. You know, a Kimberly Hancock, perhaps?"

Jimmy opened the browser again, brought the post back up, and then clicked on the name, which brought up a short profile.

Krissy Hancock. Owner/operator of Death by Coffee.

Oh boy.

"I didn't do this," I insisted. I paced away from the computer, as if distance would make it go away. "Someone is setting me up."

"For what?" Jimmy asked. "I get it. This place is falling apart. We've tried to keep up maintenance, but funding is practically nonexistent. Even our fundraisers for the library have failed. People just don't care about us anymore. I'm sure your store is doing just fine—"

I cut him off. "That's not fair. You know it's not."

Jimmy huffed and glared hard at the post before making a disgusted sound and closing the browser. "If you didn't do it, then who did?"

"I don't know, but this isn't the first bad thing to happen to me this week." I thought of the phone call with the breathing, and the texted photograph. "But I think someone is trying to get at me, make me look bad."

Jimmy looked skeptical, but at least he no longer appeared as if he might throw me out.

"I'll look into it," I said. "It could be a joke in bad taste." Though I didn't know who would do such a thing. "I promise, I didn't write that. You have to believe me."

With a sigh, Jimmy stood. "I suppose I do." He glanced across the room, toward his wife. "Would you mind leaving anyway?" Before I could protest, he went on. "Let me talk to Cindy and get her take. She was pretty upset when she saw the post. She thought you'd turned on us."

"I would never do that."

"Yeah, well, these days, you never know about people, especially online. They believe they're protected from repercussions to what they say there, as if their vitriol doesn't affect real life."

"If I had something bad to say about you or the library, I'd tell you directly."

It didn't come out quite the way I'd intended, but Jimmy seemed to get what I was going for. "Come back tomorrow. We'll see about getting you a new library card. Your current one has been revoked."

Jimmy didn't ask for me to hand over my old card as he escorted me out of the library. I felt like a criminal, despite not having actually done anything.

"I need chocolate," I muttered, climbing back into my Escape. It was a comfort food. No matter how bad things ever got, I knew I could make myself feel a whole lot better by one quick visit to Phantastic Candies.

And a whole lot unhealthier.

I'd just started my vehicle with an intent on driving over to the candy store and eating half their stock when my phone rang. I froze, almost certain it was going to be from the breather. When I checked the screen, I was relieved to see the call was from Paul.

My relief, however, was short-lived.

"Krissy?" he asked, sounding tired and a little cranky.

"Paul." I swallowed a lump that had already grown in my throat. *Let this be a friendly call.* "What's up?"

"We need to talk."

Uh-oh. That did *not* sound good. "About?" *Please don't say Shannon.*

"The Banyon Tree." He cleared his throat. "It's about last night."

"Okay?" He was being awfully careful with what he was saying, which didn't bode well at all. "What does that have to do with me?"

"One sec." There was a scratchy sound and a thump, as if Paul had set the phone face down on a desk. I could hear voices in the background, but they were so muffled as to be unintelligible.

I wanted to pace, but was sitting in my Escape,

so I simply jigged my leg up and down instead. I tried to come up with some reason as to why Paul would need to talk to me about the Banyon Tree since I hadn't been there in forever. The owners didn't like me all that much, so I tended to avoid the place unless it couldn't be helped.

Could Judith Banyon be behind the post? It made sense, I supposed. She'd had it in for me since I'd arrived in Pine Hills, and perhaps she'd finally had enough of me "stealing her customers," as she put it, and was trying to drive me out of town.

But that didn't explain why Paul had been called to the Banyon Tree last night, or why he would need to talk to me about it now.

Was Judith dead?

I was nearly hyperventilating with worry by the time Paul returned. Before I could ask him the horrible question that had become lodged in my mind, he spoke.

"You need to come down to the station. I can't talk about why. This is something that needs to be talked about here."

"Am I in trouble?"

There was a moment of silence before Paul said, "Just get here quickly."

And then the line went dead.

5

"Hi, I'm here to see Pau—I mean, Officer Dalton."

The cop glanced up at me, but before he could speak, Officer Becca Garrison appeared. While we were normally cordial with one another, I often found myself on her bad side. From her tone, I had a feeling I was there again.

"Krissy. This way."

I followed her down a short hallway I'd become far too familiar with over the years. This conversation wasn't going to happen in the parking lot, or in Chief Dalton's office.

She was taking me to the interrogation room.

"Can you tell me what happened?" I asked. My nerves were jumping, and even though no one was really paying us any mind, I felt eyes on my back, following me. "Paul never told me. I just know he went to the Banyon Tree last night, so I assume it has something to do with that?"

"In here." Garrison's face was a mask as she opened the door.

I entered, but Paul wasn't waiting for me inside. I turned to ask Officer Garrison another question. The words died on my lips as the door closed, and I was left alone.

"Well then." I swallowed with some difficulty and eyed the coffee machine in the room. While it was classified as the interrogation room, the place looked far more like a lounge. There was a couch, a dartboard, and, of course, the coffee maker. I imagined when they didn't have a suspect, most of the cops would come in here to relax.

Instead of presuming and making myself a cup of coffee, I sat down in a plastic chair pushed under the table in the middle of the room. The chair rocked slightly, thanks to a missing foot, but otherwise seemed steady enough.

My mind raced through all the reasons why Paul wouldn't have met me at the door. He'd called me in, so it was natural to think he was the one who wanted to talk to me. He could have been in the Chief's office, discussing whatever had happened at the Banyon Tree. Or perhaps he got called out to another scene and I was going to be stuck in here until he got back.

But that didn't explain Officer Garrison's attitude toward me. She'd seemed closed off, distant. We weren't the best of friends or anything, yet I'd assumed we were on good terms.

I drummed my fingers on the table and tried to remain calm. The longer this took, the more nervous I felt. What if Judith or Eddie Banyon had died? What if someone had killed them? What if it had nothing to do with the Banyon Tree, and Paul's mention of it was simply to get me here?

By the time the door opened, I was half to believing this was some elaborate breakup talk where Paul and Shannon would walk through the door to break the news, with Paul telling me that I'd be spending the rest of my life behind bars so I wouldn't interfere with their relationship.

"Paul I—"

But it wasn't Paul.

Detective John Buchannan stepped through the open doorway, a pair of Styrofoam cups balanced in his hand, and a folder tucked under one arm. He placed one of the cups, which was filled with water, in front of me, and kept the other for himself, before he returned to the doorway and retrieved a laptop from someone just out of sight.

I watched it all with a feeling of dread. Buchannan and I had a history. You know, something bad would happen, he would blame me, and in the end, I'd be proven innocent, but he'd still treat me like I had something to do with it.

And here we were again, though this time, it wasn't just *Officer* Buchannan. He was a full-fledged detective now, the first in Pine Hills. He'd only had the job for a few months, and I doubted he'd investigated much more than a petty theft here or there. Pine Hills wasn't known for its crimes.

At least, it wasn't until I'd shown up in town.

"Ms. Hancock," Buchannan said, his deep voice reverberating as he closed the door. He took the seat opposite me. He kept the laptop closed, but he did rest a hand on it.

"What's going on?" I asked. "Where's Paul?"

"We thought it best if he sat this one out."

"Sit what out? Why am I here?"

Buchannan arranged the folder in front of him, but like the laptop, he kept it closed. "Can you tell me where you were last night?"

"Where I was?"

He gave me a flat look. "As in, your location. From, let's say, five p.m. until the time you went to bed."

"Have you talked to Paul?"

The skin around Buchannan's eyes tightened. "Let me ask the questions, all right? Where were you last night?"

"At work," I said. My stomach was trying to climb up through my throat, so I took a long gulp of water. It was blessedly cool. "Then I went on a date with Paul."

Buchannan nodded, as if that was what he'd expected me to say all along. "What time did you leave work?"

"What?"

Buchannan sucked in a breath. Right. He was to ask the questions.

"I'm not sure. We closed early because of a mishap at work." No need to tell him about the roaches. I was certain he'd use it against me somehow.

"You're not sure?"

"No. I didn't look at the clock. Both Beth and Jeff were working. I sent them home and Vicki came in briefly. We talked, we left, and then I went home." I didn't feel the need to give Buchannan last names since he knew everyone already.

"And then Paul picked you up? Or did you meet him?"

"He picked me up."

"Right as soon as you got home?"

I almost said yes before I realized that wasn't the case. "No. I had time to clean up." Another thought. "And I went next door to talk to my new neighbor. Her name's Caitlin."

"How long did the two of you talk?"

"I don't know. A few minutes." I was getting frustrated, and let it show in my voice. "Why are you asking me these questions? I didn't do anything."

Buchannan stared at me long and hard before he pulled the laptop around in front of him. He lifted the lid, pressed a few keys, and then spun it around to face me.

The image was black-and-white and grainy, and was quite obviously security footage. The angle was weird, as if someone had bumped into the camera at some point and knocked it askew, but I could tell it was of the front of J&E's Banyon Tree. I was looking at the parking lot and a small portion of the front of the store.

"I didn't know they had a security system," I said, more to myself than to Buchannan.

His mouth twitched in what I took for a near smile, which couldn't be good.

Nothing moved on the image at first. The time ticked away in the corner, putting it at just after six, which was when I was at home, and about an hour before Paul would arrive to pick me up.

"What am I supposed to be—" I cut off as a figure entered the frame. The woman's hair was done up just like mine, and she was wearing a Death by Coffee apron.

Dread worked through me. My entire body went cold and hot at the same time.

The woman paused at the front of the store, reared back, and sent a brick flying through the window of the Banyon Tree. She vanished briefly inside, where she remained for only about twenty seconds, and then she all but ran from the scene, vanishing out of the frame.

Buchannan leaned forward, tapped a key to pause the recording, and then sat back with his arms crossed in a clear, nonverbal, "Well?"

"I have no idea who that was."

He frowned.

"Seriously. That wasn't a Death by Coffee employee."

"She didn't look familiar?"

"No."

"Do I need to get you a mirror?"

The dread turned into a full-blown panic, but I somehow managed not to start babbling or screaming. "That wasn't me."

"It fits well within your timeline," he said. "You left Death by Coffee, drove over to the Banyon Tree, busted the window, tossed coffee beans all over the place, and then headed home for your date with Paul."

"Coffee beans?"

"Why would you do that?" Buchannan asked.

"It wasn't me. I was talking to my neighbor. She saw me and can confirm that I was there."

"We'll see about that." He closed the laptop and pulled it away from me like he thought I might try to steal it. "Or you can admit it now. Tell me why you'd vandalize someone else's property, and perhaps the Banyons will be willing to drop any and all charges."

Charges? "I didn't vandalize anything." My legs screamed at me to stand, to pace the room, but knew Buchannan would use that against me too. "I was at home. I left with Paul afterward. I'd never do something like that!" And then, a new thought. "Wasn't the Banyon Tree open?"

"They were closed."

"Why?"

He just stared at me.

"I didn't do it. I didn't know they'd be closed."

Buchannan wasn't moved. "Was it because of the cockroaches?" At my surprise, he smiled. "Of course, I know about them. Were you so upset that your place might be closed down for an extended period of time that you decided to ruin the competition?"

"No."

"Why spread coffee all over the place?" He opened the folder and spun a photograph toward me. It was of the floor of the Banyon Tree. Coffee beans were scattered around the room like confetti. In the center of the photo was a torn bag of French roast coffee.

"That's not mine. We don't serve that brand at Death by Coffee and I don't have it at home."

"But the Banyons do. You could have destroyed their stash, but you didn't. Maybe you purchased some to bring with you, a brand you conveniently don't stock. Perhaps your conscience got the better of you."

Now that the fear had a chance to take root and then ebb away, anger started to take its place.

"Are you trying to pin this on me?" I asked. "Seriously? After all I've done to help find bad people in this town? I've tried to be nice to you, have tried to do what's right, and this is how you repay me?"

This time, I did stand, rocking the chair back on its back legs as I did. It was a wonder it didn't fall over.

"Sit down, Ms. Hancock."

I didn't. "Are you going to arrest me?" I asked, planting a hand on my hip. "Because, if not, I'd like to go now."

Buchannan sat silent for a long moment before he stood and gathered his things. "Not at this time," he said. "Just make yourself available if I need to speak to you again."

I huffed and stormed out of the room, which probably didn't do much for Buchannan's opinion of me. At that point, I didn't care. He was accusing me of something I didn't do. I had an alibi. All it would take was for him to talk to my neighbor and this whole mess would be cleared up.

I didn't look at anyone as I left the Pine Hills police station. My angry march turned into an ashamed shuffle as I made for my car. I just wanted out of there. It appeared as if yesterday's bad day had followed me into today.

"Krissy."

I jerked to a stop. Paul was standing beside my car, hat in his hand, looking embarrassed.

"Why didn't you warn me?"

"I couldn't." He set his hat on the hood of my car and then took my hands. "John was standing right there and told me not to tell you anything about what we found. He was even angry I mentioned the Banyon Tree to you in the first place."

"I didn't do it."

"I know you didn't. I told him as much, but you know how he can get."

The word "stubborn" drifted through my mind, but since it described not just Buchannan, but myself, I didn't utter it.

"My neighbor can vouch for me."

"And he'll talk to them. All of them. I know John rubs you the wrong way, but he *is* good at his job. If someone is trying to set you up, then he'll figure it out."

"You saw the video?"

He nodded but didn't say anything.

Something in Paul's eyes bothered me. He was holding both my hands, rubbing his thumb against my skin, but he wouldn't look me in the eye.

"You believe me, right?"

Paul managed a smile. "Of course."

"Because right now, I'm starting to wonder."

He sighed, dropped my hands. "Go home. Get some rest. John will talk to your neighbors, and he might decide he needs to talk to you again. If he does, just come in, let him ask his questions. Answer them honestly, and you'll have nothing to worry about."

Won't I? While it might not be about the Banyon Tree, something was most definitely bothering Paul. *Shannon?* That photo popped into my mind and I was half a second from bringing it up on my phone and showing it to Paul to see how he'd react.

Before I could, Paul rested a hand on my shoulder. "I'll call you later, okay?"

"Yeah, all right."

"You have nothing to worry about, Krissy." He squeezed, and then, he was gone, back into the police station where they were looking at me as a possible vandal.

I should have said something about the library post.

Then again, wouldn't that have made me look worse? I couldn't prove I hadn't posted it, which meant, they had no reason to believe me when I said I didn't do it.

"This can't be happening." I threw myself into my Escape and was about to pull out of the parking space when I saw that Paul had forgotten his hat on the hood of my car. If I were a vindictive person, I might have driven off, letting it fly off into a puddle somewhere.

But that wasn't me.

I retrieved the hat and set it onto the passenger's seat next to me. Paul could get it when he saw me next. Maybe by then, I'd be ready to ask him about the text I'd been sent.

But if the last two days were any indication, I wasn't so sure I wanted to know the answer.

6

"You look like something your cat dragged in."

I dropped into the chair with a grunt. "It's that obvious?"

"I couldn't have missed it, even if I tried. Let me get you some tea."

I nodded absently as Jules Phan busied himself around the kitchen. He'd been outside with his white Maltese, Maestro, when I'd pulled up in front of my house, so I'd decided to pay him a visit in the hopes that he could improve my mood.

"Lance at the store?" I asked.

"He is. While I like time away from Phantastic Candies, I often don't know what to do with myself once I'm here alone. I miss being social."

I almost suggested we jump into Jules's car and head to the candy store. Chocolate sounded really good right about then. And I hadn't gotten it since the first craving had hit earlier that day.

"Care to tell me about it?" Jules asked, leaning

on the counter while the water heated up. "I wasn't kidding; you look awful."

"It's been a bad couple of days." I went on to explain, making sure Jules understood how targeted I felt. "It's like someone is intentionally trying to make my life miserable, and I don't know why."

"I can't imagine." The teapot whistled and he paused to get our teabags steeping. "You say Caitlin was standoffish toward you?"

I nodded. "She acted like I'd done something to her, even though we hadn't met before yesterday."

"That's strange." He placed two small teacups on the table and then sat down across from me. The sugar and cream were already on the table, though he added neither to his own cup. "When I met her, she was friendly and open."

"I wish I could say the same." I blew on my tea, added a lump of sugar and stirred. "I don't know what I'm going to do. I'm feeling overwhelmed and there doesn't seem to be an end in sight."

"Let me talk to her." Jules patted my hand. "I'm sure it's just a misunderstanding."

I wondered, but didn't say anything. There was no way this many bad things happening to me all at once could be a coincidence. "Do you think someone is setting me up?"

"For?"

"For everything. I mean, it's pretty obvious someone was trying to pin the vandalism at the Banyon Tree on me. Why else wear a Death by Coffee apron?"

"I can't believe someone would do that." He tsked and took a sip of tea. "It's like one of those movies where an evil twin shows up to ruin the heroine's life." He paused. "You don't have an evil twin running around, do you?"

I cracked a smile. "No. Not that I know of."

"Good. I'm not sure this town could handle two Krissy Hancocks." He winked.

As it was, I was beginning to believe Pine Hills already had its hands full with the one.

"What if everything that's happened is connected?" I asked. "The roaches, the way Caitlin acted toward me, the vandalism, the phone call." *The text with the photograph.* Out of everything, that was the one thing I'd left out. I didn't want to drag Paul's name through the mud, especially if this were all some sort of conspiracy.

"I don't know," Jules said. "It sounds like a lot of unconnected events to me." He considered it a moment. "Though, I suppose it's possible that something does connect them. I'm not sure what that might be."

Maestro yawned as he entered the room. He looked from me, to Jules, and then climbed under the table, where he stretched out and readied himself for a nap. Just looking at the dog made me tired. I had to fight back a yawn of my own.

"You might be right," I said with a sigh. "It was a man who called the store and the video was most definitely a woman." The image kept playing over and over in my mind. While I thought the woman to be stockier than me, I could see why Buchannan would assume I was the one who threw the brick through the window. And they did say the camera added a few pounds, right?

"The truth will come out. It always does." Jules' brow furrowed and he tapped a perfectly manicured finger on the table. "You don't think Caitlin could have been the woman in the video, do you?"

I closed my eyes and tried to picture it. "I'm not sure," I said. "If she wore a wig, perhaps it could be." *And a little extra padding beneath her clothes.* "Do you really think she'd do such a thing?"

Jules spread his hands. "Hard to say. I've only met her the once. If she has it out for you, who knows what she might do."

We drank our tea and conversation drifted onto more pleasant topics, though my mind was stuck on what he'd said about Caitlin. Could she have pretended to be me? If so, why? I know absolutely nothing about her; not even her last name.

Conversation wound down and I thanked Jules for the conversation and tea. A few moments later, I was walking across the yard, back to my own place. I shot a glance toward Caitlin's house, and jerked to a stop when I saw the car sitting in her driveway.

Buchannan's car.

I had half a mind to head over, just so I could see his reaction when my neighbor told him that I'd been talking to her when the vandalism at the Banyon Tree was taking place.

Which would give her an alibi, just the same as me.

I was almost disappointed when I realized that if it was impossible for me to have done it, then it would be for Caitlin as well. That meant I was back to square one, and that there was *another* woman out there who didn't like me.

I decided to let Buchannan do his job without my interference and headed inside. Misfit was stretched out on the couch, and barely lifted his head at my entrance. As soon as I was through the door, I pulled out my phone and dialed.

"Hello?" A woman's voice.

"Laura? It's Krissy."

"Oh, hi, Krissy." I could hear the smile in Laura Dresden's voice. She'd been dating my dad for a while now, and from what I could gather, they were practically married without going through the actual ceremony. "It's good to hear from you. How's Pine Hills?"

I wasn't sure how to answer that, so I pivoted. "How's Dad?"

There was a slight pause before, "He's good. He just ran down to the store for some eggs." Another pause. "Is something wrong?"

Normally, I'd spill my guts to Dad when I called California. He'd listen without interruption, and then would give me sage advice that often helped ease my mind, or would get me focused on the right path to solve whatever mishap had marred my life. I'd never done the same with Laura, and was afraid of how she'd react if I had.

But if she *did* marry my dad, it would be inevitable that she'd hear about the disasters I constantly found myself in. She probably already did.

"It's a long story," I warned her, just in case she wanted to back out.

"If you're willing to tell me about it, I'm willing to listen."

So, I did.

It was strange dumping on Laura, but it felt good to get it all out a second time. As I spoke, I could feel the tension bleed from my shoulders, and by the time I was done, I found I was smiling self-consciously. I'd even mentioned the text I'd received and was feeling particularly silly for worrying about it.

"I'm probably being paranoid and it'll all work out by tomorrow."

"Maybe." Laura didn't sound convinced. "Have you seen anyone strange around lately?"

"Strange? Like someone I don't know?"

"Or someone who normally wouldn't hang around you or your place of business. I'm not trying to scare you, but you can't be too careful. I had this one boyfriend back, gosh, over twenty years ago, who couldn't let go. He used to stalk me everywhere I went, and it got pretty scary there for awhile."

I thought of my own ex, Robert, and how he'd followed me all the way from California. While that had been frustrating, and a little creepy, it had turned out all right.

"No," I said. "Not if you don't count my new neighbor. This is a small town, so I've seen pretty much every face a dozen times over." Though that *didn't* mean I knew anything about said faces.

"Well, keep an eye out. It sounds to me as if someone is looking to get your attention, and not in a good way."

"So, you think someone is targeting me?" I paced across the room to where Misfit lay. I stroked him for comfort.

"Honestly? I'm not sure what I think." Laura sighed. "But you are well known in Pine Hills. Your dad is also a famous author. Sometimes, that's all someone needs. You've heard James talk about how some people can get."

Boy, had I ever. There was one guy, back when I was little, who'd drive by the house and then send Dad letters telling him what I'd been up to. I don't think there was any malice in it, but it was unsettling, nonetheless.

"Well, I hope whoever is doing this has already had their fun and will find someone else to pick on." I moved to the window so I could check on Buchannan's progress. His car was still there. Maybe I *would* go over and have a talk with both him and Caitlin to sort everything out.

"Me too. And hey, maybe we're both overreacting and this whole thing will blow over and we can have a laugh over it when you next fly in for a visit."

"I hope so."

Though it's hard *not* to overreact when you're being blamed for something you didn't do. I had a hard time believing it was a coincidence, that some angry woman, who just so happened to have a Death by Coffee apron, decided to vandalize a rival's store. Or that it happened at the same time I had a roach problem. Or at the same time I received a strange call and texts.

Yeah, I didn't think I was being paranoid, here. I had a legitimate cause for concern.

"Do you think—"

Before I could finish the thought, Detective Buchannan came running out of Caitlin's house and threw himself into his car. He backed out with speed, and for an instant, I was positive he was going to tear into my driveway to arrest me for a crime I didn't commit.

"Krissy? Are you there?" Laura's voice was a buzzing in my ear.

Buchannan hit the gas as his dash lights started flashing. He sped off without so much as a glance my way. A creeping dread told me that something bad had happened. Something *very* bad.

"I've got to go," I said. "Tell Dad I said hi."

"I will. What's going on?"

"Thanks, Laura." I clicked off in a daze. I was positive that whatever had caused Buchannan to rush from Caitlin's house like he was on fire, it had something to do with me.

Or the stuff that was happening *to* me.

Egotistical? Maybe. But after the day I'd had, it was understandable.

Since my phone was already in my hand, I called Paul. If anyone would know what was happening, he would.

It rang until it went to voicemail. I clicked off without leaving a message.

"This isn't good," I told Misfit, who'd roused himself and was winding around my legs. I picked him up and pet him while I watched out my window. For? I had no idea. Buchannan was gone, and I doubted he'd told Caitlin why he'd had to rush off, so it wasn't like she was going to come over and let me know.

I can't stay here.

If I stood around my house, waiting for the shoe to drop, I'd go crazy. So, instead of risking insanity, I gave Misfit a few treats, and headed out the door. In times like these, I wanted my best friend. I *needed* her.

I parked out front of Death by Coffee, a jangle

of nerves, and headed inside. My head was buzzing like it was filled with bees, and it didn't help matters that hardly anyone was inside. I made straight for the counter where Vicki and her husband were chatting.

"She's been pretty gloomy lately." Mason was leaning against the counter. Vicki was cleaning out the pastry display, listening with half an ear.

"Who's been gloomy?" I asked, thinking they were talking about me. *And honestly, it wouldn't be a surprise if they were.*

"Heidi," Mason said. "She's got a new boyfriend, I think."

"And that makes her gloomy?" Heidi used to be married to Mason's brother, before he was murdered. The brother. Not Mason. The poor woman had gone through quite a lot since then.

"Mason thinks this new guy is bad for her," Vicki said, straightening. "Even though he doesn't know a thing about him."

"I saw her just yesterday." Mason tapped a beat on the counter with his fingertips. "She was with a friend of hers, and they were having a pretty serious discussion. As soon as I approached, they both clammed right up. Who wants to bet they were talking about this new guy?"

"You're getting as bad as Rita," Vicki said with an elbow nudge into Mason's ribs.

He grabbed his side with a wince. "Oof, I'm wounded."

Now that it was clean, Vicki refilled the display with cookies and pastries, and closed it up. "Deservedly so."

"Do you know this boyfriend's name?" I asked.

Gossip was good. Gossip got my mind off of my own troubles, at least for a little while.

"Not a clue," Mason said.

"He hasn't even laid eyes on him," Vicki said. "Doesn't know his name, what he looks like, if he's tall or short."

"He's a mystery, which makes him mysterious." Mason filled a cup with coffee, snagged a cookie, dumped it into the cup, and then handed it over to me without having to ask if I wanted it. Of course, I did. "And that friend of hers . . ." He shook his head. "I'm not so sure I like her either. She seemed weasely. Is that a word?"

"You've grown protective of Heidi." Vicki gave him another playful elbow nudge. "Should I be jealous?"

"Well, someone has to be. You know what Dad's like. And Regina." He shuddered. "Those two will have her married off to some rich old guy if she doesn't choose someone soon."

"Which is a problem a new boyfriend will solve."

"Yeah, well, it needs to be the *right* boyfriend. I don't want her to end up with some jerk who won't take care of her."

Vicki glanced at her watch. "I guess I should get going. I have a lot to get done before play practice tonight, but I can hang around for a little while longer if you need me." She aimed the last at me.

"No, that's okay," I said. "You go. I can keep Mason company."

"If you're sure?" Vicki looked torn, which made me feel like a bad friend. I didn't want to be the reason she didn't do what she loved.

"Go." I smiled to show her I was okay. "I'll catch

you after practice if you're not busy?" I made it a question.

"I don't think I'm getting into anything." She looked at Mason, who made a dopey face.

"Well, I was planning a romantic evening, complete with candles and a hot bubble bath . . ."

"So, nothing," Vicki said, turning back to me with a mischievous grin. "I'll see you when we're done. Practice will end at about six tonight and I'll likely need to wind down. It's a three-hour marathon." She made a face, though I could tell she enjoyed it.

"I'll be there."

Vicki leaned over and kissed Mason on the cheek. "And *you* can keep that bubble bath warm." And with that, she was out the door.

Mason and I watched her go. As soon as she vanished from sight, he turned to me. "What's wrong?"

"Nothing," I said, looking away.

"Don't nothing me. I can tell you're upset."

"I'm being paranoid, is all." I faced the empty dining area. "It's awfully dead. Have there been more bugs?"

"No. Don't change the subject." He paused. "I heard a rumor about a certain brick meeting a certain window. Know anything about it?"

"You know about that?" Then again, that sort of thing would get around pretty quickly in a town like Pine Hills. You couldn't sneeze without someone across town hearing about it.

"Read about it online. Speculation is that you did it." Before I could object, Mason raised a hand and went on. "I don't believe it, which is why I didn't tell Vicki."

I sagged against the counter. "I'm bad for business."

"Nah. You make life exciting."

I gave him a flat look.

"Really! Not everyone comes here for the coffee or the books. Some come here just to see what mischief you're going to get yourself in next. I know I do."

"You come here because Vicki's here." I glanced upstairs, and sure enough, a black-and-white fluffball was sitting by the counter, standing watch over the empty aisles of books. "And Trouble."

Mason chuckled, but sobered quickly. "Don't let this stuff get you down, all right, Krissy? It'll all blow over soon enough."

"People keep telling me that."

"It will happen. Just like the people will start coming back here when they crave something hot to drink. It's a blip in the radar, an anomaly. It'll pass." He stretched and popped his back. "Now, if you want, we could go over some applications. I think I've found a few good candidates, but want to run them past you and Vicki."

"Even with how dead it's been?"

"It just means we'll have time to get them up to speed. If you—"

My phone rang, cutting him off.

Paul.

"I've got to take this," I said, accepting the call as I stepped away from the counter. "Paul? I saw Buchannan speed away from my neighbor's house. Did something happen?"

A heavy sigh. "Krissy. Are you home?"

"No, I left. I'm at Death by Coffee."

He was quiet a moment as he considered that. And then, "I need you to come back down to the station for another interview."

Whelp, there was the dread again. "Can I ask why? Does this have to do with the window of the Banyon Tree?"

"No." I waited for more, but he left it at that.

"Then what? I don't want to go down there again if this is something we can discuss over the phone."

Another sigh, followed by a scratchy sound that made me think Paul was running a hand over his mouth, and that he hadn't shaved. That was most definitely not a good sign.

"No, this can't be discussed over the phone. You have to come down to the station, Krissy. There's been a murder, and John thinks you might know something about it."

7

I felt like I was in a particularly unpleasant rerun. I arrived at the police station, and was once more met by Officer Garrison, who led me down the hall, into the interrogation room, where I took the same seat as I had taken just hours before.

Earlier, I was scared because I didn't know what was going on, or why I'd been asked to come in to the police station, other than it had to do with the Banyon Tree. This time, however, the word "murder" kept playing over and over in my head. *And the police believe I know something about it.*

When the door opened and Detective John Buchannan walked in, I wasn't surprised. He sat down and arranged a folder in front of him just like before, but he didn't bring a laptop this time. I guess that meant there wasn't video evidence of me murdering someone. Small victories.

"Ms. Hancock," he said, voice and expression showing not a hint of emotion. It was a far cry from the sneering Buchannan I knew. "I assume Officer Dalton told you why you are here?"

"He mentioned something about a murder."

"And that's all?"

I nodded. Buchannan answered with a slower nod. We looked like a pair of bobbleheads.

"What happened? Was it Judith?"

"The Banyons are fine." There was a brief flash of something in Buchannan's eye. Pity? Compassion? I couldn't quite tell because it was gone so fast, I very well might have imagined it. "Can you run me through your night again? The night the Banyon Tree was hit."

I took a deep breath to center myself. If this had to do with the Banyon Tree, then my alibi would save me. I just had to remain calm and honest and everything would work out. "I was at work, but due to a small bug issue, I closed early. From there, I went home, talked to my neighbor, and then went on a date with Paul."

"Your neighbor being Caitlin Blevins?"

"Yeah, she—wait. Did you say Blevins?"

"I did."

"I knew a Blevins once." I frowned as I tried to place where I'd heard the name before. Then it hit me. "June! I met her at a Christmas escape room!" My excitement about recalling her name died quickly as soon as I remembered that someone had died there as well. "Are they related?"

"I don't know," Buchannan said. "You claim you talked to Ms. Blevins once you arrived home after work?"

"Yes. I went over to introduce myself." I paused, eyes growing wide. "She was the one who was murdered?" But that couldn't be it. Buchannan was at her house when he'd sped away, likely to wherever the murder *had* taken place.

Buchannan sighed. "How about you stop trying to guess and just answer the questions."

A comeback was on the tip of my tongue, but I quickly realized snapping at Buchannan wouldn't get me anywhere but in a jail cell. I took a deep breath to compose myself, and wished he would have thought to bring me a water. My throat was growing dry, and I could use the distraction.

"All right." I closed my eyes to envision it. "Caitlin was moving boxes from her truck. It scared Misfit. I went over, tried to talk to her, but she was busy. I left, got ready for my date, and then Paul showed up. We left."

"You're sure that's how it went?"

A flare of anger shot through me, along with an urge to say something snappish. All that came out was, "Yes."

"I see." Buchannan lightly brushed a hand over the folder in front of him. "Ms. Blevins has no recollection of you approaching her. In fact, she claims to not have met you at all."

"What?" I half rose out of my chair before catching myself and sitting back down. "I was there! Our interaction wasn't exactly pleasant, but we *did* speak." I wondered if I was making a mistake mentioning how Caitlin had treated me like an unwanted guest, but Buchannan ignored the comment.

"I can only tell you what she told me," Buchannan said. And then he pivoted. "Where were you *after* your date with Officer Dalton?"

The sudden change didn't catch me by surprise because I was expecting it. "At home. With my cat. You can ask him, though I'm not sure he'll give you much of an answer."

A humorless smile flashed across Buchannan's face, and then was gone. "Can anyone confirm your whereabouts?"

"Other than my cat?" At Buchannan's dirty look, I sighed and answered the question. "I didn't see or talk to anyone, if that is what you're asking. I suppose a neighbor might have seen my lights on. And my car was in my driveway all night. Maybe Jules or Lance can confirm that."

"What about Hamish Lauder?"

"Who?" Even as the word left my mouth, the familiarity seeped in. *Where have I heard that name before?*

"Hamish Lauder," Buchannan repeated. "Do you know him?"

I frowned as I thought about it. So much had happened over the last few days, much of it was jumbled in my head. I closed my eyes and tried to will the man's face to come to mind, but it was like trying to conjure an image of a painting I'd never seen before.

"I don't think so," I said, knowing that it wasn't right, but didn't know how else to explain it. "The name's familiar though. Should I know him?"

"I don't know; should you?"

Annoyance shot through me. The question reminded me of an old English teacher who would always ask, "I don't know, *can* you?" whenever someone would ask if they could go to the restroom without using the word "may."

"I've heard the name," I said. "But I can't place it."

"That's strange." Buchannan appeared to be getting a perverse pleasure out of this. He ran his hand over the folder once again, a faint smile on his lips, as if he had the smoking gun sitting between the manilla flaps. "Because I have a witness who claims you were talking with Mr. Lauder just yesterday."

The memory hit me like a slap. "He bought Dad's book," I said, snapping my fingers. "I remember now. He wanted a signed copy, but we didn't have one on hand. He complained about wanting Dad to finish another series before starting a new one."

"Did you fight about it?"

"I wouldn't say we *fought*." Though, I suppose someone could have made that mistake if they'd seen us together. "I promised I'd ask Dad about getting him a signed copy, he said something about Dad needing to respect his readers, and then he left. Alive." I sagged in my chair. "He was the victim?"

Buchannan ignored the question. "Did you see him after that? Did you, perhaps, go to his house to deliver this book he wanted?"

"No. I haven't even talked to Dad about it yet." And now, if I was right and Hamish was the victim, I wouldn't need to.

And then it hit me. Hard.

Why would Buchannan be asking me these questions? Sure, he might be looking for answers, and I might have been one of the last people to talk to Hamish, but there was more to it than that.

Paul had said Buchannan thought I might know something about the murder.

He actually thought I was the killer.

"I didn't murder Hamish Lauder," I said, sitting up straight. "Should I get a lawyer?"

The scowl that Buchannan shot me took me aback. It made me wonder how many people in this small town ever asked for a lawyer. I mean, for most of us, the only experience we have of major crimes and lawyers would be on television. In real life, it's not something that flashes through our minds, even though it probably should.

"No," Buchannan said, abruptly standing. "You can go." He started for the door and then uttered a line I'd heard from cops on TV a million times, "Don't leave town."

He left the interrogation room door hanging open as he left. I rose, as if in a dream, and drifted out the door, to the front of the station. Eyes were on me. I knew many of the cops who were now looking at me as if I were a killer slipping from their grasp. Even Becca Garrison wasn't watching me kindly.

"I didn't do it." The words slipped out at a whisper, so no one actually heard my proclamation of innocence. Not that they'd believe me anyway. I left the station and stepped into the parking lot. The sun was shining, which felt wrong. It should be dark and gloomy, maybe with a light rain pattering my shoulders as I made what felt like a perp walk back across the lot.

Paul was waiting for me by my car.

I had half a mind to walk right by him. He could

have prepared me better for what I'd just endured. He could have stood by my side, demanded Buchannan tell me everything he knew so I could help. What good could I do with vague questions and no real answers to my own?

"Krissy, I'm sorry."

I stopped, and despite my frustrations with the situation, I let him hug me.

"I didn't do anything."

"I know you didn't."

"Buchannan thinks I did."

Paul let me go. We each took a step back so we could face one another. "John is just trying to do his job."

"Well, he needs to do it better." It came out surly.

"You can't blame him," he said, shooting a glance toward the station doors. I couldn't see anyone inside, but that didn't mean someone wasn't watching us. "There are . . . circumstances."

"Such as?"

Paul opened his mouth and then closed it again.

"You can't tell me." It wasn't a question.

"It's . . ." Another look toward the station. "Look, I can't talk about it here. How about I come over tonight. We can discuss it then."

I wanted to argue, but what good would that do? Paul was a cop. Buchannan was investigating a murder. And as much as I hated to admit it, I was a suspect in that murder, though I had no idea why Buchannan would consider me as such. I mean, I'd only met Hamish Lauder the once.

But our conversation had grown somewhat heated.

And he'd also given me his address, which meant I knew where he lived. That couldn't be the only evidence Buchannan had against me, could it? How would he even know?

"Okay," I said. "Tonight works. But promise me you won't leave anything out. I need to know why I'm a suspect."

Paul bit his lower lip, and then nodded. "I don't have all the details yet, but I will get them."

I felt kind of bad for putting Paul in that situation, but I was relieved he was willing to break protocol, even a little, to ease my mind. "Thank you." I leaned forward and kissed him on the cheek. Anything more would have been unprofessional, and admittedly, right then, I wasn't in the mood for kisses and hugs.

Paul nodded again, and then shoved his hands into his pockets. "I'd best get inside. Wait for me. Don't . . ." He frowned. "You know."

"I'll be good," I said, mentally crossing my fingers. "But if I learn anything, I'll let you know." I winked to let him know it was a joke.

It says a lot about how dire the circumstances were that Paul didn't smile. He merely turned and walked away, leaving me to stand in the middle of the police parking lot, wondering how I'd managed to get myself tangled up in yet another murder investigation. I mean, this time, all I'd done was talk to the victim *once*.

Why does this keep happening to me?

I climbed into my Escape, and realized I still had Paul's hat. I considered grabbing it and chasing him inside to give it back to him, but decided it could wait until tonight.

I sat in my vehicle, but didn't immediately start it to head for home. I had Hamish's address, and while I couldn't walk into his house and poke around, I felt the need to at least drive by. I hadn't killed him, but somehow, Buchannan thought our interaction led to him being murdered. I needed to know why.

I checked the address he'd given me, and then with one quick look toward the police station to make sure no one was watching me, I drove off.

No one pulled out behind me, so I assumed that meant Buchannan hadn't put a tail on me. Maybe I *had* watched too many crime shows on TV. I checked my mirrors every few moments, just to make sure, and was soon pulling onto Hamish's street.

The road was a straight line, as if someone had used a ruler to make sure it was perfect, and most of the yards were open and inviting. No excess trees. No shrubs or fences. The house I was look-ing for sat at the far end of the street, yet I could already see the yellow police tape across the door, telling me it was indeed the crime scene. There were no longer any cop cars there, just one old Chevy I took for Hamish's vehicle.

The neighbors might have seen something, I realized. And I was almost positive if a vehicle like my or-ange Escape were to have driven by, they would have seen it. Could I use that in my favor?

I rolled down the street slowly, checking each house as I passed. No curtains moved, but a few people were in their yards, talking, all facing to-ward Hamish's place. They watched me with wary eyes, and when I waved at one couple, all I received in return was a scowl.

Not a good sign. But it wasn't a condemnation either.

Hamish's house was a small place that looked as if it had endured quite a lot of tough years. The siding needed to be replaced, and the roof was looking as if it might only handle another year or two of storms, but that didn't mean the place appeared rundown. I could see where small repairs had been made, as if he was doing the best he could with a limited income. The yard was well tended, and a flower bed hid some of the stains on the siding. Through the window, I could see white lace curtains that, from a distance, appeared clean.

I thought back to the man in his corduroy pants and button-up shirt. He might have been short with me, but he hadn't been outright hostile. It was obvious he'd loved books, and I imagined he had a place set aside inside where he could sit and read. Perhaps by the front window, where he could look out and daydream between chapters.

Who would murder someone like that?

I felt that itch already, the *need* to get to the bottom of Hamish Lauder's murder. I didn't know the guy, didn't even know if my perception of the man was accurate.

But he'd come to *my* store, asked about *my* Dad's book. In some ways, that brought us closer, even if I couldn't tell you for sure what color his eyes had been, or if he liked wine or beer or if he preferred lemonade with dinner.

And yet, I knew if I stuck my nose where it didn't belong, Buchannan would end up grabbing me by it and hauling me off to jail.

Wait for Paul, Krissy. He'll know what to do.

And if he didn't?

Well, then, I'd just have to figure it out for myself.

8

Hamish Lauder was just another guy. He took pictures of his dinner when he went out and then posted it online. He commented on the quality of the movie he'd just watched. Sometimes, he could be grouchy, but aren't we all? He never once used social media to badmouth a neighbor or someone he'd bumped into who'd rubbed him the wrong way. In fact, his social media profiles painted the picture of a guy who didn't actually dislike anyone.

So, why would someone want to kill him?

I sat on my couch, twisted awkwardly so I could scroll through Hamish's social media posts, while Misfit snored contentedly in my lap. My shoulder was starting to ache from the angle, but I didn't want to move him. His presence made me feel better.

I returned to the top of the page. There was no mention of my interaction with Hamish. Based on the rest of his posts, our conversation was typically something he'd have commented on. He liked books, and was a bit prickly when they didn't go exactly the way he wanted. He seemed a little OCD, always wanting the books to be in the same format, same type, same spines. If a series got changed up, perhaps with a different cover style, he'd rant about it.

But he didn't threaten anyone, didn't say he planned on marching on New York and taking down the publishers who'd offended him. He just liked things to be done a certain way, and had a harder time coping than others when those things changed.

I swapped between the pages I'd found and could access. Perhaps Hamish used a social media site I didn't know about? He tweeted he was going to Death by Coffee. No other mentions of the store were made. His Instagram showed he'd made his own breakfast, commenting on his disappointment that the Banyon Tree would be closed that day. He usually ate breakfast there.

It made me wonder if that was the trigger for the brick through the window. It was hard to imagine that his murder and the vandalism were a complete coincidence.

I did find a comment by someone named Mark Cunningham that made it seem like the two of them were friends. I wrote the name down, and then tried to find information on him, but his pages were set to private, and he didn't appear to have Twitter.

I closed down my browser and leaned back, stroking my cat. I was missing something. Hamish was murdered, likely soon after I'd talked to him, or else he would have posted something about it online, as was his norm. But Buchannan had asked about my whereabouts *after* my date with Paul. Why hadn't Hamish posted anything after he'd left Death by Coffee? Had he met up with someone, like his friend, Mark, and never gotten the chance to post before he was murdered?

I must have been fidgeting because after a few minutes, Misfit looked up at me, ears pinned back in annoyance, and then he hopped down. He made it about two feet before he plopped onto his side and curled up to go back to sleep, this time on the floor.

"Well *excuse* me," I muttered, though I wasn't too upset. My back was killing me from how I'd been sitting, and I could use a few minutes on my feet. I stood and stretched, and happened to glance out the window as I did. A car in the driveway next door told me Caitlin was home, and that the majority of the moving must be done.

She lied to Buchannan.

I wanted to know why.

"I'll be right back," I told Misfit, who didn't so much as twitch. He must have had a busy morning playing while I was gone. I'd need to check the tails of his toy mice to make sure he hadn't chewed them all off like he was wont to do. Once the mouse was tailless, it was essentially dead to him and I'd need to get him a new batch so he wouldn't get bored and decide to use something of mine as a scratching post.

The walk across the yard felt like I was walking to the gallows. Maybe it was because I knew I wasn't going to be welcome. I braced myself for insults, or at minimum, a cold shoulder, as I knocked on the door. A thump and groan from inside confirmed that Caitlin was indeed home, and likely in the process of unboxing all of her things.

The door opened and a disheveled Caitlin Blevins met me with a scowl that made her look severe.

"Hi," I said as cheerfully as I could manage. "I was hoping we could talk." I glanced inside, saw the open boxes, confirming my suspicions. "If you have a few moments, that is. I promise I won't get in the way."

The frown deepened. "I'm kind of busy here."

"I could always help."

She raised her eyebrows at me.

"I don't mind. I'd like it if we could get along since we're going to be neighbors."

Caitlin heaved a sigh and then opened the door wider. "We can talk, but we're working while we do it. I've got a lot to do."

"Not a problem." I entered the house, and was shocked by how different it looked. Back when Eleanor Winthrow owned the place, you could barely move from one room to the next without bumping into clutter—usually a stack of newspapers. The carpet had been an orange shag that had a path worn in it, and made the house feel even older than it was.

Now, there was new carpet—though I had no idea when it was put in—and new paint on all the walls. A quick look in the kitchen told me the ancient appliances were still in place, but it wouldn't surprise me if that changed in the coming months.

Caitlin led me across the living room to where

open boxes sat. She gestured toward a trendy little chair that I could barely squeeze into. She took the wider couch.

"Say what you have to say," she said. "If you want to help, you can empty that box." She nodded toward one sitting just in front of me. "Just be careful."

I leaned over the box and peered inside. A bulky black box sat at the bottom, along with a few game controllers and wires. I began removing them, but paused when I saw what was sitting in the window.

A camera. The kind you could buy at any store for home security. It was small, about the size of my fist, and was aimed out the window, toward my house.

Caitlin saw me looking. "It's not hooked up. I set it there to keep it out of the way."

There were no wires, so it wasn't plugged into anything. It likely ran on batteries anyway. I had no way of knowing if it was recording or not. *Or why she'd want to spy on me.*

I pushed the thoughts aside and got to the reason I was there.

"I talked to John Buchannan today." I used his first name in the hopes that it would make her think we were close. "He's the detective who came over to ask you some questions earlier."

She nodded but didn't reply. Her box contained lots of wires. I had no idea what any of them went to, or did.

"He says you told him we didn't talk."

She hesitated before setting a bundle of wires aside. "I may have given him that impression."

"Why?" And then, because I was curious, "You acted like you knew me the first time we met. Your last name is Blevins. Are you related to June Blevins?"

"We're cousins." She let nothing show on her face.

"Is that how you knew of me?"

"It is."

"I didn't know June was mad at me. If she—"

I cut off as Caitlin shook her head. "She's not. It's just . . ." She looked at a switch of some kind in her hand, or perhaps it was some sort of pedal. For a guitar, maybe? "After what happened that Christmas, she hasn't been the same."

It was understandable. We'd gone to an escape room, and someone had died there. Murdered even. I think all of us left affected by it.

"Does she blame me for what happened?" I asked.

"No."

"Then why are you upset with me?"

Caitlin fiddled with the pedal before setting it aside. "She might not blame you, but I guess I kind of do. If you hadn't been there . . ."

"The murder still would have happened," I said. "I had nothing to do with it."

She didn't look convinced, but dismissed it anyway. "So, when the detective came asking about you, I decided I wanted nothing to do with whatever you were involved in. I told him I knew nothing and left it at that."

"You could have told him I stopped by, but we didn't talk about much."

"Yeah, well, I didn't."

I removed the black box and set it down on the floor. It had a slot that probably took DVDs, though I saw none anywhere. With the controllers, I assumed it was one of the new game consoles.

An assortment of wires lay beneath that. I stared at them, and then realized I really didn't want to be there. Caitlin was being polite enough, but it was clear she wished I was elsewhere. She wouldn't look at me, nor did she offer up anything without me asking about it.

Could she have set me up? She had a grudge against me, albeit a minor one. It wasn't much of a stretch to imagine she might have decided to get back at me by vandalizing the Banyon Tree.

No, she was with me when it happened. Or was she? I wondered if there were enough time for her to have slipped away to throw the brick through the window after I'd gone back home, or perhaps before I'd arrived. And nothing said she'd been alone the last time I was here, so the noises I'd heard later could have been made by someone helping her unload the boxes.

Someone like June.

I tried to imagine the young woman I'd known throwing a brick through a window, and just couldn't do it. Was it possible? Sure. I barely knew June, and since she was related to Caitlin, they may have conspired with one another to get back at me for a perceived slight.

But how could they have known I had a grudge against the owners of the Banyon Tree? That wasn't something June would have known, let alone Caitlin. I wasn't even sure either woman knew I worked at Death by Coffee, so the apron didn't make sense.

Still, the thought refused to relent.

"Can I use your restroom?" I asked, standing.

Caitlin shrugged one shoulder. "It's just down the hall."

I thanked her and strode down the short hallway and entered the bathroom. The space was small, cramped, and looked as if it could use a complete remodel. The tile wasn't cracked, but it was the next thing to it. Like the rest of the house, the bathroom was dated.

A flare of melancholy zipped through me. It was impossible not to think about Eleanor while in her old house. I don't think I'll ever forget about her, even if the entire house got updated.

The toilet lid was down, and topped with one of those fluffy blue covers. I made sure to make a lot of noise as I lifted the lid, before checking the bathroom for anything that might be incriminating. Yes, I was snooping. And yes, I felt bad about it. But if Caitlin—or someone she knew—had gone to the Banyon Tree, perhaps there was evidence somewhere in the house.

Unfortunately, she'd only unpacked the essentials. Toothpaste, toothbrush, shampoo. No Death by Coffee apron hung on the door, nor was there a wig that would make her hair like mine.

She wouldn't keep it in the bathroom. I went to the door and opened it a crack. I could see Caitlin on the couch, but her back was to me, and she was bent over a box.

I slipped out of the bathroom and crossed the

hall to a room that had once stored Eleanor's newspapers. She'd been a hoarder, having kept the newspapers in honor of her murdered brother. Now, the room was filled with sealed, unpacked boxes.

That left the bedroom.

I knew I was taking a risk, but I needed to know. I left the spare room and checked the bedroom at the end of the hall. Here, the boxes were open, the bed not quite made, but usable. A photograph on the nightstand showed Caitlin with a man about her age, but there was no indication that said young man lived with her. He was smiling, with brown, curly hair cut short. A boyfriend? A lost husband? I couldn't be sure.

I scanned the room, but didn't see an apron or wig or anything else incriminating. I took a step toward the closet, figuring that if they were anywhere, they'd be there.

"Ah-hem."

I jumped about three feet into the air and spun to find Caitlin standing in the doorway, hand on her hip. She didn't look angry or surprised by my snooping.

"I was, uh . . ." No excuse came to mind, so I didn't even try. It was obvious as to what I was doing, and to try to deny it would insult her intelligence.

I'd insulted her enough already.

"I was just leaving," I said, head drooping in shame.

"That would be a good idea."

Caitlin stepped aside to let me pass. She followed me all the way to the front door.

"I'm sorry," I said. "I was curious and let my curiosity get the better of me. It's a bad habit of mine."

She didn't respond, so I stepped outside. There was a moment where I thought she might say something, even if it was a scathing insult, but whatever had crossed her mind, she chose not to utter it. Instead, she closed the door in my face.

I wasn't even insulted. I deserved it.

Misfit was no longer on the floor when I got home, and I didn't go looking for him. Instead, I grabbed my laptop from the couch, and took it to the island counter. There, I looked up Caitlin and June Blevins.

It was easy to forget how many people can be affected by a murder. It's not just the victim or the killer or even the family of both. Friends. Acquaintances. Neighbors and coworkers. Even the mail carrier or waitress at a favorite restaurant can be impacted by the murder of someone they'd served.

June had been there when a man had died. We'd all been trapped together, unable to escape, with a killer. And it was reflected in her Twitter posts.

I couldn't look at them for long before I closed the laptop lid. Caitlin and June might only be cousins, but they used to spend a lot of time together. There were photos as proof. But then, over the last few months, those times became fewer and farther between. At one point, Caitlin had posted on June's timeline that someone would "pay for what she did," but I couldn't find what that was in reference to.

Could Caitlin be bitter? She admitted to blaming me. Would she go so far as to murder what, in essence, was a stranger to the both of us in order to frame me?

It was a leap, but what else made sense? That Hamish Lauder had coincidentally gotten himself killed after talking to me, and it just so happened to be on the same day on which someone busted the Banyon Tree window while wearing a Death by Coffee apron?

And the bugs. And the phone call and text.

The text.

I pulled out my phone and brought up the image again. There was Paul and Shannon, together. But how together? Who had taken the picture? Caitlin? Someone else? Why? And how long ago had it taken place? Paul looked much like he did today, but with such a blurry image, how could I be sure this hadn't been taken over a year ago?

I decided to try something I should have tried when I'd first received the text.

I pressed the little phone icon and called whoever had sent it.

I immediately got a message saying that the number I was trying to reach was no longer in service.

Of course, it wasn't. That would have been too easy.

If I needed any more proof that there was a conspiracy happening, and that I was the target of said conspiracy, this was it. A normal person doesn't disconnect their phone after sending an incriminating text. Only someone with something to hide would do that.

My gaze drifted to the window. I could see Caitlin's house, and the living room window that faced my own.

Was she looking back at me?

Or was that camera of hers on, recording my every move in the hopes of catching something that she could eventually use against me?

9

I tapped the steering wheel with my fingertips, my mind a million miles away. I was on my way to the new improved community theatre for my planned get-together with Vicki. I was looking forward to it, and hoped it would help me put the nightmare of the last few days behind me. Paul had yet to call, let alone show, and I wasn't about to sit around my house all night waiting for him.

Bitterness was seeping into my thoughts, and I had to forcefully push it away. None of this was Paul's fault, yet I kept finding myself feeling angry at him. I knew a lot of it had to do with that photo I'd been sent. And then there were my two trips to the police station where he'd waited until *after* Buchannan had grilled me before telling me what was going on.

It's not his fault. He's just doing his job.

A honk caused me to jump. The light ahead of

me was green, and likely had been for some time now.

"Sorry." I raised a hand to let the annoyed driver know I'd heard them, and then went through the light, just as it turned yellow. The car behind me was forced to stop and wait for another cycle.

Pine Hills closed down early most days, but on the weekends, was often open a little later. Death by Coffee now stayed open until eight on weekends, and many of the other businesses had followed suit. I was hoping Vicki wanted some ice cream since the little ice cream shop was still open. I surely could use some.

I parked in the lot to the side of the community theatre to wait. It was a much nicer building than the last theatre, which was still standing, but was no longer being used for much of anything. The building here was new, and it showed. The brick was that bright red that only new buildings could manage. Outside lights kept the parking lot and entrances lit, and an old-style marquee out front displayed the name of the coming play in bold, block letters. I was curious as to how it looked on the inside since I'd never been, but didn't want to interfere with practice, so I remained seated in my Escape.

After only a few minutes of twiddling my thumbs and fighting off dark thoughts, the side door opened and people began trickling out. I recognized a few faces from my ill-fated attempt at acting a few Christmases ago, but no one noticed me sitting in my vehicle since they were all too busy talking to one another. There was an excitement among the cast and crew as they left, a sure sign that the play was coming together.

A minute passed and I began to worry that Vicki had already left, when she finally appeared, talking to a woman with her hair pulled back in a ponytail. The exchange wasn't heated, but I could tell something was bothering the both of them. When they both turned their heads to follow another woman—this one a rail-thin blond who was climbing into a Camaro—I knew that she was the topic of their conversation.

They watched her check her hair in her mirror, and spend an inordinate amount of time fidgeting behind the wheel, before she finally sped off. Another couple of words were passed between Vicki and the other woman, and then they parted. Vicki was frowning as she made for my Escape.

"Hey, Krissy." Vicki's frown turned into a radiant smile that *almost* hid her frustration. "I'm glad you made it."

"Me too." I looked past her to the woman with the ponytail, who was walking slowly across the lot, shooting glances back toward where the Camero had gone. "Everything okay?"

Vicki followed my gaze. "Yeah, everything's fine. There's just a little extra drama to go along with the drama."

Ponytail must have felt us looking because she turned to face us just before climbing into her car. Both Vicki and I waved in unison, which caused the woman to shake her head, brows coming together. She got into her car and drove off with a honk that, to my mind, sounded like she was telling us off.

"Angela and I had a disagreement," Vicki said, watching her go. "I'm not a big fan of who landed the lead role, and Angela doesn't quite agree with my assessment." She paused. "Well, we agree that Nina is struggling, but Angela doesn't want to replace her. Since she's directing the play, she has final say."

"If this Nina's not working out, why not have someone else take over the lead? What about an understudy?" Admittedly, my knowledge of local, small-time plays was practically nonexistent.

Vicki shrugged. "You'd have to ask Angela. I'm guessing someone knows someone and it's become a political issue within the theatre community. We don't have understudies here, but most of us know the lines, so we could make adjustments, move Nina down to a less demanding role. I'm trying to get Angela to sign off on it, or at least, try it for a practice or two. I'm not making much progress." She patted my door, her entire demeanor shifting. "So, what's the plan?"

"Are you up for some ice cream?" I asked. "Because I could go for a double brownie dip."

"You, my friend, are talking my language."

Vicki was parked a few spaces away, and rather than riding together where I'd end up having to drive her back to her car, we decided to take our own vehicles down the street, to the local ice cream place. I waited for her to climb into her car, and then led the way to Scream for Ice Cream. Death by Coffee was on the way, and when we reached it, I slowed enough to peek inside, but couldn't see much through the glass windows. I thought it looked like there were more customers than earlier, but couldn't be sure unless I stopped and went in.

Now's not the time to worry about that. I was here to forget my troubles; not stress over things I couldn't control.

I continued on past, determined to not let my worries ruin the night.

We parked in adjacent spaces outside the ice cream parlor and headed inside for our treats. The place wasn't too busy, considering the time and temperature, but there were enough people to make it feel social. We found a table in the corner, ordered our ice cream, and sat back to relax.

Or, at least, I tried to.

"Something's bothering you," Vicki said, just as the ice cream arrived. "Is it about the"—she glanced at the waitress, who had paused as if to listen. The young woman flashed an embarrassed smile and hurried away. "The bug problem? Because that's taken care of. Death by Coffee will be fine."

"No." Though I was still worried that our reputation was already permanently tarnished. In a small town like Pine Hills, it wasn't always easy to repair a damaged image. "A lot has happened in the last couple of days. I feel targeted."

Vicki took a bite of her ice cream and spoke through it, somehow making it look demure. "Tell me."

I felt like a broken record as I told her everything that had happened since Hamish Lauder had asked for a signed copy of Dad's book. I ate my ice cream, pausing only once, with my tongue pressed against the roof of my mouth, when a cold headache tried to make my eyes pop out of my head. Vicki listened, her face growing troubled the longer I spoke.

"Detective Buchannan can't honestly believe you had anything to do with a murder," she said when I was done. "Haven't we been down this road before?"

"We have." In fact, I'd say Buchannan looked at me as a suspect in at least half of the murders that had taken place in Pine Hills since I'd arrived. Maybe twice that. "But this time he acts like he has something on me, something I won't be able to explain away."

"Such as?"

I shrugged. "Maybe something like the video from the Banyon Tree. Maybe an eyewitness who thought they saw me somewhere. And I don't really have an alibi, not unless Misfit suddenly starts talking."

"I'm not sure anyone would want to hear what he *or* Trouble might have to say about us."

That brought a smile to my face. "The poor cats are probably traumatized."

"Ain't that the truth." She winked and pushed her now-empty bowl away. She sobered. "I don't understand why all of this is happening to you all of a sudden. Things have been going great lately, haven't they?"

"I wish I knew." I glanced at my phone, which I'd set on the table while I ate. Still no text or call from Paul. "I'm hoping Paul can clear things up once he can make some time for me."

"He hasn't told you *anything*?"

"Not really. He doesn't want to step on Buchannan's toes, I guess. I don't blame him." Okay, maybe I did, a little. But if you'd had the day I'd been having, you'd want answers too. "But what about those texts? And that picture?"

"Let me see it." Vicki held out a hand.

I was hesitant, but maybe she'd see something I'd missed. I brought up the texts and handed my phone over. Vicki read the messages, and then scanned the photo with a frown.

"That's Paul." She squinted. "The quality sucks, but you can most definitely tell who it is."

"The woman is his ex, Shannon. They're at the Banyon Tree," I said, just in case she couldn't tell. "Shannon works there, so he might have been eating and she came over to talk. He likes the food there." Though much of the menu was liable to give him a heart attack. The Tree Burger *was* practically a heart attack on a bun.

"It's pretty blurry," Vicki said. "You can't really tell what's happening with any certainty."

I could hear it in her voice, so I said it. "But?"

"But it sure looks like . . ." She glanced at me, and then closed the text. "It's probably a case of bad timing. It could have been loud and he'd whispered something to her, and whoever took the photo just happened to catch them in a position that looked far more suggestive than it really was."

"Maybe. But why take the picture at all? If it was from someone I knew, they would have told me outright, not sent a text like this, and then disconnect their line."

"Does Paul have an enemy that might want to break the two of you up?"

"Not that I'm aware." Even as a cop, Paul didn't

get on anyone's bad side; outside the people he'd arrested, of course. And those people were in jail, not sitting in the Banyon Tree, waiting to catch him in a compromising position.

"It *is* odd," Vicki said. "I sure don't go around taking pictures of random people and then sending them to their girlfriends. And you're right; if I'd seen it, I would have confronted Paul then and there, and then gone straight to you. Having it show up as an anonymous text is strange."

"It has to be a setup, right?" I really hoped that's all it was. It still meant someone was out there, trying to set me up for a fall, but at least it meant I could count on Paul to have my back. "I hate feeling like he might be cheating on me."

Vicki reached across the table and rested a hand on my wrist. "I'm sure he's not. I've seen the two of you together. There's no way he'd mess that up."

"But—"

She squeezed, cutting me off. "No buts." She waved over the waitress and handed over a credit card. "Let's take a walk. The fresh air might clear both of our heads."

I tried to pay for my ice cream, but Vicki wouldn't have it. The waitress returned with the card a minute later, and then we left Scream for Ice Cream.

The night air was crisp and cool, which felt even colder after eating ice cream. I rubbed at my arms and wished Paul were there to warm me up. Vicki was probably right and I had nothing to worry about. Other than that one photo, I'd seen nothing to indicate he'd ever cheat on me.

It took me a few minutes to realize that neither of us had spoken since we'd left the ice cream parlor. Vicki was looking straight ahead, brow furrowed as if she was thinking some rather deep thoughts.

"It's my turn to ask *you* if everything is okay," I said.

"I'm not sure." She paused under a streetlight—it got dark early this time of year—and casually glanced back the way we'd come, before turning to face me. "I think someone is following us."

"What?" My first instinct was to step around her and scour the sidewalk until I found whom she was referring to. But I held back, knowing that if I did, then our stalker would know we knew about them, and would vanish. "Who?"

"There's a man leaning against the building at the corner. He's wearing a Cincinnati Reds hat and a black shirt. Can't miss him."

I peeked, as casual as you like, and there he was. The hat was pulled low, and with it being dark, I couldn't see his face, but I got the distinct impression I'd seen him somewhere before. I took the one look, and then moved so he couldn't see me.

"Who is he?"

"No clue. He came in just after we sat down at Scream for Ice Cream and took a seat across the room from us. I noticed him glance at us a few times, but thought nothing of it."

Which was no wonder. Considering Vicki's looks, a lot of men stopped and stared. A lot of women too.

"And then he followed us out?" I asked, a chill working its way through me. "It's not a coincidence?"

"It could be, I suppose. But why's he stopped

now?" She started walking and I hurried to catch up with her. "Let's try to double back and catch him unawares."

"And then?" My mind was racing. I *knew* I'd seen the guy somewhere, but without a good look at his face, I had no idea if it was because he was a customer at Death by Coffee, or if he'd cashed me out at the grocery store.

But I *did* know that a lot of bad things were happening to me lately, and having a strange, almost familiar man follow me, couldn't be a coincidence.

Could he have been the phone breather? That had been a man who'd called, and he'd known my name, so it stood to reason that the guy following us might not just know the same thing as the guy on the phone, but *be* the same man.

Vicki kept her pace brisk as we hurried down the sidewalk. I desperately wanted to look back to see if our stalker was indeed following us, or if he'd remained standing at the corner, oblivious to our paranoid flight. I resisted the urge, knowing that if we kept looking back, he'd realize he'd been made.

We reached the next intersection and we made the turn. Vicki stopped almost immediately, and spun to face the way we'd come, but she didn't turn the corner again.

"Let's wait for him to come to us," she said. I could hear the anticipation in her voice.

Seconds ticked by. My heart kept the time by beating so loudly in my ears, it was nearly all I could hear. I kept thinking of all of Paul's warnings for me to not investigate, to avoid confronting killers without police backup.

But this guy isn't a killer. He's just a creepy stalker.

Or was he? Hamish Lauder *had* been murdered. And with everything that'd happened to me lately, it wouldn't surprise me to learn that our stalker was a killer out looking for his next victim.

I pulled my phone out of my pocket. If this guy *were* a killer and thought he was going to catch me unaware, he had another think coming. I brought up the camera app and was just raising my phone into position when the man in question strode around the corner.

Three things happened at once.

Vicki gasped and took a step forward, as if she might accost our stalker physically.

I yelped in surprise, and my thumb hit the big white button that would take the photo, all while I jumped *backward*, away from the man in the Reds hat.

And he saw us and immediately spun on his heel to run.

Vicki's fingers touched his back, but before she could grab hold, he was off like a shot. She briefly stumbled, somehow making it look graceful, and then she too was running. It took me a moment to fumble my phone back into my pocket, before I started after him, but already, we were too late.

The man bolted across the street at the intersection. There was a screech of tires and someone honked their horn as he just barely missed getting struck by a pair of cars, each going in opposite directions. Vicki and I would have kept after him, but another vehicle, a rusted pickup flying a pair of overlarge flags out of its bed, shot *between* the stopped cars, straddling the double yellow line. By the time it zipped by and traffic started moving again, Reds Hat was already gone.

"Do you see him?" Vicki asked, scanning the far sidewalk while standing on her tiptoes, as if that would help her see better.

I looked both ways, and while there weren't many people on the street, I couldn't find him. He must have slipped into one of the businesses. We could search for him, but I had a feeling that by the time we'd found whatever building he'd entered, he'd have already snuck out the back.

"No. He's gone." I pulled my phone from my pocket. "But I did snap a picture of him."

Vicki moved to stand at my side as I brought up the gallery on my phone. I clicked the thumbnail, and groaned when I saw what I'd captured.

The photo, like the one of Paul and Shannon, was blurry, which was no wonder considering I hadn't meant to take it when I did. A majority of the photo was of Vicki's shoulder where I hadn't gotten the phone into the correct position. The only thing of the stalker you could see was his Reds ballcap.

And a tuft of long, curly brown hair sticking out from underneath it.

10

The clock ticked ever closer to nine. After our encounter with our stalker, Vicki and I had parted, with her warning me to be careful, just in case he returned. It was obvious something sinister was happening in Pine Hills, and I was at the center of it.

Lucky me.

All attempts to reach Paul had been met by voicemail. I guess I shouldn't have been surprised, considering everything that's been going on around town. Buchannan probably had him chasing leads on the murder case or the vandalism. I was worried those leads would eventually lead to me through no fault of my own. The video already had.

I was stuck waiting at home, alone, with no idea as to what to do with myself.

Every few minutes, I'd get up and check the windows. I kept hoping to see Paul pulling into my driveway, while simultaneously worrying that the guy who followed Vicki and me was hiding in the dark somewhere. And then there was Caitlin's camera to consider. Was it turned on? Was she recording me peeking out of my window even now?

Curly hair. Didn't the guy in the photograph I'd seen at Caitlin's bedside have curly brown hair?

I closed my eyes and tried to bring the image to mind, but it was fuzzy, much like the picture I'd been sent. I was pretty sure he'd had curly hair; I just wasn't positive.

I was considering the merits of going next door to further ruin my relationship with my new neighbor when an urge to check the photo of Paul and Shannon one more time struck me. Maybe both Vicki and I were wrong and it was someone else in the photo. Maybe it was a setup.

I opened the text, studied the photograph, and then swapped to the picture I'd taken, hoping I'd spot some sort of similarity between the two men. A Reds hat and curly hair in one. The other was Paul. No amount of looking and hoping would change that. I closed my hastily taken photo and instead stared at the text, the one with Paul and Shannon together. Jealousy is an ugly thing, yet I couldn't shake it, no matter how hard I tried.

The photo vanished as my phone rang. My heart leapt, thinking it was Paul, but one look at the screen showed me Rita's smiling face instead.

This should be fun.

"Hi, Rita," I said by way of answer. I braced for whatever juicy piece of gossip that had my name written all over it. "What's up?"

"Oh, my Lordy Lou!" she said, voice loud and boisterous, much like the woman herself. "What have you been doing with yourself lately? Why, the internet is abuzz with tales of your misdeeds, Krissy. And I thought the creepy crawlies at the coffee shop were bad enough. Destruction of property? Libel? *Murder?*" She tsked, which gave me a chance to speak.

"I didn't do any of that." I paused. "And libel? What are you talking about?"

"Is it libel? Or am I thinking slander? I can never remember which is which." She sighed. "Anyway, I heard all about that post you made about the library. Someone took it down because, quite frankly, it needed to be. But it's still out there, floating around. You should have known that once you post something on the internet, it'll live forever."

"Rita," my tone was firm, "I had nothing to do with any of that. I didn't break the window of the Banyon Tree. I didn't make that post about the library. And I most definitely didn't murder anyone."

"Well, I know *that.*" She said it like she hadn't just told me she'd heard all about *my* misdeeds. Sometimes with Rita, it was hard to know what rumor she believed, and what she spread just because she could. "But you have to know something about it. I mean, things like this don't just happen to people. You must have done something to trigger it."

"I'm not sure what to tell you." I returned to the window and glanced outside. Still no Paul. No stalker. "Have you heard anything else about me that I should know about?" Best to get ahead of whatever fresh disaster awaited me instead of having Paul call and ask me to come down to the station once more.

"Why? Did you do something I haven't read about yet?"

"No, I—wait. Did you say 'read?' "

"Of course, dear. I *do* know how to read, you know? Speaking of which, have you heard anything about that early copy of James's book? I've been thinking about it all day. I could get word out about it early. You know, an early review to get the buzz going."

I refused to be distracted by her change in subject, not when it was my life we were talking about. "Where did you read about me?" Pine Hills no longer had a physical newspaper to speak of; hadn't had one for a long time. I knew there was an official online site, but the news there was, to put it mildly, hardly newsworthy.

Rita huffed, clearly put off at my lack of response to her request, but she answered anyway. "*The Eyes of the Hills.*"

"The what?"

Another huff. "Haven't you been keeping up with local happenings? I swear, sometimes I don't think you take your role as a citizen of this town seriously. We all need to be kept informed or else how can we do our part?"

"Sorry. I guess I've been a little busy." I winced at my harsher-than-intended tone, but Rita didn't seem to notice.

"Well, as long as you start to make an effort, all will be forgiven."

"Thanks."

"Anyway, *The Eyes of the Hills* is a local news site

run by a concerned citizen, not some politician or newsperson who has an agenda. It's online where everything seems to be going these days. How long before you can only read books online? Or get music? Why should I have to go online to listen to the Beatles when a record works just as well?"

Convenience? Storage? "The online site?" I pressed.

"It's been around for about a year now," Rita said. "They post about local happenings, everything from the small stuff to the big-time. Did you know there's a push to bring a Denny's to Pine Hills? I don't know why anyone would want to do such a thing, but apparently there are people who'd rather go to a chain than a local diner, like the Banyon Tree."

"I've never heard of this site," I said, refusing to be drawn off topic. With Rita, you had to be careful of that.

"Well, it's a valuable resource. I get a lot of my news from there."

You mean rumors and gossip. I bit my tongue to keep from saying it. I did wonder though; was this an actual news site? Or was it a gossip and *opinion* site disguised as news?

"I see. And they've posted about what's been happening to me?"

"They have. I'm not sure where they get their information, but they are pretty detailed about what they write." Rita sounded proud, as if *she'd* written the articles. "Why, they knew all about what happened at the Banyon Tree, complete with a description of the culprit."

I frowned. "Have the police made that public?"

I could almost *feel* Rita's shrug. "No idea. I

wouldn't be surprised if the author of the article knew more than the local cops." She paused. "Now, I'm not badmouthing the police, of course. How are you and Officer Dalton getting along? When I was out with Johan the other day, I saw him looking rather forlorn and wondered if it had something to do with you? Officer Dalton, not Johan. He's been great. Johan, I mean."

I so wasn't getting into my relationship with Rita. Besides, I was anxious to check out the website and see what I could learn. "Hey, I'm sorry, Rita, but I've got to go." And then, to be sure I had it right, "*The Eyes of the Hills*, correct?"

"That's it. It's kind of like the movie, dear, just rearranged. I think it's rather clever."

I suppose it was, if not a little creepy, especially considering my stalker. "I'll take a look and try to get caught up on the local news."

"You do that. And if you hear anything about that book . . ."

"I'll be sure to let you know."

I clicked off and immediately went to my laptop and brought up the browser. I had to skip past a lot of articles written about the movie, *The Hills Have Eyes*, but eventually found what I was looking for.

The page was rather plain, with a white background and a header decorated with a grainy photo of the hills that Pine Hills was named for. There wasn't any kind of "sort" function, or way to search for specific terms. The page was more like a blog than an actual news site, though the post pinned at the top did claim it was "THE #1 NEWS

SOURCE FOR THE ENTIRETY OF PINE HILLS!"
in all caps.

The next post down was a piece talking about
the Banyons and their wedding anniversary, which
was, apparently, the reason they'd closed for the
day. It was, of course, accompanied by a photo of
the diner pre-vandalism. As I read, my mouth fell
open in shock.

> *After finding her establishment to be below sani-*
> *tary standards, Ms. Hancock took it upon herself*
> *to ruin Judith and Eddie's celebration by destroying*
> *the business that rivaled, and surpassed, her own.*

"What?" I scrolled to the next article, which was
a puff piece about Too Le Fit to Quit and new exercise equipment, to find a story about my involvement in Pine Hills's worst crimes.

"A Criminal Among Us?" was the headline. Like
the bit within the article about the Banyons, this
entire article was nothing more than a hit piece,
intent on ruining my name. Apparently, I'd been
seeding misinformation among the populace in
order to aggravate people to murder one another.
Then, I'd casually insert myself into the investigation, and "solve" the crime to further my celebrity.

I made it most of the way through the article before I couldn't take it anymore. There was no real
news to the article, just groundless speculation
presented as fact. I scrolled back to the top to
search for the name of the article's author. Whoever wrote this had it in for me, and I wanted to
know why.

A quick glance told me the story—as well as *all* of the articles on the site—was written by Abby Kohn.

I immediately googled the name and came up with the same articles and site I'd already found, but nothing else. There were other Abby Kohns out there, but none of them were from Pine Hills, or the surrounding area.

"Who are you?" I wondered aloud, returning to the articles. I scrolled through them, finding my name more than a few times. It seemed like every other article mentioned me in some way. Here, it talked about my involvement with the Christmas play, and how I'd ruined it. There, it went into detail about my involvement in a Halloween gone bad. These references were all imbedded in more recent articles about the community theatre and a benefit being held at the old mansion where the Halloween party in question had taken place. At least I'd been left out of the Denny's article.

I returned to the main hit piece and reread it, searching for some clue as to who this Abby Kohn might be to me. There was no photo, of course, no address or phone number I could use. Just the words on the page, and that told me nothing other than the fact that Abby Kohn didn't like me one bit.

> *Ms. Hancock loves the attention. These crimes that have plagued our town since her arrival all have the same thing in common: Krissy Hancock. Without her, none of the murders would have happened.*

"I didn't kill anyone."

Misfit paused in the hallway to look at me before he continued on toward the litter box. I went back to reading.

> *Evidence in all these crimes points to Ms. Hancock being involved in more than an investigative and periphery manner. The only reason she is not currently sitting in a jail cell is because she has formed a relationship with the local police department. They have since covered up her crimes in order to protect the police chief, Patricia Dalton, and Ms. Hancock's partner in these crimes, Officer Paul Dalton.*

I closed the laptop with a snap.

I'd had people badmouth me before. Some of it was online. Some behind my back. Others, to my face.

Yet, these articles were different. Every other time, there was a reason for the insults, even if that reason might have been misinformed or prejudiced. These articles were simply out to get me, to paint me in the worst possible light.

And I hadn't the slightest idea why I'd become a target.

Headlights lit up my front window. I hurried over to peek outside, and was relieved to see I might finally get some answers.

Paul had finally arrived.

I didn't want to appear too eager, but I couldn't help myself. I jerked open the door, and was nearly dancing from foot to foot as he climbed out of his car.

"I'm sorry it took me this long to stop by," he said as he entered the house. He had dark circles under his eyes and his hair was a mess atop his head. He looked like he'd spent hours tearing at it, and considering the predicament I was in, he probably had.

"It's all right." I led him over to the island counter, where he took a stool. I put on the teapot, figuring a hot drink might do us both some good. "I found your hat."

"I see that." It was sitting on the counter next to him. He picked it up, inspected it, and then set it aside. "I wondered what happened to it."

I pulled down two mugs and got the teabags ready. "Please tell me you've figured this whole murder thing out," I said when I was done.

"No, not yet." Paul yawned and rubbed at his face. "But I do need you to do something for me."

I crossed my arms. Something about the way he said it made alarm bells start clanging in my head. "Oh?"

"Remember when you went to that convention out of town?"

I nodded. "JavaCon."

"You bought a mug there. Can I see it?"

"Why?"

"Please, Krissy. Humor me."

I studied him, but he gave nothing away, so I opened the cupboard to retrieve my mug. It sat among the chipped mugs I'd personally chipped myself—trust me, it's a long story—but I had never been able to bring myself to put a chip in the JavaCon mug. It held some sentimental value to me and I was afraid I'd break it if I tried.

I moved a couple of mugs aside, a frown forming, before I checked the dishwasher. "It's not here."

Paul heaved a sigh that sounded as if it had come straight from the depths of his soul. "All right. I need you to check on a book. *Victim of the Heart.* The one your dad sent you."

"My signed copy?"

He nodded and looked down at his folded hands as if he couldn't bear to look at me. Either that, or he was afraid of what I'd see in his eyes.

I left the room, my heart in my throat. Before I'd reached the bookshelf in the spare room where I kept a copy of all of Dad's books, I already knew what I'd find.

Victim of the Heart was gone.

"What's going on, Paul?" I asked, returning to the kitchen. "Why are my things missing?"

He fidgeted a moment before he answered. "You can't repeat this to anyone. Buchannan's not releasing the information to the public at the moment, but since they're your items, it's not like we can hide it from you."

"Hide what?"

"The book and mug were found at the murder scene."

I eased down into a stool across from him. The teapot whistled, and if it weren't so annoying, I would have ignored it. I rose and took it off the burner, but instead of filling our mugs, I returned to my seat. "How?" Before he could answer, a thought hit me. "Wait. Misfit was acting strange yesterday."

"Strange how?"

"He was hiding and acting nervous, like something had spooked him. I dismissed it, thinking that it was because of the noises coming from next door." A new thought. "My neighbor doesn't like me. She was acting strange when I talked to her and she didn't tell Buchannan the truth about my visit. Could it be because her boyfriend, or husband, or whoever he is, was in my house? He could have stolen the items because they are setting me up for crimes I didn't commit. I mean, he has curly hair. Or I think he does. I might be wrong and—"

"Slow down, Krissy." Paul patted the air. "Take a breath. Then tell me everything you know. Slowly."

I took that breath, tried to calm my racing heart, and then I told him.

The story was disjointed and I kept having to repeat myself or backtrack to add something I'd forgotten. So much had happened, I wasn't even sure I was keeping it all straight, even though I'd lived it.

"And the guy got away," I said, winding down. "Then I came home, heard about a website from Rita, and then you showed up."

"What website?"

"I can show you. And I have a bad picture of the guy who'd followed us, but maybe something in it will tell you something." I snatched up my phone and unlocked the screen.

Both of us went completely still.

"What is that?" Paul asked.

I was stuck between wanting to close the image on my phone and to shove it in his face. When I'd gotten the call from Rita, I'd forgotten to close the text messages, and now, before I'd had a chance to tell him about it—I'd left it out of my tale. For, you know, reasons—here it was, staring us both in the face.

"You tell me," I said, choosing to hand the phone over to him to do with as he pleased.

Paul studied the picture a moment before turning off the screen. "Where did you get this?"

"Why were you with her?"

"It's complicated."

The words struck me like a punch to the chin. A right hook maybe. My eyes started watering, and I'd like to think it had to do with the mental image of being sucker punched, not that I was starting to cry.

"Paul . . ." I didn't know what to add, so I fell silent.

He reached across the counter and put a hand on my own. "It's not what it looks like. I . . ." He frowned. "It's not my place to explain. But it's not anything you need to be worried about."

And you can't explain it to me? I wanted to shout it at him, but knew if I did, I'd be bawling like a baby.

Paul seemed to realize there was no way he was going to win without a solid explanation, so he stood. "You'll have to trust me on this, like I'm trusting that you had nothing to do with the murder or the vandalism."

"That's not fair."

He winced. "I know. I don't want to betray Shannon's trust." He rounded the counter, forced me to stand so he could wrap me in a hug. I let him. "And I don't want to betray yours either. Give me a couple of days to work it out with her and I'll tell you everything, all right?"

I nodded. "You'd better." And then, despite how crappy I was feeling about, well, everything, I added, "You can stay here tonight if you want."

He was silent for a long moment before he stepped back. "Actually, I'd better go. There's a lot I need to do, and I don't think it would help your cause any if I hung around too much. You know how John can be."

"I do." But I didn't see how having a cop around to make sure no one else broke in, or stop the stalker if he were to return, would be a bad thing.

"I'll check in tomorrow." He kissed my forehead. "Text me that website address. And anything else you might think of, all right?"

"I will."

Paul searched my eyes a moment, and then grabbed his hat. He paused halfway out the door. "What kind of tea are you making?"

I was confused as to why it mattered since he was leaving and wasn't going to be drinking it, but I answered him anyway. "Spiced chai."

His face darkened, and then he nodded and walked out the door, leaving me to wonder if somehow, my choice in tea had made things a whole lot worse.

11

A lanky kid with heavily lidded eyes that made him look like he was seconds from falling into a deep sleep entered Death by Coffee, took one look around, and then made a beeline for Mason, who'd waved him over. They shook hands and then the kid sat, legs and arms sticking out like he didn't know where to put them. He looked kind of like a character in one of those Tim Burton animated movies. *A Nightmare Before Christmas*, maybe.

Mason had spent most of the day doing interviews in the hopes of finding a couple of solid workers. I'd come into work a short time after he'd started, determined to focus on the good things in life. Buchannan would find Hamish's killer, as well as whoever had busted the Banyon Tree window. Paul and I would work things out in regard to Shannon, and we'd spend a weekend lounging around somewhere well away from distractions.

I just had to be patient.

"I can't just sit around and do nothing," I said with a huff.

"What?" Beth rounded the counter, cleaning rag in hand. We'd been busier today than we had yesterday, which was a good sign that the cockroach incident wasn't going to ruin our reputation permanently. We still weren't back to pre-roach levels, but we were getting there.

"I think I'm going a little bit stir-crazy." I rubbed at my temples, but without a headache coming on, it did little to help my agitation. "Don't mind me."

Beth carried the rag to the backroom, and then returned. "I've heard about what you've been going through. And that man who died . . ." She shook her head. "I can't believe it."

"Did you know him?"

Another head shake. "No. Well, not really. He's been in a few times before, but I never knew his name. He liked the books."

"Yeah. He asked about Dad's book when he was here."

Beth winced as if that somehow made his death worse. "He seemed like an okay guy. He was polite to me, anyway." She stared off into the distance briefly, like she was remembering a memorable encounter with Hamish, before she managed a smile. "I suppose we can't ever know what's going on in someone's life, can we?"

I wasn't so sure Hamish's murder had anything to do with his own life but nodded anyway. "Did you notice anything strange while he was here?" I asked. "Like, did he meet with someone when he left or perhaps someone acted like they knew him?"

Beth thought about it a minute before answering. "Not really. There was one guy, I guess, who watched the two of you talking, but most of us were doing the same thing since it sounded like you two were fighting, or close to it."

Which hurt to think about. "Did you know the guy? The watcher, I mean?"

"No, sorry. He was sitting at the table by the door. He took off as soon as that woman started screaming about roaches in her coffee."

Which wasn't strange in the slightest. Most of our customers had vanished when that had happened.

But I couldn't dismiss the watcher out of hand. If the guy was watching us because he was interested in Hamish, he might have been involved in the murder. It was a stretch, but at least it was something to go on.

"What did the guy look like?" I asked.

Beth considered the question before she shrugged. "Just a regular guy, I guess. He didn't stand out. He might have been wearing a hat." She frowned. "I think."

"A Reds hat?"

She spread her hands. "I'm sorry. I can't remember."

"That's all right. If you see him again let me—" A shriek from the direction of the restrooms cut me off.

A trio of teenaged boys ran from the men's room. One was giggling, while the other two were acting like they'd just walked in on a body. I was moving before Mason could so much as turn his head out in the dining area.

"What happened?" I asked, waving Mason back down when he tried to rise. Whatever it was, I *knew* it was going to have to do with me, and I wanted to keep him out of it.

One of the boys turned away without speaking, while the giggler turned red in the face. The other, a plump kid with the start of what was going to be a serious case of acne, pointed to the rest-room.

"Roaches. There's cock-a-roaches in there, lady!"

My heart sank straight down into my feet. "Where?"

"In there." He pointed again. One of his buddies snorted.

"Was anyone else in the men's room while you were there?" I asked. If there was, I was going to need to send Mason in to check on the bugs. Otherwise . . .

"Nah, was just us."

I pushed past the kids and entered the men's room. I was hit by the smell of cleaner, which, for a restroom, was a good thing. My eyes immediately found the bugs scattered across the floor. There had to be two, three dozen of them.

And none of them were moving.

I frowned and approached the nearest cock-roach. It was nearly the size of a stick of gum, but fatter. The bright restroom lights reflected off of its surface. I nudged it with my toe, and when it didn't start wiggling, I crouched down and touched it with the tip of my finger.

Plastic.

"Those little . . ." I spun and hurried out of the restroom, but the three kids were already through the door and running down the sidewalk, laughing and bumping into one another.

All eyes were on me as I emerged. Mason was standing by the table with the lanky kid still lounging with his limbs akimbo. I could see the question in Mason's eyes. And the worry.

"False alarm." I spoke loud enough for everyone to hear. "They're toy bugs. The kids were playing a prank on us."

"I'll get a broom," Beth said, turning away, just as her face broke into a grin.

I noticed Mason was smiling as well.

"It's not funny," I said, hiding my hands behind my back. They were shaking.

"It is. Kinda."

Some of the tension bled from me as I thought about it. No one was hurt, and it wouldn't mar the reputation of Death by Coffee to know it got hit by a trio of pranksters.

I took a breath and my trembling subsided. "Okay, maybe it is a little."

Mason sat back down for his interview with a chuckle. I was happy to note that no one threw away their drinks or slunk out the door because of the prank. If this was the worst that came out of the roaches from the other day, then I would take it.

Beth slipped past me with her broom and an

empty trash bag. "What do you want me to do with them?" she asked.

"Save them. If the kids come back, maybe we can get them back."

Her eyes brightened. "I'll think of something." She grinned as she entered the men's room to clean up the fake bugs.

I was on my way back to the counter when the door opened and Rita Jablonski walked through with her boyfriend, Johan Morrison, on her arm. Her eyes found me right away.

"Krissy! Just the person I was hoping to run into," she said, tugging Johan after her as she made for me.

"Rita. Johan." I nodded to each.

Johan smiled at me and that old nervousness about him returned. There was nothing sinister in the smile, but something about it bothered me. Johan seemed friendly enough. And yet, I couldn't shake the feeling that he was hiding something from not just me, but everyone else—Rita included. He had no online presence, and I knew nothing of his past, let alone who he was outside of Rita's boyfriend. He was a stranger in more ways than one, and since Rita was my friend, it made me nervous.

I continued on toward the counter, wanting to put it between us. I didn't think Johan would attack me or anything, but it felt, I don't know, safer.

"I can't believe you didn't say anything to me when we talked earlier," Rita said, following me over. She paused, and then pivoted. "I'll take a plain coffee today. Johan would like the same."

"Didn't say anything about what?" I asked as I poured the coffees.

"About the book and coffee mug, of course!" She rolled her eyes as she took her coffee. "I hear it was the JavaCon one. Why on earth would you choose to take that mug with you to that poor man's house? I mean, if you were going to give him a gift, wouldn't a Death by Coffee mug be better?"

"Wait, hold up. You heard about the mug?" So much for Buchannan keeping a tight lid on the evidence. Was this his way of putting pressure on me? If so, it was working.

"I did." Her smile was almost smug as she sipped. "I also read that the murder weapon was a teapot filled with spiced chai tea. You've started drinking that, haven't you? I can't abide it much myself. I prefer mint, or maybe Earl Grey like Johan's favorite captain drinks." She nudged him with her shoulder.

"Hot," Johan said with an affected British accent.

My entire body felt the polar opposite of hot. "He was killed with a teapot?" First my book and coffee mug. And now, my tea? If I ever questioned whether or not this was a setup, I had my answer.

"Struck right on the head. Multiple times. It must have taken some work." She gave me a pointed look, as if I was supposed to read something in the comment. "Not that this is something we should be discussing here." She glanced behind her at the people sitting at the tables. The nearest couple were watching us, not bothering to hide the fact that they were listening in.

"I had nothing to do with any of that," I said. "Those items were stolen from my house." I paused. "Not the teapot. Mine is still right where I left it."

"Well, that's good, I suppose. I was shocked when I read about it," Rita went on, ignoring her own reservations about talking about the murder in public. "Didn't someone get murdered by getting struck with a teapot years ago?"

I nodded, unable to speak. Hamish was killed the same way as another murder victim whose crime I'd solved. It made me wonder if perhaps the two incidents were connected. Could someone involved back then be targeting me now?

But the killer was behind bars, and as far as I was aware, no one held his incarceration against me. I mean, I was sure there were family out there who were unhappy, but to blame me for the killer being punished for what they did?

And then something else Rita had said struck me.

"Wait. You read about this?"

"Of course, dear. I told you about *The Eyes of the Hills*. They ran a story on it just this morning. I swear, sometimes I feel like you don't ever listen to me."

"I listen." I grabbed my phone and tuned her out as I brought up the page. Right there, front and center, was a new article: "Death by Teapot".

It was all there. Hamish beaten to death in his own home with a teapot. My book sitting at his side, two coffee mugs filled with spiced chai tea—one of them my JavaCon mug. And my name was, of course, tied to the entire shebang.

"You're not listening, are you?"

I glanced up. "How did they know about all of this?" Buchannan was supposed to have kept the details under wraps, yet here they were, online for everyone to read. While the cynical part of me wanted to blame Buchannan for leaking the information to put pressure on me, it didn't seem like something he'd do.

Before Rita could respond, the door opened and Paul Dalton walked in, dressed in his police uniform. He removed his hat when he saw us, smoothed down his hair, and then joined Rita at the counter.

"We should get going," Johan said, taking Rita by the arm. He hadn't touched his coffee.

"You're right. We best leave these two lovebirds alone." She looked Paul up and down and I could see the wheels turning behind her eyes. She had questions, and wasn't thrilled about being pulled away when many of them could be answered by sticking her nose in our business.

Yet she went at Johan's gentle urgings. As he led her from the store, he glanced back, but his smile was gone. In its place was a nervous look targeted at the police officer who'd interrupted us.

Guilty conscience? I wondered.

Paul sighed heavily and set his hat on the counter. "I have one question for you. Did you tell someone about what we discussed last night?"

"No, of course not," I said, and then spun my phone around to show him. "Remember the website I mentioned?" The one I'd completely forgotten to text him about like he'd asked. "It's all here, including some things you never told me."

He took my phone and read the article. His brow furrowed and a frown marred his features as he read. He scrolled back to the top and checked the name there, much like I had when I'd first found the site.

"Do you know who Abby Kohn is?" I asked. She, like she had all the others, had written the article.

"No idea, but I'm going to find out."

I asked him the same question I'd asked Rita, "How did she know all those details? You told me Buchannan was keeping a lot of this stuff under wraps, yet here it is."

"No clue." Paul handed back my phone. "But if you didn't tell anyone about our conversation, then—"

"She must know the killer," I finished for him.

"Or," he said, "we have a leak at the department."

That sounded more plausible. "Who would leak something like this? Why?"

"I wish I knew." Paul sighed and rubbed at his face. "John is on the warpath because of this, so he didn't say anything. He believes I told you about it and then you went around blabbing it to everyone who would listen. We didn't know about the website."

"Why would I spread this around?" I asked. "It implicates me in the crime!"

He spread his hands. "Like I said, we didn't know about the article. The phones were ringing off the hook this morning with people asking about Mr. Lauder's murder, and they kept mentioning details that weren't supposed to be public. John assumed Rita and her friends had caught wind of it, via you, and were spreading it all over town."

Which was a reasonable assumption. Anytime a rumor started spreading like wildfire, Rita was normally involved. "I didn't tell anyone," I said, just to reinforce it. "I didn't even know about the teapot or tea. You kept that from me."

A flash of pain shot across Paul's face. "I'm sorry about that. After you showed me that photo on your phone, I . . ." He trailed off and picked up his hat. "I need to get back to the station and let John know that you had nothing to do with this before he comes looking for you."

"None of it," I said. "Not just the rumors; but the murder either."

"Noted." He managed a smile and rested his hand upon my own. "And I still plan on talking to Shannon. I'll get back to you as soon as I'm sure I won't be upsetting her by talking to you about it. Hang tight, all right?"

"I'll try."

He squeezed, and then left Death by Coffee.

I sagged against the counter, head in my hands. Why was someone targeting me? Did it have to do with an old murder investigation? Was someone bitter about my involvement in the old cases? Was it something new? And while I *had* helped solve those old cases, much to the annoyance of people like Detective John Buchannan, I'd also hurt a lot of feelings along the way. I could be bullish at times, sticking my nose where it most definitely didn't belong. Did someone believe I'd learned something about them that could get them into trouble?

But was that reason enough to murder what was essentially a complete stranger to me? All to get back at me for being an occasional nuisance?

It was suddenly hard to breathe. The walls of my little bookstore café felt too close, the space behind the counter like a prison.

"I need to take a break," I said as Beth returned with a trash bag filled with plastic cockroaches. "Do you have this?"

"Yeah," she said. "You look like you need some air."

Oh, did I ever. "Thanks, Beth. I just need to clear my head. Let Mason know I'll be back soon."

I started for the door, but stopped when I realized I was still wearing my Death by Coffee apron. After that surveillance video from the Banyon Tree, I didn't think it would be a good idea to wear it out around town. As far as I knew, the video was already all over the internet and someone would take it upon themselves to arrest me for the vandalism.

Buchannan could be putting pressure on me. That had to be it, didn't it? If he truly thought I killed Hamish Lauder and busted the Banyon Tree window, he might have released the information in the hopes I'd break.

And if the pressure becomes too much for me to bear?

That's not going to happen. I balled up the apron and tossed it into the office. Krissy Hancock does *not* break.

I kept that thought firmly in mind as I left Death by Coffee, praying that I wouldn't get pushed hard enough to find out if I was right.

12

The church was as magnificent as when I'd first laid eyes on it years ago. It was the only church in all of Pine Hills as far as I was aware. While there were many denominations in town, most everyone came here when they needed to worship or to find guidance. This church turned no one away, even if other churches might have done so.

In a way, it was a lot like Pine Hills itself.

The red brick was clean, as were the large, stained glass windows. The hedges out front were meticulously trimmed so that not a single leaf or branch stuck out. The flowers along the sidewalk were in bloom, and provided a rich array of colors to anyone approaching the building.

I stood outside it, unsure I wanted to go in. I knew from experience that the interior wasn't as immaculate as the outside. It happened when a building was used for nearly every indoor event in town; weddings, group meetings, bingo, and so on. The writers group used the church for their meet-ups, and a part of me longed to return to those get-togethers. Writing did get done, but most of the meetings ended up with the local authors jabbering about their day.

But those meetings weren't until later—and were on a different day. Nor were they the reason I was there. I didn't need to test them to know the doors were unlocked. They always were. Someone was likely inside, working on setting up for the next group event or perhaps the next sermon. Would they appreciate me interrupting them?

Heels clicked on the sidewalk behind me, making up my mind for me. While I knew I'd be welcome inside, I had no reason to be there, other than to ease my mind, which I could do anywhere. I wasn't all that religious, so seeking guidance from above wasn't something I did often. But right then, I was feeling overwhelmed, and if someone *were* looking down on me, I hoped they'd step in and give me a little help navigating the mess I found myself in.

I stepped aside to let whoever had approached pass, but she'd already stopped and was staring at me.

Elsie Buchannan was a tall, thin woman, with sharp green eyes. She organized events at the church, which I supposed meant she was a member of said church, and when we'd last met, she was friendly, despite how I often clashed with her husband, Detective John Buchannan. When she smiled, she lit up the room. Well, if we were in a room, and not outside.

And if she were actually, you know, smiling.

"What are you doing here?" she asked, planting a hand on her hip. She was wearing a black, ankle-length dress, a golden cross around her neck, and black heels.

What now? From her expression and tone, she was most definitely not happy to see me. Either she followed the online news like Rita, or her husband had fed her a serious dose of anti-Krissy rhetoric. Honestly, with everything that had happened recently, I didn't blame him.

Much.

"Hi, Elsie. I was just passing by." Chipper. When she didn't respond, I went on, filling the air like a guilty person afraid of silence. "What brings you to the church?"

"Really? That's what you have to say to me?"

I blinked at her, heart sinking. Yup, someone had gotten to her too. "Whatever you heard, it's not true."

Those pretty green eyes narrowed.

"Someone has been trashing my name," I said in a near pleading tone. "They've been telling lies about me, causing trouble and making it look like I was responsible for it."

"Why would someone do that?"

"I wish I knew. The police have evidence that points to me as the culprit in more than one crime, but I swear, I didn't do any of it. Whatever Buchannan told you—"

"Nothing. He keeps his job separate from his home life."

Then that meant . . . "What happened?"

Elsie studied me for a long moment before

some of the tension bled from her shoulders. Her hand remained on her hip, but at least now she wasn't staring daggers at me.

"I received an email from you just this morning. Suffice it to say, it wasn't pleasant. When I saw you standing there, I thought you'd come to reinforce what you'd said in person."

"I didn't send any emails; to you, or anyone else."

She stared at me for a long couple of seconds before she nodded slowly. "I don't know why, but I believe you. It didn't seem like something you'd do." She paused. "I would steer clear of John until I can talk to him, however. I told him about the email, and he wasn't very happy about it."

Uh-oh. Considering he was already annoyed—and suspicious—that could be a problem. "What did the email say?"

"That John needs to drop his investigation. You—I mean, whoever sent it—claimed that if he didn't, he would end up with a pen through the eye and would be left where the hedges die. Whatever that means."

I got it immediately. "Ted and Bettfast." Ted and Bett Bunford ran a bed and breakfast out of an old mansion they'd purchased years ago. Age and a lack of funds had caused repairs to slow in recent years, and the hedge animals out front were overgrown where they weren't outright dead.

And the place was connected to a murder or two, and by association, me.

"I see. And how on Earth would you know that?" Elsie asked.

"The animal hedges there are dying, and that whole bit about the pen . . ." I felt myself pale. "Someone was murdered that way in Ted and Bettfast." Someone who was close to my dad. I wondered if that was a warning meant for me, as much as it was to Buchannan. "Was my name actually *on* the email?"

"Well, no, but it was implied. The sender used the name, *KHDbC*, which John assumed was—"

I finished for her, "Krissy Hancock, Death by Coffee."

She nodded. "He was prepared to hunt for you right away and arrest you on the spot, but I talked him down." Finally, the hand left her hip. "Why would someone do this? It doesn't make sense."

"I wish I knew." But I was getting an idea. Everything tied back to my past, which might mean that someone from my past was responsible. "Did the email say anything else? Something that might indicate who'd really sent it?"

"No, just the warning." Elsie stepped closer to me. "What have you gotten yourself into, Krissy? John thinks you might have had something to do with a murder. He might not talk about his job, but I see the reports, hear him talking on the phone when he thinks he's alone."

"Someone is setting me up. I'm going to find out who." And why.

"That might not be such a good idea." Elsie glanced at her watch, which was a tiny thing that looked more like a bracelet than something that had a function. "I really need to get inside." She put a hand on my shoulder and looked directly into my eyes. "Keep your head down, Krissy. John is determined to solve this, and if you get in the way, whether you're guilty or not, you could end up in some serious hot water."

I wasn't so sure things could get much worse, and almost said so. *Don't tempt fate, Krissy . . .*

"I'll be careful," I said.

Elsie gave me a sharp nod, and then headed for the church doors. She paused just before going inside. "Sometimes it's better to let others do their jobs, even though it is often hard to walk away when our reputation is on the line."

And then she was gone.

I huffed out a breath. Sitting back and letting a detective investigate me wasn't something I was keen on doing. Paul repeatedly told me that Buchannan was good at his job, but the detective targeted me so often, it was hard to believe he would do the right thing now. Too much evidence pointed my way. The video. The email. The online posts. The actual evidence found in a murder victim's house. It was a wonder I wasn't already sitting in a jail cell, awaiting trial.

Maybe laying low would be the smart thing to do.

I turned to head back to Death by Coffee to do just that when I caught sight of a head of curly brown hair, hurrying down the sidewalk away from me. My breath caught and my heart leapt into my throat.

Could it be my stalker? Had he been watching me as I stood outside the church? If he'd sent the email, he might have been checking up on me to see how Elsie would react. How he'd know we'd run into each other wasn't clear. I wondered which of us he had been following and if he'd gotten what he'd wanted.

There was only one way to find out.

I hurried after him, but instead of calling out, I decided to see where he went. If he could follow me around town, then I could do the same darn thing.

The sidewalk wasn't too busy, so it was easy to keep track of Curly Hair, even though he was a good ways ahead of me by now. He wasn't wearing a Reds hat today, but was instead wearing a pair of gray sweats and a loose T-shirt along with sneakers that hid much of his shape. It was a change, sure, but it wasn't much of a disguise. If I could get a good look at his face, then I'd be able to describe him to Buchannan. *Or know who to look for the next time he appeared.*

We passed by Phantastic Candies, and I started to wonder if he would keep walking until I ran out of steam. I was admittedly poor when it came to keeping in shape, and walking long distances like this wasn't something I did, well, ever. By the time he slowed, I was panting and sweating like I'd run three miles.

Curly Hair never once looked back. He checked his wrist, which was bare, and then, with what appeared to be a frustrated huff, he turned into a shop, vanishing inside. I took a moment to catch my breath before I approached.

"You've got to be kidding me," I muttered, noting the name of the place. I'd been there before.

Too Le Fit to Quit was a fitness shop that catered to those with a penchant for exercise. I'd never actually shopped there, but I knew one of the employees. A murder that had happened years ago had brought me here once.

And, apparently, my stalker was doing that now.

I pushed through the doors and entered a world of supplements and yoga mats. I swear there were more pill bottles stacked by the door than what could be found at the local pharmacy. These pills promised to cut fat, create muscle, and turn your body into something to be worshipped. The men and women on the labels were made of nothing *but* muscle. The sight of them made me feel like a blob.

There wasn't a lot of people inside Too Le Fit. A couple stood by one wall, perusing hand weights, while an employee hovered not too far away, waiting for the moment when he could pounce and make the sale. A child of about ten was playing with a jump rope a few feet from them. I assumed she belonged to the couple.

And across the room, standing by a rack of stretchy bands, back to me, was Curly Hair.

"Got ya." I took a step toward him, just as he turned to look at another rack, giving me my first good look at his face. Or should I say, *her* face. She had a cleft chin, and her hair was done up much like Sigourney Weaver's in *Alien*, which was to say, wasn't masculine at all.

The woman found a band she liked, and then she made her way over toward a wall filled with fitness watches. She never once glanced my way since she wasn't interested in me in the slightest. She never had been. This wasn't my Reds hat-wearing stalker.

I felt like an idiot. I couldn't spend my life chasing after every curly-haired person I met, yet here I was.

Even though no one else knew I'd just tracked an innocent woman halfway across town, I wanted to sink through the floor and vanish. But since I was there and didn't want to appear as if I'd wandered in accidentally, I crossed the store to look at some ankle weights I'd never buy.

"Krissy?" I jumped at the sound of my name. When I turned, I found Heidi Lawyer approaching, an inquisitive expression on her face. She was wearing her work outfit, which was basically the same thing as workout attire, though it looked less functional than it was revealing—without actually revealing anything. Every curve and dimple could be seen through the lightweight cloth. It made me embarrassed for Heidi every time I saw her in it.

"Heidi," I said, fighting down the urge to squeak it. "It's good to see you."

She looked confused for a moment before she managed to smile. "What are you doing here?" she asked, coming to a stop next to me. "I didn't think you worked out."

"I don't," I admitted. "But I've been thinking of starting up." And had been thinking about it for the last couple of years with no actual progress in doing so.

"Well, I wouldn't start here," she said, motioning toward the weights which had numbers on them that seemed a little high. Who'd wear twenty-pound weights on their ankles? "I suppose it couldn't hurt, but if you're just starting out, you

DEATH BY SPICED CHAI   141

might want to start with the lighter weights over
here." She sounded almost apologetic as she motioned toward another shelf. The numbers there
were in the low single digits. "Maybe a fitness watch
might be a good idea." She turned toward the
watches, which was still being perused by the woman
I'd followed.

"No, that's all right." And then, because I desperately wanted to change the subject, I said, "I
heard you had a new boyfriend."

Heidi's entire demeanor instantly changed.
Gone was the saleswoman and acquaintance, and
in its place was someone who wanted to be anywhere else but there.

"I do." She looked away as she said it.

"Are you happy?" When she didn't respond, I
moved so she was forced to look at me. "Heidi, is
everything okay?" And then, because my concern
might not be enough, I added, "Mason's worried."

That brought a smile to her face, albeit a small
one. "Mason is always worried. It's sweet."

"He looks out for you."

"I know." She sighed. "It's just . . . I don't know.
I'm happy, but my boyfriend can be overbearing at
times."

"Overbearing how?"

Her eyes darted around the room before settling on the customer by the watches. "He likes to
keep tabs on me. If someone were to be rude to
me, he'd fly off the handle, make a scene. We were
having dinner last week and some guy bumped
into me as I was sitting down, and he started yell-
ing at the guy as if he did it on purpose."

"It sounds like he's protective of you." Albeit too protective. There's a fine line between protectiveness and controlling.

"I guess. It's frustrating at times. He's great and all, but he thinks I walk on water and should be worshipped as such. While that's nice every now and again, sometimes I just want to be me without worrying that if I talk to the wrong person, he might take it the wrong way."

"He's jealous?"

She made a face and wobbled her hand back and forth. *So-so.* "He doesn't think I'd ever cheat, but . . ."

The door opened, drawing both our eyes. The woman who walked in froze midstride when she saw us staring at her. Heidi opened her mouth to say something, but the woman spun on her heel and scurried away without a word.

"That was strange," Heidi said, brow furrowing. Before I could explain it to her, however, the curly-haired woman headed for the counter, fitness watch in hand. "I've got to get to work. It was nice seeing you, Krissy. Tell Mason I'm fine, all right?"

"I will."

"And . . . thanks for your concern." She flashed me a smile, and then hurried over to the counter to help the woman check out.

I left Too Le Fit to Quit feeling strangely unsettled. I checked both ways in the hopes of spotting the woman who'd left so abruptly, but she was already out of sight. It was the same woman who'd found the roaches in Death by Coffee, and I'd hoped to let her know that the bug problem was a thing of the past, and that if she wanted a free week of coffee, she could have it.

But it appeared that would have to wait. The woman was already long out of sight. It was as if she were afraid the roaches had followed me all the way to Too Le Fit to Quit and she'd fled as fast as her legs would take her.

Besides, I needed to get back to the bookstore café. I'd had a chance to clear my head, and while I wasn't completely settled, I *was* feeling a little bit better. I couldn't leave Mason and Beth alone to handle the store. Perhaps our luck was about to change and I'd walk in on a rush of customers filling Death by Coffee to the brim.

I put on my mental walking shoes and started the long trek back to work, where I belonged.

13

"It's going to take days to clean it all up, maybe weeks. I'm not sure they'll be able to get it done in time."

"Do you think they'll cancel?" Mason had a hand on Vicki's shoulder. Every few moments he would squeeze.

"I don't know. From her tone, I think Angela is considering it."

"What's going on?" I asked, joining them behind the counter. Only a few customers were in the dining area of Death by Coffee, but no one was paying the couple any mind, despite Vicki's agitated state.

"The theatre . . ." Vicki heaved a sigh, and couldn't seem to go on, so I looked to Mason.

"Someone made a mess of the stage," he said.

"A mess?" Vicki laughed. She sounded near hysterics. "The sandbags were all cut down, then slashed open. Pumpkins were smashed across the seats. And eggnog was smeared all over the curtains and left overnight to spoil."

"Eggnog?" I asked, nose scrunching. The smell had to be awful. "Are they sure?"

"As sure as they can be. I guess a thermos of the stuff had been left in the middle of the stage. I can't imagine what the place must look like."

"You haven't been to the theatre?"

"Not yet." She sighed again and rubbed at her forehead. "Angela called the cast and told us that practice is canceled tonight. It sounded as if she has an idea who made a mess of the stage, but she didn't fill me in. Clearly, she's not happy, and I felt . . ." She frowned. "I guess I felt targeted by her anger. She snapped at me before she hung up."

My mind immediately went to the rivalry between the director of the play and the lead actress, Nina. Could something have happened between them? Something that Vicki triggered when she'd mentioned her dissatisfaction with Nina's performance? I hoped that was it because I really didn't want to consider the alternative.

"I know what you're thinking," Vicki said, eyeing me. She always could read my thoughts as if I'd spoken out loud.

"And?"

"And I honestly don't know. It's not like Angela fired her, so Nina has no reason to cause trouble like this."

"Maybe she realized she wasn't working out and didn't want to lose the role to you." Mason said with a nudge to Vicki's shoulder. "So, she destroys the stage so no one can have it. Can't get fired if there's no play to be fired from."

"Maybe. But I doubt it. Nina is pretty self-absorbed. I'm not sure she even realizes the rest of us think she's underperforming." She closed her eyes, brow scrunching as if she was in pain. "I was really looking forward to this play and now . . ."

I felt bad for Vicki. She loved the theatre, especially small plays such as this. And I had a sinking feeling that this latest disaster was going to end up being my fault.

"You said eggnog?" I made it a question. "And it was in a thermos?"

"Yeah."

"And there were smashed pumpkins? And cut sandbags?"

She nodded, and then paled, catching the connection. "Wait. You don't think . . ."

"I'm not sure what I think." But all of those things sounded awfully familiar. If this were an isolated incident, I could play it off as a coincidence. After everything else that had happened, however . . .

A pattern was forming. French roast coffee at the Banyon Tree. Smashed pumpkins. Eggnog in a thermos. The threat of a pen through the eye. The JavaCon mug. The dented teapot. I could go on and on.

Every one of those incidents and threats connected back to murders I'd solved.

"Do you need to sit down?" Mason asked, moving toward me as if he thought he might need to catch me if I fainted.

I shook my head, but leaned against the counter for support anyway. Someone was targeting me. If

I had any doubts about that before, the destruction of the stage sealed it.

But why mess with the play? I had nothing to do with it. And the only play I'd ever been in had been ages ago, and I'd only filled in because of Rita. It wasn't like I was an actress who did this sort of thing for a living.

But Vicki is my friend. And whoever was doing this, wasn't targeting me directly.

They were going after the people and places around me.

"I need to go," I said, straightening. I might have wanted to get working again, but Death by Coffee was slow, and there was something else I needed to do. "If you two have this, that is?"

"Go. We'll be fine."

I rested a hand on Vicki's upper arm. "I'll get to the bottom of this."

"I know you will."

I left Death by Coffee, worried I'd just made a promise I wouldn't be able to keep. So far, I'd learned almost nothing about whoever was causing all the trouble in town, and the longer it went on, and the more it kept leading back to me, the more likely it would be that Buchannan would show up and arrest me for one of the myriad of crimes I was being framed for.

I could have walked to the theatre, but since I'd already done my fair share of walking for the day, I decided to drive. If I was right and the saboteur had it in for me, I had a feeling I wouldn't be welcome when I arrived, and might want to make a quick getaway. I wondered what "evidence" would be found that tied the vandalism to me, beyond the callbacks to the old murders. Another one of my dad's books? My fingernail clippings? At this point, nothing would surprise me.

There were only two cars in the parking lot when I arrived at the theatre. One of them was Angela's. The other I knew all too well.

I parked next to the familiar car and then headed for the side door, which was propped open. As soon as I neared, the pungent scent of spoiled eggnog hit me. It was really bad, and I could only imagine how much worse it must have been with the place closed up tight for the night. The vandal had to have used gallons of the stuff. At least the building had a chance to air out a little, so I was only getting a fraction of the stench.

Still, it was bad enough that I held a hand over my nose and mouth as I stepped inside.

The theatre was much nicer than the last—barring the smell and mess Vicki had mentioned, of course. There were designated spaces for props, racks and hangers for costumes. An open door gave me a glimpse into a room that looked a lot like a break room. I could see a microwave and a long table, where I imagined the cast would break for a snack after long practice sessions. I couldn't see the stage, or the seats, from here.

Voices reached me and I followed them to the front. The curtains were closed, and I could see dark splotches on the thick red fabric. The closer I got to the stage, the worse it smelled. It was all I could do to keep from gagging.

"This is going to cost thousands of dollars." A

woman's voice. Angela, I supposed, considering it was her car in the lot. "And without a play, we're going to struggle to make enough money to pay for the cleaning. But if we don't clean this up, we can't have a play."

"I understand." Paul sounded stressed, and it was no wonder. The police had been pretty busy recently. "You're sure the cameras didn't pick anything up?"

"I checked them twice. No one approached the theatre. No one was inside. And then the cameras cut out. All of them. At once. You can't tell me that's a coincidence."

I went around the curtains, taking a side door, rather than stepping up onto the stage and risk touching the spoiled eggnog. Paul and Angela were standing on the stage. Paul was scanning the mess—and it was a mess. Sand—or whatever was in those sandbags—made the stage appear as if it were set for a desert scene. Wet clumps of it piled up near the curtains where eggnog had run down into it. To my right, pumpkin guts were strewn across nearly every seat. Whoever had done this must have brought a dozen pumpkins with them. Maybe twice that.

"You!" Angela noticed me first. She jabbed a finger my way. "It was you, wasn't it?"

Paul turned and he immediately grimaced when he saw me. "Krissy? What are you doing here?"

"I heard about what happened," I said. I eyed the stairs, but decided not to join them on the stage. Angela appeared angry enough to toss me right back off of it. "Vicki told me."

Angela started to say something, but Paul raised a hand, cutting her off. She glared at him, before turning her angry stare on me.

"Let's talk." Paul clomped down the stairs, and took me by the arm. He led me down the aisle a short distance, stepping carefully over pumpkin guts as he went. "Okay," he said, once we were out of earshot. "Let me hear it." He crossed his arms.

"Hear what?"

"I know you didn't come down here because you were concerned about the play. You know something."

I mirrored his stance. "And how do you know that? Vicki *is* my friend. And she's upset. I want to help."

Paul must have realized how standoffish he looked, because his arms dropped to his side. "Then tell me anything you know about what happened here."

"All of this." I spread my arms to encompass the room. "It's meant for me."

"How so?"

"The pumpkins. Remember that Halloween party we both went to? The one where that woman died?"

He frowned. "How could I forget."

"Well . . ." I pointed toward a smashed pumpkin. "And the eggnog ties back to the Christmas play I was in before it was canceled, as do the sandbags. I was almost killed by one of them. Did I tell you that?"

Of course, it made me wonder if the person who'd destroyed the theatre had something to do with the Christmas play. Who else would know about the sandbag nearly falling on my head?

I had a brief thought that the old theatre's owner might have decided to get revenge on the new theatre, but that seemed a tad farfetched. As far as I knew, the old owner had left town, moving on to greener pastures or some such nonsense.

"So, this is a setup?"

"It has to be. All of it. Someone is going to great lengths to make me look bad."

"Yeah, but why?" Paul sounded skeptical. "Does this have to do with the murder? Should I call John in?"

I almost blurted, "No!" but reconsidered. "Probably. I think it's all one case."

Paul pinched the bridge of his nose. "Great." He looked back toward the stage, and then lowered his voice. "What can you tell me about this?" He produced a baggie with a single sheet of paper in it.

I took it and squinted through the plastic. I recognized it immediately. "That's my stationery."

"I figured as much."

The Death by Coffee logo was at the top of the page. The writing below it was printed carefully, as if to disguise who had written it.

Nina is not *lead material. Vicki Lawyer is your only option, and unless she is given the lead role, your play will be put on permanent hiatus. This is your first and only warning.*

K.

K, as in Krissy. Of course.

"I didn't write this."

"I didn't figure you did, but it doesn't look good. Who has access to this paper?" He took the baggie back.

"Me. Everyone who works at Death by Coffee."

"And?"

I shrugged. "That's it as far as I'm aware. We just got the stationery in and I've only ever used it to scribble notes to myself."

"You don't lend it out for other people to use?"

"I haven't." I paused. "I did hand one page out to a woman who was curious about Dad's books, but she's not responsible for this."

"You're positive about that?"

"Not unless you think a little old lady has a vendetta against the theatre."

He sighed. "So, no one else has access?"

"I can't speak for anyone else at the store, but I haven't been handing it out. But it's not like it's behind lock and key or anything. Anyone could have snuck behind the counter and grabbed a sheet."

He nodded as if that was exactly what he expected. "All right. I'm going to call John. I don't think you'll want to be here when he arrives."

"No kidding." Buchannan would likely arrest me on the spot.

"I'll stop by Death by Coffee and ask around about the page. I don't want you getting involved, so don't say anything to anyone." When I opened my mouth to protest, he held up a finger. "I mean it, Krissy. If you go snooping around, asking questions, John is going to bust a gasket."

"I hear you." But I so didn't like it. Someone was

out to sabotage *me* and I was supposed to sit on my hands and do nothing?

"If you think of anything that might help, call me. I'll pass word on to John." He took in the seats and the pumpkins smashed over them. "And I'll smooth this over with him. As long as you keep your head down, this won't come back on you."

He waited until I promised to be a good girl before he returned to the stage. I was nearly to the side door when Angela caught up with me.

"I was told all about you, you know."

I turned to face her, resigned. "Don't believe everything you hear."

"Are you saying you had nothing to do with this?"

"That's exactly what I'm saying. Who have you talked to about me?"

She shrugged. "You hear things here and there. And you . . ." She shook her head. "I couldn't even escape your name during the interview."

"Interview? What interview?"

"About the play." Angela frowned, which caused every line in her face to deepen. It made me wonder if she was older than she'd first appeared. "I was asked if I knew what caused the last theatre to be shut down."

"I had nothing to do with that." Sure, someone had died, and I'd been involved in the investigation—and the play that year—but it wasn't the reason the new theatre had been built, nor was the murder the reason the old theatre had been closed. That was all on the owner and his refusal to put any money into it.

"Yeah, well, she was pretty insistent. Told me to watch out for you, that you'd make everything all about you." She glanced back toward the stage, where I imagined Paul was making his call to Buchannan. "And then this happens."

"You said she," I said, not missing the reference. "Did she give you a name? What did she look like?"

Angela turned back to me. "She did, but I never saw her. It was a phone interview with Abby Kohn for her online paper, *The Eyes of the Hills.*"

14

Abby Kohn.
Who was she? What made her start her online paper? Do we have mutual friends? Enemies? What's her real name?

And, most importantly; why does she hate me so darn much?

I spent far too long sitting at my table, scrolling through Abby's online stories. Not everything was about me, of course, but far too many of the stories took pot shots at me, even when I wasn't involved in whatever she was writing about. It was like I was stuck in her head, and no matter what it was she wanted to discuss, my name insisted on popping up.

But why?

Nothing I read gave me any hint as to who Abby was. She put nothing personal in the articles, no clue as to where she lived, if she had family, or if she was alone and angry at the world. I couldn't tell if she was young or old, or if she was even a woman at all, though Angela's phone conversation proved that well enough.

I thought of the woman I'd followed to Too Le Fit to Quit. I'd mistaken her for the curly-haired man who'd followed Vicki and me. Could it be possible that the man and this Abby Kohn were related, and that I'd been right and the woman *had* been following me? Could I have mistaken Reds Hat for a man, when in reality, *he* was a *she*?

I rose from my table with a popping of knees and a sharp crack from my back. I waddled over to the window, shaking out my tired joints, and peered outside. When I'd come home, Caitlin's car hadn't been in her driveway. One look told me that it was still the case.

Is she out there now, doing something else that will be blamed on me?

It was hard not to think of my neighbor as a suspect. She hadn't liked me from the start, and she had a connection to one of the murders I'd helped solve. And then there was the camera, and the curly-haired man in the photograph by her bed, and the online posts where she'd said that "someone would pay for what she did." Was I that someone?

Misfit rubbed up against my leg, and then fell over onto his side with a huff. He remained lying there for a couple of seconds before he glanced up to make sure I'd noticed his sudden weakness.

"All right," I said, giving him a quick belly rub. His body snapped closed, claws at the ready, but I'd removed my hand before the trap could spring. "I'll feed you."

As soon as I took a step toward the kitchen, he popped up and rushed ahead of me, completely cured of his weakened state. I fed him and then wandered back over to my laptop. *The Eyes of the Hills* site was still up, but I was in no mood to keep reading. There was nothing in it that would help me anyway.

I closed the page and then stared at my laptop, not quite sure what to do with myself. I couldn't just sit around and wait for Buchannan to show up and arrest me. Evidence was piling up against me, and while someone like a police detective *should* see that it was an obvious setup, that doesn't mean they *would* see it that way.

But what could I do about it that wouldn't get me into more trouble than I was already in?

I mentally sifted through what I knew, looking for some sort of direction. The theatre sabotage, the Banyon Tree window, the post about the library. They were all attempts to mar my name through places I had a connection to.

But in all those attempts, no one was physically injured.

Hamish Lauder, however, was.

Could everything else be a distraction from the murder?

Whoever had killed Hamish, had left some of my items at the scene. They had to have known about his desire for a signed copy of Dad's book. They also knew I'd taken to drinking spiced chai tea, though that could have been a coincidence. I doubted it, considering everything else, but I couldn't just assume that it was connected.

So, what did I have? A murder with evidence

pointing to me. The killer had to have overheard Hamish asking me about Dad's book, or Hamish himself had to have told them. If I was merely a convenient target, then the killer—and, quite possibly, the person trashing my name—must have been someone close to Hamish himself.

I couldn't go to Hamish's house and poke around. I mean, I *could*, but if Buchannan caught me breaking into a murdered man's house, he'd have me sitting in a jail cell before I could blink. I could talk to Hamish's neighbors and find out what they might have seen or heard, or instead . . .

I brought up a search engine and typed in a name I'd recently come across in connection with Hamish Lauder. In seconds, I had a phone number and address. I wrote them down, closed my laptop, and then was out the door.

Calling ahead would be the polite thing to do, but I didn't want my quarry to rabbit on me. Or, if they were involved in the murder, be prepared for my sudden appearance. So, instead, I typed out a text to Paul, complete with phone number, address, and time, but didn't send it to him quite yet. I saved the draft, and if I were to be attacked, I could hit "send" and he'd know what happened to me.

Paranoid? Maybe. But with the way my life had been going lately, I'd say it was warranted.

I pulled into a paved driveway a short time later. The house was a cute ranch, with a half dozen windchimes hanging from the front patio. A handful of birdfeeders peppered the yard. As I came to a stop, the sky filled with bright feathers as the birds who'd come to eat scattered.

A man stood from his seat on the patio. He wore a sunhat, though the sun was going down, a pair of flip-flops, and light-tan slacks paired with a flower print button-up shirt. He shaded his eyes and squinted at me, despite the hat and lack of bright sun.

"Mark Cunningham?" I asked. My voice was accompanied by the tinkle of the chimes as a breeze picked up briefly before calming.

"Yes?"

"My name is Krissy Hancock." I strode toward him and extended a hand. "I was hoping we could talk."

We shook, and then he removed his hat briefly to scratch his head. I took note that he was balding, and unless he'd once had a perm, he'd never had a curly hair in his life.

"About?" He frowned as he replaced his hat. "I'm not interested in whatever you have to sell."

"Oh, no, I'm not trying to sell you anything." I flashed him a reassuring smile that likely had the opposite effect than what I'd intended. "I was hoping we could talk about Hamish."

Mark deflated. "Oh." He eased down into the wicker chair behind him. "I thought you might be from that power company that's always trying to get me to show them my bill so they could sign me up for their program."

"I'm most definitely not trying to scam you," I said.

"I get that now." He motioned toward another wicker chair across from him. "Please, sit. There's lemonade on the table if you'd like some. I come out here to unwind, usually with a book." His smile was sad. "But I couldn't read, not after what happened, so I didn't bother bringing one out."

A trio of upside-down glasses sat next to the lemonade, which had ice floating in it to keep it cool. I took one and filled it halfway.

"Thank you," I said, taking a polite sip. The lemonade was a tad bitter, but was good nonetheless.

"My wife made it. She's lying down right now. What happened to Hamish . . ." He shook his head. "It was hard on the both of us."

"You were friends?"

"We were. Hamish kept to himself mostly, but my wife and I were part of his trusted circle, as he called us. If it wasn't one of us with him, he'd normally be alone. He liked it that way since most people got on his nerves. They tended to talk when he was trying to enjoy his meal, or would distract him from whatever he found important that day— often a good book."

"Hamish didn't like people?" I asked.

"Oh, he liked people well enough," Mark said. "But he'd had some troubles with friends in his past. They turned on him, I guess. These days, he liked to keep most people at arm's length, just so it wouldn't happen again."

"Turned on him? How?"

Mark leaned back, eyes drifting toward the birdfeeders. The birds had returned and were picking out the seed, with one little guy tossing them onto the ground where his friends gobbled them up. "I don't know the details since it happened before we became friends, but Hamish never really got over it. He didn't like to talk about himself, and since it was obviously painful for him, I didn't pry."

"Do you know why someone would want to kill him?" I wondered if those old friends, and whatever had happened between them, might be responsible, though I was still uncertain how it could possibly tie back to me.

Mark shook his head. "Hamish wasn't a bad man. He kept to himself, yes, and while he could be off-putting at times, it was often an act so people would leave him alone."

"When was the last time you saw him?"

"A week ago, maybe? He'd been keeping to himself more than usual over the last few weeks, but I'd talked him into meeting me for a late lunch. We made plans to meet up again a few days later, but . . . I . . . he . . ." Mark took a shuddering breath. "We were supposed to meet on the day he died."

He looked away and dabbed at his eyes.

My heart broke as Mark fought to keep control of his emotions. It was clear he'd really liked Hamish. Could this be an act to throw me off? I supposed, but I found it unlikely. Mark seemed genuinely broken up about his friend's death.

"I'm sorry," I said. "This has to be hard."

"It is." He sniffed and managed a weak, sad smile. "I keep thinking that maybe I could have done something. We were supposed to meet, and when he didn't show, I figured he'd blown me off like he sometimes did when he was feeling less than social. I ate without him, and then went on with my day like usual."

A bird hopped over toward us, regarded Mark a moment, and then returned to the feeder. I wondered if the birds knew Mark was the one who provided the feed and if they were curious as to why he was so sad.

"It wasn't until later when I realized how unsettled I was," he went on. "I kept thinking that something was wrong, something I couldn't put my finger on. I eventually couldn't take it any longer and called Hamish, thinking that talking to him would ease my mind."

"He didn't answer." Which would have had the opposite effect.

"Oh, no; Hamish answered the phone."

That caught me by surprise. "He was at home?"

Mark nodded, eyes growing distant once more. "He apologized for standing me up, but said something had come up and he'd forgotten to let me know he wasn't going to make it. He'd done it before, so it really wasn't much of a surprise, to be honest."

"Do you know what it was that came up?"

"No idea. He seemed distracted, as if he was only half listening to me. I tried to engage him, but I quickly realized I wasn't getting through to him and ended the call."

My mind was racing. Hamish was alive later into the evening than I'd assumed. Since he hadn't posted about his encounter at Death by Coffee, and hadn't shown up for his lunch date with Mark, I'd thought he'd been murdered sometime within that window.

But if what Mark said was true, Hamish was still

alive hours after he'd left my store. Distracted, yes, but alive.

"What time was this?" I asked. "When you called, I mean?"

Mark thought about it a moment. "I'd say it had to have been close to six, maybe a little later. I didn't look at the clock."

If Hamish was alive that late, what did that mean for me? Buchannan had specifically asked about my whereabouts just after my date with Paul, but this had happened before. I assumed that meant they had an approximate time of death. Was there evidence Buchannan was holding back, something Paul didn't know, or hadn't told me?

Before I could ask Mark if he'd talked to the police yet, he went on.

"The whole series of events was strange," he said. "Not Hamish blowing me off. Like I said, he did that often enough; so much so, I wasn't even offended by it."

"But?"

"But when I called him, he wasn't alone."

A cold chill seeped through me. Had Mark called while Hamish's killer was in the room? Or could there be a witness out there? Someone who knew what really happened that night?

Someone who could clear my name.

"Really?" I asked, taking a sip of lemonade to moisten my suddenly dry mouth. "He had company? Like a girlfriend?"

"I can't say for sure," Mark said, "but Hamish wasn't in a relationship as far as I was aware. He didn't have interests of that sort. My wife and I had tried to set him up with dates, but he steadfastly refused, claiming he was perfectly happy alone. And, honestly, I believed him."

"But he wasn't?"

Mark shrugged. "It's hard for me to know for sure. I'd have sworn he was content, but since someone was with him, at his house, I could only assume they were close."

"Do you know who it was?"

Mark looked down at his hands, which were trembling. "No. I don't think I've ever heard the voice before."

"You heard a voice?" My excitement spiked. If he could place that voice, or describe it well enough so that maybe *I* could place it, then perhaps Hamish's killer could be caught.

Mark removed his hat and focused on it, as if searching for answers there. "It was faint, like it came from another room. And I suppose it could have been the television, though Hamish wasn't one to watch TV. He always preferred reading. The TV only ever came on when he couldn't sleep, but his eyes were too tired to read. We used to talk about it . . ." He trailed off, squeezing his eyes shut against more tears.

I waited him out. A voice wasn't evidence, but it was *something*. It might help Buchannan turn his attention elsewhere, toward the real killer, and not me. It might help narrow the time of death. Even if his guest wasn't Hamish's killer, they could have seen something, or perhaps heard something important. If Hamish feared for his life, he might have let it slip, along with who he was afraid of.

Mark took a deep breath to center himself before setting his hat aside. "It was a woman's voice."

My heart leapt. "A woman?" *Please don't say it was my voice. Please don't say it was my voice . . .*

"It was faint, like I said, but I'm pretty sure it was a woman I heard in the background. It was quick, like she was angry about something and had raised her voice." Mark looked toward the birds, just as something spooked them and caused them all to take to the skies in a flurry of wings and chirps. "And I believe someone else answered her."

15

At least two people were involved in what happened to Hamish Lauder. I'd suspected as much, considering how I was almost positive my stalker was male and the person in the Banyon Tree video was female, yet it was good to have it confirmed by what Mark overheard.

And, yes, it was entirely possible Hamish had guests over who had nothing to do with his death. But for now, I was willing to run on the assumption that the woman Mark heard speaking was indeed Hamish's killer—or an accessory to such.

I left Mark a short time after his revelation when it became clear he had nothing else for me. I found it strange Buchannan had yet to talk to Mark, so I made him promise to contact the detective and tell him everything he'd told me—leaving out my name, of course. No sense in giving Buchannan more ammunition against me.

A gloom hung over me as I made my way back

home. What if I were right and the murder had nothing to do with me? What if I was just a convenient patsy and Hamish's private life was where the real evidence could be found?

If that were the case, I'd been going at this all wrong. Could the killer have created chaos in order to hide their real motive? It made far more sense than someone committing a murder just to make me look bad.

But who would do such a thing? I knew practically nothing about Hamish Lauder. There had to be a connection somewhere, something more than his being a reader of my dad's books. I just had to find it.

My mind drifted in a new direction. There was a new person in my life, someone I knew just as little about as I did Hamish Lauder.

Caitlin Blevins.

She had a problem with me, thanks to a murder I'd solved that involved one of her relatives. There was the curly-haired man in the photograph. The camera pointing toward my house. Her online post about making someone—a she, in fact—pay. That was a lot of little connections for one person *not* to be involved in some way.

As I turned onto my street, I was happy to note a light was on in Caitlin's house, and her car was in the driveway. It was time we had a little talk, and this time, I wasn't going to walk away until I got some answers.

I parked in my own driveway and walked across the yard to Caitlin's property. A wail, followed by what I could only describe as an explosion of discordant notes, boomed from Caitlin's house. Someone screamed something completely unintelligible, and a blast of drumbeats interrupted the guitar, before it all came to an abrupt halt. Three heartbeats later, it started up again.

I approached the door, almost expecting it to come flying off its hinges as another failed guitar solo echoed throughout the neighborhood. There was a very unladylike curse from inside, and the whole thing came to another crashing halt. I took the brief lull in sound to knock.

"Caitlin?" I called when she didn't answer. "It's Krissy. From next door." I waited a beat, and when she still didn't respond, I added, "I was hoping we could talk."

The door jerked open with a little too much force. Caitlin was wearing a black tank top and shorts that clung to her in a way that spoke of vigorous exercise. Sweat beaded her brow, and she was rubbing at her left wrist as if it pained her. "What do you want?"

I glanced past her, expecting to find an entire band lounging in her living room, but she appeared to be alone. "I'm not interrupting, am I?"

"Kind of. I'm practicing."

"With?"

"*Rocksmith.*"

I stared at her.

Caitlin heaved a sigh and wiped a hand across her forehead. "It's a game. It teaches you how to play guitar."

I had to take her word for it, and since hers was the only car in the driveway, I assumed she was telling the truth. "Been playing long?" I asked.

Caitlin scowled at me and repeated her earlier question. "What do you want?"

So much for small talk. "I was hoping we could, I don't know, get to know one another better," I said. "We *are* neighbors, and I figured it we should at least try to get along."

The scowl continued unabated. "We've gone through this already. I just want to practice before it gets too late."

"And you can." Though I hoped she'd turn down the volume a tad before she started up again. I had a feeling poor Misfit was hiding under the bed, wondering if the world was about to come to a screeching, banging end. "I just want a minute of your time." I took a step toward her, hoping she'd step aside to let me past.

She didn't budge.

Okay then. We could talk outside. "I happened to notice something the other day," I said, trying to sound as innocent as I possibly could. "There's a photograph in your room, right beside the bed."

"There is." Her eyes narrowed. "Which you only saw because you were snooping around my house."

"I'm truly sorry about that." And I was. Sometimes, it takes common sense a few minutes to catch up to my brain. "I was curious. You know how it is. New, mysterious neighbor." I tried on a smile, but Caitlin was having none of it.

"What do you want?" she asked for a third time. "I really want to get back to practice. It's been a long day and I do this to unwind. This," she waved a hand between us, "isn't helping."

I took a breath and bit back a retort. I was trying

to be friendly, and yet it appeared as if she *wanted* to be enemies. "I was just curious as to who was in the photo with you."

"And that's your business because . . . ?"

She had me there, but that didn't stop me from pressing. "We tend to keep an eye out for strangers in this neighborhood," I said, making it up on the spot. "I wouldn't want to confuse your boyfriend for a stalker."

She didn't flinch at the word "stalker." Good thing? Bad thing? Hard to say.

"He's not my boyfriend."

"An ex?"

She just stared at me.

"I know it's none of my business, but I'd hate to call the cops on someone who doesn't deserve it." I sounded like one of those overly paranoid neighbors that spends my day watching the neighborhood like a hawk, but it wasn't like I could just come out and ask her if she and her boyfriend had killed Hamish Lauder and if they were trying to blame it on me.

Well, I mean, I *could*, but I doubted it would get the result I was looking for.

"You call the cops whenever your neighbors have company?" she asked, crossing her arms. She wasn't buying my explanation for a second.

"No, but if . . ." I trailed off. This wasn't working. "It's better to be safe and informed than to be caught by surprise." She could take that how she liked.

Caitlin scoured my face, and must have seen something there—honesty maybe—because she sighed and slumped against the doorframe. "The man in the photograph is my brother. And no, he won't be visiting any time soon."

"Estranged?"

"He's out of the country. He only visits once or twice a year, and usually stays with our parents, which means he won't be anywhere close to this neighborhood." She paused, then straightened. "Is that all?"

"Do you know anyone by the name Abby Kohn?"

Once again, she didn't flinch. Either she was really good at controlling her emotions, or she wasn't the mysterious article writer. "No. Should I?"

"What about Hamish Lauder?"

Caitlin spread her hands. "Is this some kind of test? I've never heard of the guy." She glanced back, toward her living room. A black-and-white electric guitar was leaning against the couch. A cord ran from it, toward her television, which was sitting out of sight.

"Looks expensive," I said, nodding toward the guitar and hoping to win a few points, but once again, I'd missed the mark.

"It's a piece of crap. I want a Gibson, but I can't afford it." She scowled at the guitar, then at me, as if the price was my fault.

"I've taken up enough of your time," I said. "I'll let you get back to your practice. Thank you for talking to me. Maybe we can sit down and have a real conversation sometime?" I made it a question.

"Maybe." Caitlin didn't sound like she had any intention of talking to me any more than she had to. Honestly? I didn't blame her. I'd made a nuisance of myself, and peppering her with nonstop questions wasn't making it any better.

"You sound pretty good." I said, plastering on a smile. "You'll be playing arenas any time now."

"Uh-huh." Caitlin stepped back. "Goodbye, Krissy." She closed the door in my face.

I deserved that.

I slunk my way toward my house, pausing long enough to check Caitlin's living room window. Sure enough, the camera was still sitting there, pointed toward my place. Either she'd yet to get it hooked up, or it was indeed there to spy on me.

But why? To monitor my movements? It *would* make it easier to frame me if she knew when I was home alone, without an alibi.

What if she's not guilty? I could be making a life-long enemy because of my paranoia. The thought made me sick to my stomach. I trudged back home, positive I was making more than enough mistakes on my own. I didn't need my harasser's help making myself look bad.

I jangled my keys and unlocked the front door. "Misfit?" I entered my house, and as expected, my orange fluffball was nowhere in sight. "I'm home."

I found him lying on the bed, snoozing away. The music coming from next door was muffled, barely there, so it wasn't as loud as I'd thought it would be. I spent a few minutes petting my cat before I grabbed my laptop and headed for the couch. Here, the music was a little louder, but not so much as to be annoying. The only reason I could hear it was because of the complete silence in my own home.

I clicked on the TV and turned to an old movie I didn't plan on watching, just so I'd have something playing in the background. I then opened

The Eyes of the Hills, but there were no new articles about me, or anything else connected to the series of crimes happening in Pine Hills.

Was that because Caitlin was too busy practicing her guitar to write the article? It might be a good idea to wait for the music to stop, and then see if something popped up soon after. I had a feeling that if she were indeed Abby Kohn, after my little visit, Caitlin would have a lot more to say about me.

But until then, I had research I could do.

I clicked over to Caitlin's social media and perused it more carefully than I had the last time I was there. I checked every photo for a curly-haired brother, but I found nothing. The same went for her cousin's photos. And when I checked their friends and followers, I couldn't find anyone that looked like the man in the photo, though my memory of him was a tad fuzzy since I'd only gotten the one quick look.

Even though it was entirely possible Caitlin's brother didn't have a social media profile, I found it suspect. If I were running around, committing crimes in Pine Hills, I wouldn't want someone to be able to go online and find a picture of me. And with how every app seemed to want to know your location these days, it would be best not to have a social media profile at all if you were skulking about.

As I scrolled, Misfit sauntered in from the bedroom. He paused in the kitchen to give me a longing look, before he headed over to his dish, just in case I didn't get the hint.

"All right, I'm coming." I set my laptop aside. I needed a break anyway. I wasn't having any luck, and I had a feeling that staring at the screen for much longer would only result in giving me a headache. "But this is it for today."

Misfit wound around my legs as I filled his dish yet again. He'd become much calmer in his old age—not that he was really that *old* for a cat. But when he was younger, he used to be an absolute terror when he wanted something, often climbing the walls or tearing around the house with the sound of ripping carpet. He was now past that hyperactive kitten stage, and I found I kind of missed it.

"We all change," I said, stroking his back, before retreating from the kitchen. I probably should have fixed something for myself to eat, but I wasn't hungry. I think a part of me was waiting for the next blow, something that would send me careening down an even darker path than the one I was already on. I hated not trusting my neighbor. Hated thinking that someone was out to get me. Or that someone was using me as a scapegoat for their crimes.

It took me a moment to realize the house was quieter than it had been a moment before. I turned off the TV and listened, and sure enough, no more wails were coming from next door. I peeked out the window and saw that Caitlin was still home. From the looks of it, the television was still on. There was a constant flicker that made me think she'd graduated from her game and was now watching the television. Perhaps the movie I'd just turned off.

I stepped back from the window and returned to my laptop. What were the chances?

I opened my browser, clicked on my history, and reloaded *The Eyes of the Hills* site.

"Should the Questioner Be Questioned?"

I stared at the title, heart hammering. There was no way, not after what I'd just asked Caitlin. She couldn't have . . .

But she had.

Or Abby had.

The article was all about me and my penchant for asking questions that were best left for the police. It didn't mention a specific incident, just that I'd been seen running around town, talking to people. It speculated that I was using my standing within the community to distract them from what I was really doing.

My mouth was hanging open by the time I finished reading. It was yet another hit piece on a website that was supposed to be dedicated to local news. I wondered if I should contact someone, or if something like this was even illegal. Could I sue? Should I?

My phone rang, startling a scream from me. I slammed my laptop closed, as if ashamed that I'd been caught reading the article, and then snatched up my cell. One look told me it was coming from Death by Coffee.

I groaned. *What now?*

Fully expecting Vicki to tell me that a swarm of cockroaches had infiltrated the store, or that my reputation had finally killed any interest in the bookstore café and we'd have to close for good, I answered with a nervous, "Hello?"

"Ms. Hancock?"

I paused. "Jeff?" That was *not* who I'd been expecting.

"Yeah." He cleared his throat and I imagined him looking away, as he was wont to do whenever he talked to me. "I thought I should call you."

"Okay?" My heart was pounding, and his tentativeness only made it worse. "Did something happen?"

"I'm not sure." There was a scraping sound and a click. The background noise, which had been a dull murmur, vanished. "I talked to Mr. and Mrs. Lawyer about it and they tell me it's okay, but . . ." No matter how many times we told him he didn't have to use our last names, Jeff always reverted to Mr. and Mrs.

"What happened, Jeff?" I asked it kindly, even as I braced myself for the next gut punch.

"The police were here," he said. "They were asking about the notepad."

"The store stationery?" *It's about the theatre.* I wondered if Paul had been the one to stop in, but if he was, I had a feeling Jeff would have said so. He knew about my relationship with Paul. *Buchannan then.*

"Yeah." He took a deep breath, and seemed to hold it as he spoke. "They asked if I knew anything about it, like who had access to it and whatnot."

"Sounds reasonable. Someone used one of the pages from the notepad to leave a nasty message at the community theatre."

"That's what the police said. And Mrs. Lawyer was pretty upset about it." He paused, and I waited him out. My pulse beat in my ears, a rhythm not far removed from what Caitlin had been playing a short time ago. "I'm afraid I made a mistake. I don't want to lose my job." He sounded panicked, like he thought I might fire him on the spot.

"Jeff, you have nothing to worry about. You're a valuable member of our team."

"I guess." He didn't sound convinced.

"What happened?" I asked. "I promise I won't be mad."

There was a pause before he answered. "It happened a few days ago, maybe a week. I was working upstairs and some guy asked me for a piece of paper so he could write down the name of a few books. I had the pad in my hand, and I didn't think anything of it, so I tore off a sheet and gave it to him."

"The stationery?" I asked, just to be sure.

"Yeah. Right off the pad. I didn't know I wasn't supposed to. I didn't mean for it to mess up Mrs. Lawyer's play."

"Jeff, you're not in trouble. Giving someone a piece of paper isn't a crime." And then, "Do you know who this guy was?"

"I didn't get his name. I'm sorry."

"It's all right." I wished I were there so I could pat him on the shoulder or give him a hug. Jeff sounded miserable.

He cleared his throat, took a deep breath, and seemed to calm down. "I do remember what he looks like a little," he said. "It's not much, and the police didn't seem to find it all that interesting, but when I told Mrs. Lawyer about it, she sounded excited. She told me to tell you."

"Okay, I'm listening." Had my harasser finally made a mistake? If I could link that single sheet of paper to someone, then I very well might have, not just the vandal, but Hamish's killer—if they were one and the same. "Tell me what you saw."

"I didn't pay much attention to his face." Jeff spoke carefully, like he still feared a reprimand. "I was busy, and you know how it can get. But I do remember that the guy was wearing a baseball hat that he kept pulled low to hide his eyes. He didn't look up, so there wasn't much to see."

"That's all right. Any little bit could help."

"I hope so." Jeff took a deep breath, and then hit me with it. "It was a Cincinnati Reds ballcap. And brown hair curled out from underneath it."

16

I stood in a wide-open space, surrounded by images I couldn't quite make out through a haze that obscured everything but my own body. A Death by Coffee apron hung around my neck, and it was splattered with blood that was not my own.

Someone stepped forward, out of the haze. Curly hair. A face that started as unfamiliar, but then began cycling through faces of people I knew. Paul. Will Foster. Robert Dunhill. Thomas Cole.

My own.

"You are not to be trusted." A man's voice.

I turned to find Raymond Lawyer and Regina Harper standing behind me. Mason's father was shaking his head as if disappointed with me, while Heidi's mother was scowling, as she always seemed to be. I'm not sure I've ever seen either one of them smile, and this time was no different.

"I didn't do anything." My voice came out disconnected, and echoed in a way that it most definitely shouldn't have in such a wide-open space.

In the background, a window shattered, and an image solidified. The library stood with a sign claiming it to be permanently closed hanging from the door. One of its windows was busted, much like the Banyon Tree's had been.

"She never should have trusted you." This from Regina. "You bring pain."

"I'm only trying to help."

Raymond opened his mouth, but instead of words, a blast of music burst from between his lips.

And just like that, the strange space, and everyone in it, was gone. Misfit leapt from my bed and bolted out the door as the music continued. My heart was hammering, and it took me a long moment to realize the music was from my phone.

My new ringtone.

I'd changed it just before bed.

I fumbled, half-blindly, for my phone. My eyes were heavy with sleep, and I was so disoriented, I wasn't even sure if it was light out or if it was the middle of the night. I should have realized that I was able to see without turning on a light, but that's what happens when you're startled awake after a nightmare.

"Hello?" I said through gummy lips. "Who's this?"

"Hey, Buttercup? Did I wake you?"

"Dad?" I rubbed my eyes, and once they focused, I looked at the clock. *10:30!* "I guess I slept in."

"I'm sorry. I should let you go."

"No, I need to get up." I swung my legs over the edge of the bed with a yawn. "Why'd you call? It's what? 7:30 there?"

"It is. Laura wanted to go for an early morning run, but my knee is acting up, so she went alone. And since I was already up and moving, I decided to call."

"I'm glad you did." I stood. My back popped and cracked with every movement.

There was a pause. "Is everything all right? You sound off."

"I'm fine." Though I desperately wanted to brush my teeth and take a shower. The nightmare had left a bad taste in my mouth, and I felt strangely cold. "Just tired."

"Laura told me you called. I wanted to call you back right away, but she insisted you were fine and that there was no reason for me to bother you." Another pause. "Are you fine? Really?"

There was a moment where I considered telling him everything. It was what I did. And he liked hearing about what was going on in my life, especially if it involved solving a murder. As a mystery writer, he lived for this sort of stuff.

But if I told him about Hamish and all of the bad things happening to me, he'd only worry. And right then, with how everyone in my life was becoming a target, I didn't want that.

"It's under control," I said. "Did I tell you that John Buchannan is now a detective?"

Dad made a sound I couldn't quite decipher over the phone. A scoff maybe? My best guess was that he didn't believe me when I said I was fine and was debating on whether or not to press me for information.

Thankfully, he chose not to.

"You did. I take it he's taking care of this prob-

lem of yours? Laura didn't go into detail about
what the two of you talked about, so I don't really
know what's happening." He sounded almost offended that I'd shared something with Laura that
he wasn't privy to. I felt bad, but not *too* bad.

"Nothing is happening." And then I decided to
give him something, just so he wouldn't feel left
out. "Someone *was* murdered, but that has nothing to do with me."

"You're not looking into it?"

"No, not really." I padded out into the kitchen
and poured some dry cat food into Misfit's bowl.
He gave me a dirty look, likely because I'd made
him wait so long, before he chowed down. That
cat. He'd slept in just as long as I had.

"Well, if you need any advice . . ."

"You'll be the first I call."

There was a moment of silence where I *knew*
Dad was thinking of prying. I could almost feel his
curiosity through the phone, so I decided to cut
him off before he gave in and started peppering
me with questions.

"Rita was asking about your new book," I said.
"She would like a signed copy of *Victim.* I also
promised her I would ask you about getting her
early copies of *Scars* and *Fear* as well."

"I don't see why not. I could send her early
copies as soon as I have them, and then follow
those up with signed copies of the releases when
they are in my hands. Should I deliver them personally?" I could hear the smile in his voice. He
knew just as well as I did that Rita had a near obsession with him.

"I don't think that will be necessary, but if you

want to come to Pine Hills for a visit, I'm not going to complain."

"I might just do that. It's been too long."

"Yeah, it has."

A wash of melancholy fell over me. Sure, all of my friends were in Pine Hills, my life. But of my family . . . Dad was all I had left. I missed being able to see him whenever I wanted. Talking over the phone just wasn't the same.

"We should look into using video chat," I said. "Zoom or whatever program everyone is using these days."

"We should. Laura uses those things quite often, though I admit, I'm completely at a loss when it comes to them."

"Talk to her about it," I said, imagining Dad fumbling with his computer like one of those hopeless old men you hear about. Dad was anything but hopeless, but the thought did bring a smile to my face. "Let me know what she says. She might have to walk us both through the setup since I have no idea what I'm doing."

"You and me both." Dad chuckled. "I suppose being technologically savvy isn't a family trait."

"No, it's not." I glanced at my laptop, and then looked pointedly away. "I should probably go. I've got to get cleaned up before I have to head in to work." I'd hoped to get a few things done before work, but now, I didn't think I was going to get a chance. That'll teach me to sleep in.

"All right." Dad sounded less concerned than when he'd first called, but I could still hear it in his voice. "I'll talk to Laura about the video chat stuff and see what she says. And I'll make sure Rita gets a copy of *Victim*, and maybe a signed photo. What do you think? Shirtless?"

"Ugh." I squeezed my eyes closed, but it didn't stop the image of Dad flexing shirtless for the camera from invading my mind. "Please, no."

He laughed. "Have a good day, Buttercup. And if you need anything . . ."

"I'll call."

We said our goodbyes and I hung up to go about my morning routine. I hated not telling Dad the truth about the person going out of their way to make my life miserable, but the thought that he could spend *his* day without worrying about me made up for it. Right now, I'd take all the small victories I could get.

Once I was showered and had a hot breakfast—including two cups of coffee—I was ready to head in to Death by Coffee. We were planning on doing second interviews today, and both Vicki and Mason had asked me to do them. They wanted my perspective on who we hired, though I was skeptical I would be much help. It was going to be hard to replace Lena Allison.

As I picked up my purse and keys, my eyes drifted toward my laptop. What I really wanted to do was sit at home and do some research on people involved with Hamish Lauder, Abby Kohn, and Caitlin Blevins. Someone had to be committing those crimes, and it stood to reason that it was someone connected to one of those three.

Let the police handle it. I gritted my teeth and turned toward the door, just as there was a knock, followed by, "Krissy, it's me."

Paul? I hurried over to the door and jerked it

open to find that, indeed, Paul Dalton was standing on my doorstep, in full uniform. There was a flash of worry that he was here to arrest me, but when he took off his hat and smiled, I realized that wasn't the case.

"I wasn't sure you'd be home," he said, eyes flickering to my purse, which was hanging from my shoulder. "And it looks like you won't be for long." He stepped back. "This can wait."

"No, come in," I ushered him into the house, and to the island counter. "I have a few minutes."

"I can't stay long anyway," he said. He seemed to waffle over whether or not to sit, before choosing to stand. "I'm sorry I didn't stop by last night. Or call. Chief had me running errands for John's investigation." He paused. "And John doesn't think I should see you."

Of course, Buchannan wouldn't. I tried not to bristle when I asked, "Did he say why not?"

"He says it's a conflict of interest." Paul shrugged. "I guess he's right, but at the same time, I don't see you as a suspect. You're a victim in all of this."

"Thank you for saying that, but Hamish Lauder is the real victim." And then, just to reiterate, "I barely knew him."

"I know." Paul sighed and rubbed at the bridge of his nose. "But you know how John can be. He wants to make sure you're totally cleared before dropping you as a suspect. That video of the Banyon Tree is the major sticking point with him. And he said something about an email to his wife?"

"I had nothing to do with that either," I said. "I talked to Elsie about it and we've cleared the air."

"Well, John still thinks you're holding out on him and that you might be involved more than you're letting on. You aren't poking around in this are you?"

I felt myself redden, so I turned away. "I might have spoken to a friend of Hamish's." And then, because I was feeling defensive, "Buchannan hasn't spoken to him yet, even though he has information that might help the investigation."

Paul rounded the counter and took me gently by the arms to spin me around to face him. He looked concerned. "What information?"

"That this guy, Mark, talked to Hamish the night he was murdered. Mark heard a voice in the background. He thinks it was a woman's voice, but said it was muffled. He also thinks someone else might have been there, and that they might have been arguing."

"Did he know who these people were?"

I shook my head. "And the timing of the call puts it just before we went out on our date. I'm not sure if it happened before or after I was supposed to be breaking the Banyon Tree window, but I have a feeling it's close enough to clear me for one of them." If I was getting my timing right, that was. "If the person Mark overheard killed Hamish, then . . ."

Paul frowned as he thought about it. Sure, there were holes. I wasn't positive the murder had happened soon after Mark's call with Hamish. He could have been killed hours later, long after my date, when I was alone in my house with no alibi outside my cat. Mark could have lied to me, though unless he was involved in the murder, I didn't see why he would.

But right then, it was the best I had. And if it took the pressure—and suspicion—off of me, all the better.

Paul must have thought the same, because he nodded. "All right. I'll tell John to talk to this friend. You said his name was Mark? Do you have a last name?"

I did him one better; I gave him Mark's last name, phone number, and address. The police would have no reason not to get in touch with him now. "I know Buchannan is trying his best, but he really needs to stop trying to lay this on me. It's causing him to make mistakes."

Paul winced as if I'd insulted him, rather than his colleague. "I'm sure he has a reason as to why he hasn't spoken with this friend. He might not have known about him. From what I can gather, Mr. Lauder didn't seem to be the sociable type. His neighbors don't recall him ever having guests."

"Not even that night?"

Paul hesitated. "I'll have to double-check that. If he did, it's entirely possible nobody saw them, especially if they weren't there for long."

I had my doubts about that. How long had Hamish been entertaining his guests? He'd missed a lunch with Mark, which could mean he'd come across his murderer long before he was killed. And then there was the tea. The way the scene was laid out—not that I'd seen it personally. But from the sound of it, it didn't appear as if the murder happened quickly.

He knew his killer. If those voices in the background of the call did indeed belong to Hamish's murderers, then he'd let them into his house, had sat down with them for tea.

"I was thinking . . ."

I jerked myself out of my own head at Paul's nervous tone. Unsubstantiated speculation could wait. "About?"

"Dinner. Tonight."

Something in his voice had my own nerves jumping. This didn't sound like he was inviting me to a romantic dinner at Geraldo's, or a quiet evening at his house.

It sounded more like he was inviting me to my own execution.

"I should be free." My voice came out only slightly choked.

"It . . ." He frowned. "It won't be just the two of us. Shannon and I thought it best if we all sat down and talked."

Shannon and I? The dread was pooling. "I see."

"She wants to explain herself. I told her about the photo and your concerns." He paced away, ran his fingers through his hair. "It was her idea. I was planning on asking you out tonight anyway, so —"

"No, it's a good idea," I said, cutting him off before he could withdraw the offer. If this dinner spelled the end of our relationship, I'd rather get it out of the way now than drag it out for weeks more. "We *should* talk."

Paul looked torn, but after a few long moments where he just stared at me, he nodded. "I'll let her know. Is Geraldo's all right?"

The fancy restaurant didn't sound like a great place for what could be the worst night of my life, but I wasn't about to object. If he dumped me, at least I'd get a good meal out of it.

"Sounds great."

Paul checked his watch, and then put on his hat. "I'd best get going. I don't want to keep you."

I walked with him to, and out, the door. I wasn't sure what to say, so I said nothing. I didn't want to believe this was the date where he left me for his ex, but with the week I'd been having, it was hard not to at least consider it a possibility.

"I'll pick you up at seven."

"I'll be here."

We stopped between our cars. After a brief hesitation, Paul leaned forward and kissed me. It was warm and kind and just what I needed. When it was over, his hand lingered on my cheek before he stepped back and climbed into his vehicle.

That hadn't felt like a goodbye kiss.

But if it were, it was one heck of a good one.

17

"I think coffee is important. Like, people need it and stuff. You know?" Eugene—the lanky kid Mason had interviewed yesterday—grinned from across the table at me. "It's like, something I could do. Provide it. And I know how to use a register, so I won't really need training there."

"Uh-huh." I scribbled a note onto the pad of Death by Coffee stationery. I was listening, I really was, but it was hard to remain focused. I kept thinking about Paul and Shannon, about Hamish and his mysterious guests. I was doing a terrible job at conducting the interview, and I think Eugene knew it.

"My eyes are normally like this, natural-like."

"Hmm?" I looked up from the pad where I'd circled the Death by Coffee logo. "I'm sorry?"

"My eyes." He blinked them so slowly, it looked as if he were falling asleep. "People think I'm into drugs or don't get enough sleep or something. But that's not it. I'm like, just made this way."

And likes the word "like."

I squashed the thought and smiled to show him that I was okay with him, no matter what his eyes were like. *And now I'm doing it too.* "Oh, I didn't even notice your eyes." I had.

"It's cool if you did. I get it all of the time. Teachers used to yell at me in class, saying I was nodding off during their lectures. I wasn't, but they didn't know that." He winked, which involved a twitch of his right eyelid. The kid really did have squinty eyes.

"Did you get into trouble a lot?" I asked.

He shrugged, causing his entire body to move like someone had yanked on a string holding him upright. Those long legs and arms looked like they were connected to his body by rubber bands. When he'd walked in, it had reminded me once again of *The Nightmare Before Christmas*. I wondered if he'd dressed up like the lead character—or perhaps as a scarecrow—for Halloween, but decided it would be rude of me to ask.

"Some, I guess. But it was all nothing, like total miscommunications and misunderstandings. I've never done drugs, and I don't drink. I'm out of school, so I can work whenever. I've got myself my first apartment lined up if I get the job." There was so much hope in his voice, I'd have felt horrible for turning him away.

Good thing that I liked him and had no intention of giving the job to someone else.

"Well, I'd say your chances are good," I said,

flashing him my biggest smile. It faded quickly as the door opened and my ex-boyfriend's current flame, Trisha, walked in. She glared a hole straight through me, and then marched upstairs, toward the books, with one last glare that told me I was to join her as soon as I was done. "But I'll need to talk to the other owners first."

"Sweet."

I already knew Mason preferred Eugene to the other applicants, though he did say that he'd like to hire one other newbie, outside of Eugene, to make our lives easier. As it stood, Mason, Vicki, or I always had to be on hand, and with Vicki's plays, and my penchant for chasing crimes, it fell on Mason to be around more than his fair share.

Upstairs, Trisha paced between a pair of shelves. She shot looks my way every few seconds, and to say they were dirty would be an insult to dirt.

"We've got your number," I said, rising. "As soon as we've made a decision, someone will call and let you know one way or the other." And because I couldn't hold back, I added, "I'd get that apartment deal sealed up."

"Yeah. Thanks!" Eugene popped to his feet, grinning so wide, it almost made all my other troubles fade away.

Almost.

We shook and Eugene practically skipped toward the door. He shot someone outside a thumbs up, but I didn't peek out the window to see who. Instead, I turned toward the stairs to where Trisha was waiting, arms crossed, foot tapping, and a scowl a mile long plastered across her pretty face.

Here we go again.

I could sometimes be slow on the uptake, but it didn't take a genius to figure out that my harasser had gotten to Trisha. The only question was; what did they do to her? I had a feeling that Robert would be involved because of our history, but in what way? I was about to find out.

I headed for the stairs, each step dragging worse than the last. I so didn't want to do this, but had no choice. If I left Trisha to stew, it would end up blowing up in my face down the line.

As soon as I reached the top step, I opened my mouth to proclaim my innocence, but before I could utter much more than a, "Tr—" she shoved a bag under my nose, nearly hitting me in the mouth with it.

"What is this?" she demanded, shaking the bag, which rattled in a way that was all too familiar.

I stepped back so I could see to be sure. Yup, they were exactly what I thought they were. "Chocolate covered espresso beans," I said. "Look, Trisha, I—"

"How dare you," she said, cutting me off with a stamp of her foot. "I thought we had an understanding." Trisha raised her hand even with her mouth, which caused not one, but *two* rings to sparkle. "Robert and I are married. I know you two have a history, but that doesn't mean you can come in and try to ruin our relationship."

It took a moment for my mouth to work. *They're already married?* Last I knew, they'd gotten engaged, at my house no less. But married? I totally missed the memo on that one. "Trisha, I'm not—"

"Don't try to deny it!" Tears leaked from her eyes and I noted her hand was trembling. "I saw the note. He *showed* it to me. You didn't think he'd do that, did you? He cares for me. I know that's hard for you to understand, and I know you two had your issues, but those issues do not extend to our relationship now."

"Trisha, stop!" I rested a hand on the hand holding the bag of espresso beans. She didn't jerk away, which I took as a good sign. "I didn't send those to Robert. Someone has been attacking me by going after people I know and making them think *I* did it."

She gave me a skeptical look, but I could tell she wanted to believe me. "But . . ."

I squeezed her hand, and then dropped my own. I could do this. I could make things right. "Do you have the note with you?"

Trisha wiped at her eyes and nodded.

"Can I see it?"

She studied me a long moment, as if trying to determine if this were some sort of trick, before she reached into her purse and removed the note. I'd expected it to be written on the Death by Coffee stationery, but it was just a lined sheet of yellow paper, torn in half. She handed it over.

The writing was fluid and, in a word, pretty. It was nothing like my own, but it wasn't like I'd ever written notes to Robert *or* Trisha, so they didn't know what my writing looked like. Either my stalker was getting desperate and was making mistakes, or this was done by someone else.

There wasn't much to the actual note. Just a declaration of love and a desire to put the past behind us to forge a better future. It wasn't signed by someone claiming to be me, but it indicated that I was indeed the author. It referenced Robert travel-ing halfway across the continent for love, so there really wasn't anyone else it could be from.

"He was flattered, as expected," Trisha said. She sniffed, and then removed a tissue from her purse to dab at her nose. "But shocked at the same time. He couldn't understand why you'd do such a thing, especially now of all times."

"I swear to you, it wasn't me." I took Trisha by the elbow and led her toward the couch, which was currently empty of guests. She let me guide her to it. "This has been happening all over town."

"Why?"

"I wish I knew." I found myself staring at the bag of espresso beans. It was yet another example of something that tied back to an old murder investi-gation. "When did these arrive?"

Trisha took a breath and let it out slowly. "A few days ago. Robert wasn't sure he should tell me in my, as he called it, 'delicate state,' so he kept them hidden."

"Delicate state? Are you ill?"

Trisha finally smiled. "Not ill. But . . ." She touched her belly.

My eyes widened as the realization struck me like a punch. "Oh!" There was a strange twinge I couldn't decipher. It wasn't jealousy, but some-thing else, something that did tie back to the fact that I'd dated Robert, had a history with him, and now someone else was having his child. "Congratu-lations!"

"Thanks." Trisha caressed her stomach before pulling her hand away. "It came as a shock, but not a bad one."

I wanted to reach out and hug her, but didn't know if she'd want that, so I just sat there and stared. Robert and Trisha. A baby? I could imagine her as a mother, but Robert as a dad? No way.

"I guess it's why I overreacted so much when he finally did tell me about the note. I thought you must have found out about the baby and realized that he was going to stay with me, so you decided to try to break us up. It was stupid, but my mind has been going to some pretty strange places lately."

"I'd never do such a thing," I said, still stunned by her declaration. "I didn't even know the two of you had gotten married."

This time, her smile was embarrassed. "We decided to have a little ceremony with just the two of us and a friend of mine to witness. It saved us a ton of money, and it meant we didn't have to coordinate things with both our families." She shrugged. "It was nice and quiet, and if given the chance, I'd do it again."

"I don't blame you." Weddings were expensive. And in Pine Hills, who knew what would happen. Just ask Vicki and Mason.

"I should have known you wouldn't do something like this," Trisha said. "I saw the letter, knew that you two had a history, and then nothing else mattered. I was so angry, I didn't stop to think."

"It's all right. You couldn't have known what was going on."

Trisha dabbed at her nose once more before shoving her tissue back into her purse. She considered the espresso beans, and jammed them inside as well. "No sense in wasting them, I guess."

"Nope. You two could eat them while laughing about this whole mess." Now that my shock over her pregnancy announcement had ebbed, I had questions. "You said the note arrived a few days ago?"

"Yes. I think Robert said it was three or four, but I can't be sure without asking him. I kind of blacked out when he told me and might be confused over what he'd said."

I had a feeling she had it right. Three or four days ago would put it just about the same time the cockroaches appeared in the restroom here, as well as the same time the Banyon Tree window was busted. *And don't forget about Hamish's murder.*

I buried the thought before it could show on my face. "How did they arrive? Through the mail?"

Trisha shook her head. "Robert says he found them in my car." She frowned. "Which probably should have raised some questions. Why my car and not his?"

Because whoever planted them, wanted you *to find them, not Robert.* "Did someone break into your vehicle?"

"The window wasn't broken, if that's what you mean. I sometimes forget to lock my car, especially lately. I mean, we live in a safe neighborhood. There's no reason to lock it. At least, there wasn't before." She shuddered. "Robert was going to borrow my car that day, I guess. He sometimes prefers to drive it since it gets better gas mileage and we aren't exactly rich, especially with . . ." She touched her belly. "Every little bit saved helps."

"I bet." I was once again amazed thinking of Robert as a dad. He'd always struck me as the kind of guy who would date around and never settle down and have a family, yet here we were. "Did you or Robert ever see someone strange hanging around your place? Or maybe a car driving up and down the street you didn't recognize?"

Trisha started to shake her head but paused. "There was this one woman, I suppose. I saw her walking the neighborhood a week or so ago, but haven't seen her since."

"Can you describe her?"

"Short hair, I guess. Glasses." She gave me an apologetic look. "Sorry. I didn't really pay much attention. I only thought of her because no one really walks around our neighborhood and she passed by our place at least a dozen times over two days. Could she have been watching us?" Trisha straightened, eyes widening. "You know, when I came in, I swear I saw someone watching this place."

"The same woman?" I asked, adrenaline spiking as I shot to my feet.

Trisha joined me. "No, another. She was sitting in her car and had a camera. It struck me as strange, but I was so angry at you, I didn't think much about it until now."

"Where?" I started for the stairs, and after a moment, Trisha followed me. My heart was pounding, and I was half ready to leap through a window if it meant putting an end to the harassment.

I burst out onto the sidewalk, startling a middle-aged man who was talking on his phone outside of Death by Coffee. There were a dozen cars parked on the street, but as far as I could tell, none of them were occupied.

"Huh." Trisha came to a stop beside me, one hand shielding her eyes from the sun. "She was right there." She pointed to an empty space across the street. "But she's gone now. Maybe she was just out sightseeing."

I stared at the empty space like it had personally offended me, and then to the building behind it.

Lawyer's Insurance.

Where Raymond Lawyer, father of Mason Lawyer, worked.

The man didn't like me. And he'd invaded my dreams recently. Could that have been a sign that he was the culprit behind everything that had happened to me recently?

Raymond wouldn't do that. Would he?

I wanted to march across the street and ask him if he'd hired the woman to spy on me, or if he'd sent people out to ruin my reputation, all because his former employee, Beth Milner, now worked for me. He was vindictive enough to do it.

But murder? I'm pretty sure that was where even Raymond Lawyer drew the line.

As much as I ached for the confrontation, I had other things to worry about. A quick glance at my watch told me my next, and final, interview of the day was due to arrive at any minute. Raymond could wait.

I thanked Trisha for understanding, and once more promised her I had nothing to do with the espresso beans, before I headed back inside Death by Coffee. I glanced toward the counter, where Mason was working. He looked up at me, and I could tell he was curious about Trisha, but right then, I couldn't talk to him. If I tried, I'd bring up his dad. If Raymond *weren't* involved, then I didn't want to drag Mason into it.

But if he was?

Then I was afraid his involvement might actually succeed in tearing the Death by Coffee family apart.

18

The teabag sat on the counter, mere inches from the mug. The water was hot, ready to be poured. A spoon was sitting beside the sugar bowl. All I had to do was mix it all together.

But I couldn't bring myself to do it.

When I'd readied the tea, my mind had been elsewhere. Raymond Lawyer had already left Lawyer's Insurance by the time I'd finished with work, and I hadn't had the energy to track him down. So, instead, I'd gone home. I'd walked in, petted Misfit, put on the water, and set everything out for my tea, all while I considered the interviews I'd done earlier in the day, as well as the crimes that had been committed in my name. I'd gone into the bedroom, had gotten cleaned up and changed for my date with Paul and Shannon.

And then I'd realized what I'd done.

The water whistled and I'd taken it off the burner. Then, I'd just sat.

Spiced chai tea, my latest drink obsession, was now ruined. Someone had used it to pin Hamish's murder on me. Had they known I'd been drinking it lately? Had Hamish simply had some on hand, and it was a mere coincidence?

As much as I wished that to be the case, I knew the killer had taken the tea with them. It was all part of the setup.

I had hours yet before Paul would arrive to pick me up. The tea would settle my stomach, while coffee would make me jittery. I wanted the warmth, but I didn't want to be bouncing off the walls later. I was holding out hope that tonight's festivities would end with a calm, quiet evening alone with Paul, despite Shannon's presence at the start. I didn't want to be overly caffeinated for that.

I reached for the teabag, paused, and then withdrew my hand.

It's just tea. It didn't commit the crime.

And, honestly, it wasn't even the murder weapon. I was being silly.

I rose from my stool and poured the water, added the teabag, and then returned to my seat to let it steep. If the thought of drinking the spiced chai still bothered me when it was ready to drink, I could always dump it out and make coffee instead.

I turned my back on the mug and tried to focus on something else. I wasn't sure what to expect when I had dinner with Paul and Shannon. Should I take a box of tissues, just in case it ended badly? An overnight bag? Mace?

The rational part of me knew that Paul wouldn't just up and dump me. Even if he was planning on doing just that, he wouldn't do it in front of others, especially an old girlfriend—even if their romance had rekindled.

No, Paul had a good reason as to why we were all getting together like this. If he'd asked for a private meeting, then I'd have reason to be worried. A public dinner and shaming? That wasn't his style.

I thought of the photo I'd been sent, and its implications. Maybe, just maybe, Shannon knew who had sent it to me and why they'd taken it in the first place. She could explain what was going on in the photo as well, something Paul could have done, but hadn't for whatever reason that led to our meeting tonight. Perhaps we'd all have a good laugh over this whole mess by night's end.

Unless I was wrong about Paul.

I can't sit here and stress over this. A glance at the clock told me a whole five minutes had passed since I'd begun worrying over the tea. If I kept thinking about Paul and Shannon, I'd have an ulcer by the time he arrived to pick me up.

So, what could I think about then? The murder?

It was as good of a use of my time as any.

Without considering what I was doing, I rose and spooned a small bit of sugar into my tea, before carrying it back to the counter. No cream or milk for me, at least, not this time. I was still experimenting and hadn't quite figured out the way I liked it best.

Which did make me wonder how Hamish preferred his tea.

No, that wasn't the right question.

Whose tea was found at the scene? I couldn't imagine a stranger whipping out teabags to drink on the fly. Had it been Hamish's idea? Or did he do this sort of thing often? Tea with companions. Just because Mark didn't think Hamish had much in the way of friends, it didn't mean he didn't have *some*.

So, was the killer a friend then?

If not a friend, I knew he'd had a guest, perhaps more than one. Could they have been new friends? People he'd just met and had hit it off with well enough to invite them back to his home?

Or had old ones come back to haunt him?

I remembered what Mark had said about friends turning on him in his past. Could that be why Hamish was killed?

I snatched up my phone and found Mark's number. There was only one way to find out . . .

Mark answered on the second ring, sounding mildly distracted.

"Hi, Mark," I said. "It's Krissy. I paid you a visit yesterday."

"Yes, I remember. We talked about Hamish."

"We did. I have a question about something you told me about Hamish and his friends."

Mark was silent a moment before he said, "I don't really remember much of the conversation. I was mourning—still am—and ever since Hamish died, I've been forgetting things. Simple things. It's like a part of me died, which sounds stupid since we were just friends and not soulmates or anything, but I can't help it."

"I'm sorry for your loss," I said, knowing it wasn't nearly enough. "Losing a friend has to be hard."

"It is. Even though Hamish could be trying at

times, frustrating at others, he was a good friend. It'll be strange moving forward without him."

Mark sounded as if he might cry, which, in turn, made *me* want to cry. He was trying to be strong, much like we all do whenever something horrible happens and we have to put on that brave face just to get through the day. I wondered how much my conversation with him had torn him up, and if by calling him now, I was making it worse.

"I'll be quick," I said. "It's just one question."

"I'll answer if I can."

"You mentioned that something bad had happened to Hamish when he was younger. Something about his friends turning on him?"

"Oh, yes, I remember." He sucked in a breath and let it out through his nose in a huff. "It shaped his entire life."

"I know you said you didn't know much about it, but anything you could tell me about what happened could help," I said. "Could it have led to his"—I almost said murder, but realized how harsh the word would sound, so I amended it on the fly—"death?"

There was a hitch in Mark's breathing, and he didn't answer right away. I let him consider the question, to decide what to tell me, without prodding. As much as I wanted to get to the bottom of the murder for my own sake, I did need to consider the feelings of everyone else involved. I might have been framed for the crime, but a man *was* dead, and those who loved him were hurting. Being pushy wouldn't help—or solve—anything.

"As I said before, I don't know the details," he finally said. "Hamish didn't like to talk about it and had only let little bits and pieces slip out over the years I'd known him. We weren't friends back when it happened. I didn't even live in Pine Hills back then, which means it wasn't something I'd lived through."

"That's all right. Anything you could tell me might help."

I could almost see Mark's nod on the other end of the line. "All I know is that when Hamish was younger, there was an accident. One of his friends died, and the others . . ." A pause. "I can't say for sure, but I got the impression that they blamed him for it. I don't know if that meant publicly, or in private, only that Hamish retreated into himself and those friends stopped *being* his friends."

"Do you know what happened? With the accident, I mean?"

"No. I asked once, and with how Hamish paled, I immediately regretted it and withdrew the question. Whatever it was, it still hurts—" Another pause, this one obviously pained. "It *hurt* him, right up until he died. I don't know if it was guilt, or just the pain of losing someone close to him. But, despite his reluctance to discuss it, I did get a name from him."

"A name? Of someone involved?"

"I'm not sure. He let it slip one day when we were hanging out. I don't think he was even talking to me, or realized he'd said it out loud. And afterward, I never looked this person up because I respected Hamish's privacy, and I guess a part of me was afraid of what I'd find. He was a good man, despite his flaws. And he *was* hurting. He'd never admit it to anyone, but I saw it in him when he'd look off into the distance. I knew he was thinking about his past, knew that when he dove into a book, he was looking for a way to escape."

I was forced to swallow a lump that had grown in my throat. I tried to remember if I'd treated Hamish with kindness when he'd been in the store, and couldn't quite bring it to mind. He had been short with me, but that didn't mean I needed to act the same with him.

You never know what someone is going through.

"Anyway, the name stuck with me," Mark said. "Abigail Abele. That's the name. I don't know if she's alive or dead or if it was someone he'd made up in his head. That's all I know. I hope it helps."

I paused as I jotted the name down. Abigail? That was awfully similar to Abby, but was there a connection? "Thank you, Mark. If I find something that might explain what happened to Hamish, I'll let you know."

"If it's something bad, I . . . I don't think I want to hear it. I don't want my image of Hamish tarnished by something he might have done in his past."

"I understand." And I did. Often, when someone died, it was best to think only of the good times, to let the worst ones go.

Sometimes, it was the only way to move on.

We said our goodbyes and I was just dragging my laptop over in front of me to see if I could find anything on this Abigail Abele, when there was a knock on my door.

A glance at the clock told me Paul wasn't due for nearly two hours. Leaving my laptop closed, I headed for the door, curious as to who it might be.

Robert's name kept playing over and over in my mind, and I wondered if I was going to have to explain the espresso beans and note all over again, but this time to a guy who wouldn't listen to a word I said.

I opened the door, and jerked back in surprise. "Caitlin? What are you doing here?" That had come out wrong—and rude. "I'm sorry. I was expecting someone else."

My neighbor looked like she wanted to be anywhere but on my doorstep. Her house wasn't on fire, and she didn't have an empty measuring cup, so she wasn't there due to an emergency or a need to borrow sugar.

"Hello, Krissy," she said, eyes flickering to my face, before settling somewhere around my navel. "Mind if I come in for a moment?"

"I, uh, sure." I stepped aside.

Caitlin braced herself, as if she were about to walk through a minefield, before she entered my house. She moved to stand in between the living room and dining room, and there, she stopped, arms crossed, brow furrowed.

"Look," she said, when I closed the door. "I know we got off on the wrong foot and all that. And I know I've been a tad harsh on you."

"It's all right. I understand—"

She cut me off with a hard shake of her head. "Let me do this."

I mimed zipping my lips, and then smiled, trying to lighten the mood, but Caitlin didn't appear as if anything could cause her to unclench.

"I've talked with the other neighbors and one of

them, Jules, assured me that you're a good person, that I need to give you a chance."

I started to tell her that she didn't *need* to do anything, but caught myself before my lips could do more than part. She wanted to do this, and she didn't need me interrupting and making it more difficult than it had to be.

"So, this is me giving you a chance," Caitlin said. "I'm sorry for how I acted. I've taken my frustrations out on you. I've blamed you for things that weren't your fault. You've helped people. I can't hold that against you."

I couldn't stop myself this time, "Even if I'm a bit too nosy for my own good?"

Her lips twitched in what I took for a near smile. "Even then." She sucked in a deep breath and let it out in a body-sagging sigh. "I got myself all worked up, thinking you were some sort of evil mastermind who manipulated people into seeing things your way. It made me feel like I was protecting June by giving you a hard time."

"I'd never hurt her."

"I know." She laughed, rubbed at her temples. "I was being stupid. Paranoid, even. After . . ." She trailed off with a frown.

"After what?" I asked, that nosiness kicking in.

Caitlin scratched at her ear and glanced toward the door, as if she was considering whether or not to make a run for it. She remained standing where she was.

"I've had troubles with people before," she said. "A friend. Or she used to be." She threw her hands into the air in frustration. "No, she wasn't. I don't know what she was, but I don't think we were ever truly friends."

My mind immediately went to Hamish and the trouble he'd had with his own friends. "Did she hurt you somehow?"

"Hurt?" Caitlin shook her head. "Nah. Not physically. But she made me paranoid." Her gaze shot to the window, like she expected someone to be standing there, peeking inside. "She'd stop by and as soon as I was out of the room, she'd go through my things. Or, if she'd crash for the night, I'd wake up and find her standing over me, staring. It was creepy."

"I bet." I tried not to think about how I'd done something similar by going through her house un-invited. I'd felt ashamed then, and was even more so now.

Caitlin hugged herself. "I caught her looking into my windows countless times. As in, I'd be watching TV or playing a game, and would look up and find her just standing there, looking in. She always blew it off as a joke, but it got to me, you know?"

I nodded. I'd never experienced something *that* personal, but after Robert followed me from California, I knew what it felt like to have someone seemingly obsessed with you, following you around.

"It got bad enough, I was afraid to change clothes in my own bedroom. I taped the blinds closed so they wouldn't part and let her peek in. There were times I would stay out all night and then sleep in my car, just so I wouldn't have to worry about her finding me."

"That sounds horrible."

"It was." Caitlin ran her fingers through her hair, bunching it briefly and tugging, before dropping her hands to her side. "It's why I have cameras facing out the windows. It's why I moved. If she finds me, I don't know what I'm going to do."

I felt bad for ever thinking Caitlin was spying on me. She sounded like someone at the edge of her sanity. I wondered if this woman was the person she'd referenced in her post to June online, the one she said would pay, but decided not to bring it up. I had a feeling that my poking around her social media profiles would come off the same as if I'd gone through her mail.

"I'm sorry I snooped," I said. "I didn't know how it would affect you." No, that didn't sound right. "I mean, I know it wasn't right, but I was curious, and I tend to act before I think—"

Caitlin held up a hand. "It's all right. Jules explained that it's something you do." She gave me a sideways grin. "But I *would* refrain from poking around my place too much. I have . . . precautions set up, just in case."

"I'll keep that in mind." I said it with a smile.

Caitlin appeared as if she might say something else, but a knock on the door cut her short. There was a flash of panic across her face, and then she seemed to realize that she wasn't at her own house, and that the person knocking was there for me, not her.

"I'll get out of your hair," she said, following me toward the door.

"I'm glad you stopped by," I said, hand on the knob. "I would really like us to get along."

"Yeah." She didn't go as far as to say, "me too,"

but I was hoping the thought had crossed her mind.

The knock came again, more insistent this time. With a "what can you do?" eyeroll, I opened it, fully expecting it to be Robert this time.

And once again, I was wrong.

"Oh, you *are* in," Rita said even before the door was all the way open. "I was afraid you might not be home, though your vehicle *is* in the driveway. I thought to myself, Rita, if she—Oh!" Her eyes widened briefly as Caitlin slipped past with a barely audible, "Excuse me."

"Rita," I said, drawing her attention back to me before she could start peppering my neighbor with questions. A quick look past her told me she wasn't alone. "Johan. Come on in."

"I can't stay," Rita said. "But I *did* have a fantastic idea. In fact . . ." She put a hand on Johan's back and practically shoved him into my arms. "I need to get going before it gets dark."

"Wait," I said, confused. "You just got here."

"I know, dear. I was there." She waved a hand in front of her face, though I had no idea why. "Anyway, Johan will keep an eye on you until I get back. He knows what to look out for." Rita turned as if she might leave.

I stepped around Rita's boyfriend, who didn't seem to know what to do with himself. "Rita, wait."

She paused halfway to her car. "Yes, dear?"

"Where are you going? You can't leave him here." I tried really hard to keep the panic out of my voice, but failed miserably. I knew nothing about Johan, and his mere presence often left me feeling creeped out.

And here Rita was, abandoning him with me. At my house. Alone.

Rita's smile was bright as she wagged a finger at me. "Don't you worry none, dear. I know what I'm doing. Everything will be better for you by morning, just you wait and see!"

And before I could stop her, she climbed into her car and was on her way.

"But . . ." I watched her helplessly as she pulled out of the driveway, honked twice, and then sped off.

I turned to find Johan standing on my doorstep, hands shoved into his pockets. He wasn't smiling. There was no emotion in his eyes at all. He merely stood there, his face an expressionless mask, waiting for me to decide whether to kick him out, or invite him in.

I might not feel comfortable around the guy, and knew little to nothing about him, but I wasn't a total jerk either.

"I guess you'd better come inside," I said with a sigh.

Johan nodded once, and then turned and entered my house.

After one look to the sky, and a quick prayer for strength, I followed him in.

19

Tick. Tick. Tick.
  "Would you like some tea? Coffee?"
  "No, thank you."
  Tick. Tick. Tick.
  "What about water? Or if you're hungry, I'm sure I have something around here you could eat."
  "No. I'm all right."
  Tick. Tick. Tick.
  I glanced at the clock. Ten minutes. Johan had been sitting in my house, in my chair, for ten whole minutes, and yet it felt like hours. Both of his feet were flat on the floor, hands resting on his knees. He looked both stiff and completely at ease at the same time. A vague smile that hadn't shifted an iota since he'd walked through the door was on his face. When I moved, his eyes would follow me, yet his head remained motionless.
  Misfit had vanished the moment Johan had en-

tered the house and I had yet to see hide or hair of him since. I was alone with a man I didn't trust, a man who was dating one of my friends, and I had no idea what to do with him.

"So . . ." I dragged out the word, desperately trying to fill the silence between us. "You and Rita, huh?"

His smile widened slightly, though it came nowhere close to touching his eyes. "Yes. It's been good."

"That's nice. Did she say where she was going? Or how long she'd be?" I asked. "I have a date later." I didn't want him to think I was uncomfortable with him there, even though I was desperate to get him out of my house.

"She didn't say."

Great. Knowing Rita, she wouldn't show back up until long after Paul arrived to take me to our date with Shannon. I wondered if he'd be okay with bringing Johan along. I mean, it's not like having him with us would make the conversation any more awkward.

"Rita mentioned you travel out of town every now and again. Is it for work? Family?"

"A little of both."

I waited, hoping he'd expand on the thought, but he just sat there, smiling vaguely at me. I didn't know what he did for a living. Nor did I know what had brought him to Pine Hills in the first place. Paul had done a little research on Johan Morrison when I'd asked him to a few months back, but he'd found almost nothing. The guy, as they said in the movies, was a ghost.

A ghost who was now currently haunting me.

I fidgeted in my seat and glanced at the clock again. Another two minutes had passed.

"If you have something you need to be doing, don't mind me. I'm fine just sitting." He did that thing where his smile widened, yet his eyes remained void of emotion. "It's sometimes good to just sit for a little while."

While I didn't like the idea of leaving Johan alone in my living room, I couldn't pretend to be a sociable host any longer. I'd end up driving myself crazy if I tried.

"If you're sure?" I asked, already rising and making my way to the island counter and my laptop. "I'll be just in here in case you need me for anything."

"I'm sure." That smile. "I'll be all right."

I rounded the counter and sat down so I could keep an eye on Johan while I worked. He was facing forward, eyes aimed toward the couch, yet I swore he was still watching me through the side of his head.

I suppressed a shudder and lifted my laptop lid. I adjusted it so I could see Johan and the screen at the same time, and then brought up my browser. A quick look at Johan to make sure he wasn't somehow able to see the screen, and then I typed in a search: *Abigail Abele*. And then, before I hit *Enter*, I added, *Pine Hills*.

I found what I was looking for immediately.

Abigail Abele was only eighteen when she'd died. Apparently, she'd been out with friends—unnamed here, but after my conversation with Mark, I knew one of them to be Hamish Lauder—and had vanished. She was missing for five days before her body was found in the woods. The cause of death was ruled as an accident, and the case was closed before it really got started. The article said she'd gotten lost, caught her ankle on a vine, and had fallen into a ravine.

As I read, my heart ached for not just Abigail, but for Hamish, as well. If he'd been with her before she'd gotten lost, then he must have felt responsible for her death. I tried to imagine what could have happened, but it was hard to do without having any more facts than the meager details provided within the article. Had she run off, crying over a fight she'd just had with her friends? Were they playing a game and she'd gotten turned around and couldn't find her way back? Had they parted for the evening, and she'd decided to take a shortcut through the woods to get home, but ended up lost and confused?

Had someone chased her and she'd been running for her life?

There was no way of knowing, not without talking to someone who was there.

I skimmed through the rest of the article, which talked about funeral arrangements and mentioned the family—a mother who'd passed two years prior to Abigail's disappearance, and a father who, at the time of the writing, was in mourning. I was about to skip the final few paragraphs and close the browser when I noticed a name I recognized.

"Abigail was a good person. Kind. She'll be missed."

The quote was from Raymond Lawyer.

I stopped breathing as I scrolled back up. Why

was Mason's father being quoted in an article about someone else's kid? It took me only a moment to find out.

He was best friends with the father, Cal Abele.

My heart started hammering. Raymond Lawyer knew the woman who'd died. Hamish was her friend.

What if Raymond, like Hamish's friends before him, blamed Hamish for Abigail's untimely death?

I ran a few other searches, but couldn't find anything on Abigail's death—or connection to the Lawyers—that explained more than what I'd already learned. Had Mason known Abigail? Were they friends? Often, when two sets of parents become friends, the children likewise grow close. You spend time with one another when you found yourselves at cookouts and picnics and parties together.

But if Mason and Abigail were friends, did that mean Mason knew Hamish as well?

It looked like I was going to have to have a talk with members of the Lawyer family, a prospect I was not looking forward to in the slightest.

A knock at the door caused me to snap my laptop closed and check the clock. Paul still had twenty minutes before he was due to arrive, yet I felt the guilt flooding my face as if he'd caught me investigating. I didn't want him, or anyone else, to know what I'd found. Not until I'd talked to Mason and Raymond. I was reluctant to get either of them into trouble if I didn't have to. And knowing Buchannan, anything I found would cause endless amounts of trouble.

The knock came again. Johan's head cocked

slightly to the side, but otherwise, he didn't glance toward the door, nor did he comment on my sluggishness in answering it.

Creepy, I thought as I rose. If he'd act even a little bit normal, then perhaps I wouldn't think so poorly of him. He was dating Rita, who'd been hurt in her past. It had taken her decades to get over her last real boyfriend. I didn't want her to be hurt again.

Those thoughts chased me across the room, to the door. By the time I reached it, I was convinced Rita would be on the other side, ready to regale me with tales of . . . well, whatever she'd done.

I jerked opened the door, but it wasn't Rita who stood on my front stoop.

It was the man I should have expected all along.

"Robert." His name slipped from my lips like a groan. I'd known he'd eventually show, but now was *so* not a good time.

"Hey, Kris." He stepped past me and entered my house without waiting for an invitation. He paused when he saw Johan, but quickly dismissed him. "Look, we need to talk."

I closed the door, praying for strength as I did. I'd been doing that a lot lately. "I've already spoken to Trisha. I didn't send the chocolates. I didn't write the note. Someone has been harassing me and they thought it would be funny to leave them for you in my name."

Robert flashed me a smile that said more than words that he didn't believe a word I said. "Seems like a strange way to get at you, don't you think?"

"Robert, I didn't—"

"Kris, it's all right." I wanted to slap him for using a shortened version of my name, one he knew I hated, but even if I did, it wouldn't make a difference. "I get it. I went through the same thing when you first dumped me. It hurt, and all I wanted to do was get you back."

I opened my mouth to object, but he continued on right over me.

"And I understand why you didn't want Trisha to know about us. We had something special." He reached out and rested a hand on my arm. "But that time has passed. I'll treasure you forever. And I'll think about what we had until the day I die."

In the next room, Johan's shoulders began to shake. Was he actually *laughing*?

"Trisha and I are together now," Robert went on. "Perhaps someday, things will change, and I will be a free man once more. But until that day, my dear Kris, we can only be friends."

And with that, Robert Dunhill stepped forward and wrapped me in a hug. I accepted it, too stunned to speak, let alone push him away.

He broke the hug and stepped back. "I'd better go." Robert touched my cheek with his palm, smiled fondly at me, and then he walked out of my house.

I stared after him, mouth hanging open, mind completely blank.

"Oh, hello, dear. Are you visiting Krissy again?" I could hear the curiosity *and* interest in Rita's voice, yet I was still too shocked by what had just happened to react. "I see you did so with your shirt this time!"

Robert said something I couldn't hear, which caused Rita to giggle. *Giggle!* And then he was gone. Rita entered the house in his place, closing the door behind her. Johan stood immediately, as if on springs, and moved to stand at her side. For the first time since I'd known him, I saw actual humor in his eyes, though he did manage to keep his smile from splitting his face in half.

"Well, that was awfully strange," Rita said, leaning into Johan's arm as he slid it around her shoulder. "I swear that boy is smitten with you and you keep leading him on, despite what I'd heard about him and that woman of his. They're married, aren't they?"

"I'm not leading anyone on." I closed my eyes and willed the headache that was building to go find someone else to torture. "It was a misunderstanding." With Robert, it always seemed to be. "And, yes, he's married."

"Uh-huh. I'm sure it was, dear." Rita winked at Johan before turning her attention back to me. "We'd better get out of your hair. Rumor has it that you have an interesting night planned."

I had no idea how she'd heard about my date with Paul and Shannon. At that moment, I didn't really care. I just wanted a few minutes alone to make sense of my life before Paul arrived.

"Thank you." It was the only thing I could think to say.

"No problem, dear. I'll talk to you tomorrow." Both Rita and Johan turned as if to go.

A new thought struck me. "Wait!" I scurried around to block off their path to the door. "What did you do, Rita?"

"Do?" She glanced around the room, as if completely flummoxed by the question. "What could you ever mean?"

"Tonight. When you left Johan here. Where did you go? What did you do?" *Am I going to pay for it later?*

Rita smiled in a way that made my heart sink straight through the floor. Yup, this was going to come back and bite me in the butt.

"You have a good night, dear," she said, patting me on the arm. "Don't worry about anything other than what's in front of you right now. Everything will work out. We'll talk tomorrow." This time, her wink was for me.

Rita and Johan stepped around me and were gone. They were quickly replaced by the one sane person in my life.

"That looked interesting," Paul said, joining me.

"I . . . I think I'm going crazy," I said. I mean, I had to be right? It couldn't possibly be everyone else in Pine Hills who was completely off their rockers, could it?

"Do I want to know?" Paul asked. I finally was able to look at him, and my toes immediately curled. Gone was the police uniform and hat, and in its place was something absolutely scrumptious, despite not being anything special. A dark-blue button-up shirt, blue jeans that were made for him. I swear he could make a unitard look sexy.

I somehow managed not to drool all over myself and smiled. "No. I'm all right."

Paul scoured my face, likely looking for the lie. I must have hidden it well, because he returned my smile and seemed to relax. "Are you ready for this?"

After everything that had happened over the last few days. After Robert and Rita and Johan.

After Caitlin and Raymond and the library. After the cockroaches, and Trisha, and Hamish's murder.

If I could handle all of that, I was pretty sure I could handle a night with my boyfriend and his ex.

"I am," I said.

And for the first time since I saw that photograph of Paul and Shannon together at the Banyon Tree, I meant it.

20

Geraldo's didn't look like much from the outside. A small parking lot in the back, brick exterior, simple sign. You could drive by it a hundred times and not realize you'd just passed the nicest restaurant in all of Pine Hills.

The inside, however, was a different story.

Light jazz played over the speakers as Paul and I entered the restaurant. The lighting was dim, the atmosphere friendly. A man in a suit approached and led us quickly to a table in the back. Almost immediately, the waitress appeared in a black dress. We ordered drinks—both going for water and a Coke—and then turned our attention to one another.

"Shannon?" I asked.

"She'll be here soon. I wanted a few minutes alone with you before she arrives."

A good thing? I hoped.

"Are you going to give me a hint as to what this

is about?" I picked up my cloth napkin and folded it into my lap, just so I'd have something to do with my hands.

"I probably shouldn't." Paul looked pained as he mirrored my movements.

The waitress arrived with our drinks. We promised to order once the third member of our party arrived. She smiled at us, and then vanished as quickly and as silently as an assassin stalking her prey.

Obviously, my mind was in a weird place.

I fidgeted with my spoon, then my fork. They were both clean, as was the knife sitting next to them. Out of the corner of my eye, I could see Paul watching me, yet I couldn't bring myself to look directly at him. I was afraid of what I might see if I studied him too hard.

"Krissy . . ." He made a frustrated sound, one not targeted at me. "This is difficult. I desperately want to tell you everything, but it isn't my place."

"I know. You've said so before."

"And I mean it." He reached across the table and stopped my hand, which was stroking the knife. "Please, look at me."

After some internal debate, I did.

Paul's eyes were soft and so very inviting. "No one is going to hurt you. That includes both me *and* Shannon."

"The photo—"

"Is nothing. You don't have anything to worry about."

I wanted to believe him; I really did. But with how my week had been going, it was hard. Every time I moved, I fully expected the floor to collapse under my feet, or the roof above my head to spring a leak.

All because someone has it out for me.

Or did they? Could this all be a ploy to distract from the real reason Hamish was murdered?

Despite the fact I was sitting across from the one man I wanted to spend the rest of my life with, I found myself thinking about another man entirely. A couple of them, actually.

"Has Buchannan made any progress on Hamish Lauder's murder?" I asked.

Paul looked surprised by the question. "He's working on it."

"Has he talked to Mark Cunningham yet? He's given me a lead, one I think Buchannan should—"

Paul squeezed my hand, causing me to cut off. "*You* should talk to John," he said. "If you have something that might be useful for him, take it to him." He frowned. "Then again . . . You aren't poking around where you shouldn't be, are you?"

"No, not really." And this time, I was pretty sure I meant it. "I already told you I'd talked to Mark."

"You did."

"Well, I called him today to clarify something he'd said about Hamish's past. He ended up giving me the name of woman who'd died a long time ago. A friend of Hamish's. I've been wondering today if perhaps that woman's death might be the reason Hamish was murdered."

"And they blamed it on you because . . . ?"

I opened my mouth and closed it again. That was the part I still couldn't figure out. I supposed if Raymond Lawyer was involved somehow, he could have decided to frame me since he considered me a thorn in his side.

But did I really think Raymond capable of murder, even peripherally? That was stretching it quite a bit. He and I might not get along, and he often treated everyone not named Regina Harper like crap, but that didn't make him a killer.

"She's here."

It took me a moment to realize Paul wasn't talking about Raymond's girlfriend or a murdered woman. He withdrew his hand and stood as Shannon joined us. She was wearing jeans and a plain T-shirt that looked as if it had been balled up in basket for a week before she'd thrown it on. Her hair was pulled back from her face, and a faint bead of sweat speckled her brow. It appeared as if she'd come straight from work at the Banyon Tree.

"Paul," she said, leaning forward and kissing him on the cheek, before turning to me. "Hello, Krissy."

"Hi, Shannon." I didn't expect a cheek peck and didn't get one.

Paul looked uncomfortable as Shannon got settled. She took the seat to my right, effectively putting her between Paul and me. Well, the table was between us, but you know what I mean.

The waitress materialized and took Shannon's drink order. Then, poof, gone again.

"So . . ." Paul cleared his throat. He was the one who was now fiddling with his fork and spoon and refusing to meet anyone's eye.

No one else jumped in to break the awkward silence that followed. Shannon picked up her napkin, and as Paul and I had done before, folded it neatly into her lap. I sipped my Coke and stared hard into my water, which was clear and clean. Even the glass was spotless, which was hard to do in a restaurant where there could be dozens of people touching it.

This is going great.

The waitress returned with Shannon's drink and we went about the routine of ordering food. We were all sitting at the same table, all knew each other in some capacity, and yet it felt like we were strangers locked away in our own little boxes. Every breath I took seemed to suck a bit more oxygen out of the room. In moments, I was near gasping like a fish.

"Excuse me a moment," I said, rising and quickly hurrying toward the bathrooms in the back.

I expected either Paul or Shannon to follow me, but they remained seated at the table, giving me space. It wasn't like I was going to go cry my eyes out or flee Geraldo's in an attempt to hide from whatever was to come. Paul assured me I had nothing to worry about. Deep down, I knew he wouldn't lie to me, that I was overreacting.

It still didn't mean this was going to be easy.

I could only imagine what Paul had gone through whenever he saw me with Will Foster. Or Robert Dunhill. My exes. He'd had his moments of weakness before, times when he'd questioned my loyalty. We all go through it for one reason or another. My weakness had to do with that one photo, while Paul had someone call him out of the blue, claiming I'd fainted in Will's arms. It had upset him.

I paused, hand on the bathroom door.

Someone had called him.

It had happened months ago, right in the middle of yet another murder investigation. I tried to remember if Paul had said whether it was a woman or man who'd called, but couldn't recall. I did know that we'd never discovered who'd called him. I'd always assumed it was someone tied to the murder back then, or perhaps Shannon or someone who didn't approve of my relationship with Paul.

Or someone who flat-out didn't like me.

Kinda like what was happening now.

I turned on my heel without ever going into the bathroom and marched right back to the table. I took my seat, and before anyone could say anything, I spoke.

"Do you remember the call from a few months ago, back when I'd sprained my wrist, and someone said Will was taking care of me even though it was Darrin?" Darrin Crenshaw was a doctor at the practice Will used to work at.

Paul looked startled by the question, but recovered quickly. "Yeah. I remember."

"Was it a man or a woman who called you?"

"The caller was male."

So, not Shannon. My gaze flickered toward her, and I felt an odd sense of relief knowing she hadn't tried to break us up back then. I returned my attention back to Paul. "What did this guy sound like?"

Paul's eyebrows rose. "Like a man?"

"I mean, did you recognize the voice? Did he sound old? Young? Did he have an accent?"

"Krissy?" Paul looked to Shannon, who shrugged. "What is this all about?"

"Someone called you and tried to break us up by telling you that bogus story about me fainting into Will's arms. Someone has been framing me for crimes happening around town. They called *me*. Breathed into the phone. And then there was the guy who followed Vicki and me from Scream for Ice Cream."

"But that call happened months ago," Paul said, though I could tell he was considering it.

"It could have been the start of all of this." I waved my hand over the table, as if every problem that had been blamed on me was lying in front of us. "This stuff could have been going on for months, and we just didn't notice." Which could be why it had escalated to murder. My harasser could have been tired of being ignored.

"It's possible," Paul said, brow furrowing. "I don't really remember the man's voice, but I can tell you it wasn't one I recognized offhand at the time."

Not Raymond then. That is, unless he used a voice changer or something. Could you even buy those?

Shannon sat quietly by as I considered what I knew, or what I thought I knew. After only a few minutes of churning over the facts, I realized I was being rude. We weren't there for me. This was Shannon's night, and if I ignored her, I would only make our relationship worse.

"I'm sorry," I said, forcing myself to set aside my theories. I turned to face Shannon. "You had something to share?"

She flinched as if I'd taken a swing at her before she nodded. "I do, I suppose." She glanced at Paul, and then turned her attention to the empty chair across from her.

"I told her about the photo," Paul said, jumping to her rescue. Whatever she had to say, she was struggling to say it. "Explained that someone took it and was using it to try to hurt us."

"There was nothing to it," Shannon said. "I needed comforting and Paul was there for me. He's a good friend." She reached out, touched his hand, and then pulled her own hand back into her lap as if she feared I might bite it off like a protective wolf-mother might for her pups.

"I don't want to pry," I said. I suddenly felt like a horrible person, like I was forcing Shannon to admit some deep dark secret, all because I was insecure. "You don't have to tell me anything you don't want to."

"No, it's all right." Shannon took a deep breath. When she let it out, her lips flapped, and she managed a smile. "Keeping it in is harder than just admitting it to the world, and it's not like I can hide it forever."

"Whatever it is, just know, I'll do what I can to help." I felt like I owed it to her. I had, I supposed, stolen her boyfriend. Not on purpose. They'd broken up on their own, without my intervention, though I supposed it was possible Paul had left her because of his feelings for me. That was something I'd never ask him.

Shannon picked up a water glass and downed half of it before setting it aside. She looked ready to burst, and her nervousness was making *me* nervous. I picked up my own water glass to take a drink. I'd just filled my mouth when she spoke.

"I'm pregnant."

Water went down the wrong tube and I choked, spraying the table in a fine mist. I coughed, eyes watering, and set the glass aside before I could dump the rest into my lap. About half the people in Geraldo's turned to see what was happening, as I hacked and coughed up what felt like an ocean of water.

Pregnant?

The only boyfriend I knew Shannon had was sitting across from me.

"It's not mine," Paul said, correctly guessing my line of thought. He half rose from his seat, but I waved him back down. I was done choking and didn't need to be saved.

"I was stupid," Shannon said. "Made some bad choices that I'm perfectly fine living with."

"The father . . . ?" I supposed I was asking who the father was, but then again, my brain wasn't working quite as it should.

"Who knows?" Shannon said with a shrug. "Well, I know *who* it is. But not exactly *where*. He flaked on me. I was upset, didn't know who to call. My family wouldn't understand, and most of my friends would give me the 'I told you so' lecture."

"So, you called Paul?"

Shannon nodded. "We might have broken up, but we are still friends. I needed someone who wouldn't treat me like I was a leper. He made me feel better, promised to be there if I needed him." She looked at me then, dead in the eye. "I'm not trying, and never would, to take him from you. I knew, even while dating him, that he cared about you. I realized it early on."

I felt like a dolt—and a jerk—for ever thinking that Shannon was looking to steal Paul from me. "Are you okay?" I asked, genuinely concerned. Being a single mom couldn't be easy, not that I had experience as such. Handling my cat by myself is hard enough for me.

"I am." Shannon smiled and then sagged in her seat. "It does feel good to get that off my chest, because, quite frankly, I'm not ashamed." She touched her belly, which was still as slim as it ever was. "But people have a tendency to shame you, nonetheless."

"And the photo?" I asked.

"I was giving her a peck on the cheek before I left," Paul said. "To see you."

Which meant, yes, it was indeed a kiss. But not a romantic one. Just a goodbye peck between friends. "I'm an idiot."

"Someone wanted you to feel that way," Paul said. "I can't blame you for wondering."

"I wish I knew who took it," Shannon said. "I don't remember seeing anyone that day. Though I suppose I was too mentally wrapped up in myself to notice if someone was watching us."

Which was completely understandable. "If you ever need anything . . ." I left the rest unsaid. She understood what I meant.

"Thank you."

Our meals arrived a short time later. We ate, and now that the secret was out, I found the conversation pleasant. There was no further talk of phone calls or of missing soon-to-be fathers or murder. All in all, it was an enjoyable experience.

Once we'd finished eating, and before dessert, Shannon left. This time, I'd earned myself a peck on the cheek, as did Paul. Through it all, I'd somehow managed to make myself a new friend, and was looking forward to meeting her baby when the time came. *Maybe her baby could be friends with Trisha and Robert's.*

It made me wonder when Vicki and Mason would end up having children, and if, someday, I would ever be ready for kids of my own.

Getting a little ahead of yourself there now, aren't you, Krissy?

"I'm sorry I didn't tell you before now," Paul said. "But, as I said, it wasn't my place."

"No, it wasn't. I shouldn't have pried."

"We got through it."

"We did."

He paused, a smile playing on the corners of his mouth. "Speaking of my place," he said. "Would you mind if we headed there after our tiramisu? That is, if you don't need to get back home right away."

"And miss out on the chance to see your doggies?" I grinned. "Not a chance."

"Kefka and Ziggy miss you."

"I'll be sure to give each of them sufficient cuddles to make up for lost time."

"I hope I can snatch a few of those cuddles."

"Oh, I think you'll have all the cuddles you can handle."

Paul's eyes gleamed as he picked up his fork. "Well, then, we'd best hurry and finish off dessert."

And together, we dug in.

21

"Someone's in a good mood."

I didn't even pause in my whistling as I flashed Beth a smile. For the first time in five days, I felt fantastic. No, better. I felt like nothing anyone could do could touch me. I was invincible, completely immune to my tormentor. And my night with Paul . . .

Bliss.

The morning rush had come and gone, and Beth and I had managed it just fine, despite it being just the two of us. Eugene, along with a young woman who insisted on being called Pooky, had been hired, but didn't start until next week. Until then, we were going to be running bareboned shifts. It meant people had to wait for their books longer than usual, and the tables weren't cleaned as often as I liked, but we got through it.

I was busy sweeping up the front, while Beth handled the counter. We'd barely had time to speak until now. As soon as I'd opened the doors, people were clamoring for their morning caffeine fix. It appeared as if our lull due to the cockroaches had ended.

But that didn't mean they were entirely forgotten.

I'd just scooped the last of the debris from the floor when I noted the trio of boys outside. They were huddled together, not paying me any mind, but were intent on whatever the bigger kid was saying. He was hiding something in his shirt, something, I was sure, that was meant for my store.

"Beth," I said, motioning toward the kids with my broom. "We've got company."

One look, and she was grinning ear to ear. "Got it." She scurried into the office.

The dining area was empty, which was a good thing considering what was about to happen. Upstairs, a pair of women were chatting about a book they'd both read. They didn't seem to agree on it, because one was talking animatedly, while the other was shaking her head and waving a hand in a warding gesture.

Originally, we'd planned on using the plastic cockroaches against the boys if they were to ever come back. I wasn't sure how we could do so, and before long, we scrapped the idea. How do you freak out a bunch of boys who were intent on messing with you without resorting to unkind methods?

It was Beth who'd come up with a plan.

It's funny, but when I'd first met Beth, I'd looked at her as a fake; bottled blonde, slept with a married man, played dumb when asked simple questions. She'd worked at Lawyer's Insurance, and back then was the mistress of Brendon Lawyer—Raymond's murdered son. It made me wonder how Mason handled working with her all the time, considering her history, but then again, I'd never seen him complain, and he wasn't vindictive, so it likely wasn't that difficult for him.

I supposed he understood that Beth wasn't to blame for how things had gone back then. It took me a long time to realize that she wasn't that ditzy person she'd pretended to be while she'd worked for Raymond. After seeing how he'd hounded her once she'd left, her behavior made more sense. Raymond liked to control everything, and that included the personalities of the people who worked for him.

Beth returned behind the counter, just as the three boys entered Death by Coffee, vainly trying to act like they were innocent angels out for a stroll. One of them was snickering, while another looked ready to bolt the moment someone as much as looked at him funny. He kept shooting me worried glances, like he thought I might come charging at them with my broom and beat them out of my store.

"Hi, guys," I said, turning my cheery disposition into a dour drawl. I scuffed my shoe on the floor and pouted out my lower lip. "I'm sorry we can't serve you."

The boys stopped just inside the door, with the bigger kid with the acne in the front. He had a hand over a bulging pocket that I suspected held more fake bugs or some other plastic critters.

"Huh?" he said, frowning. He looked around at

the empty tables, which were sparkling clean by now. They looked as if no one had sat in them all day.

"We've had more troubles." Out of the corner of my eye, I saw Beth bend, and then straighten. "Big ones."

And on cue, a rat the size of a man's shoe zipped out from behind the counter, straight for the boys.

The snickering kid shrieked so loudly, *I* jumped about a foot, even though I knew it was coming. His nervous friend saw the rodent next, and was out the door so fast, it was a miracle he didn't go through the glass. The bigger kid was slower on the uptake, but when he saw the rat, which was now inches from his shoe, he leapt atop one of the nearby chairs, spilling plastic spiders all over the floor in his haste.

The rat zoomed past, spun around, and then scurried back to Beth, who picked it up and clicked the off button on its underside. She was desperately trying not to laugh, her face a bright red, as she set the remote-control rodent down onto the counter.

"Got ya," I said, unable to hide my own smile.

Needless to say, I earned myself about a hundred points in those kids' books. We spent the next twenty minutes laughing over the prank, with each of the kids—including the one who'd run— taking a turn with the rat. By the time they left, they'd promised not to bring any more fake bugs into my place of business, but I had a feeling they'd find some other way to get back at us, but in a good-natured, friendly way.

A few customers trickled in after that. When I went upstairs to assist a teenager who was looking for books on astrophysics of all things, the women who'd been discussing their book rose and waited for me to finish helping him. Once he was gone, they came over to join me at the counter.

"Where's the kitty that's usually here?" one of them asked with a pointed look toward the cat bed behind the counter.

"Trouble? He's not in just yet."

"I see," the other said with a frown. "We were afraid he wasn't coming back."

"Oh, he'll be back," I said. "His owners bring him in when they come to work, so he's not here all of the time."

The two women glanced at one another, nodded, and then turned and walked away.

Strange, I thought. But I guess it wasn't *too* strange. Trouble was a popular fixture of Death by Coffee, and since Vicki was busy with the play, he didn't always get to come in since Mason sometimes left him at home. I wondered if I should start bringing Misfit in his place, but nixed the idea almost immediately. He'd have the books off the shelves in minutes, and since he wasn't much of a people kitty, he'd likely never forgive me for dragging him into a place often full of people who'd want to pet and hold him.

I began straightening up the shelves, moving a few misplaced books back to their rightful home, and then turned to pick up the books left on the table in the seating area. I noticed Beth was giving me a meaningful look and slowly set the books back down. She nodded her head subtly into the dining area, and when I looked toward where she'd indicated, I immediately saw what had caught her attention.

A man wearing a 49ers cap.

A zing of adrenaline shot through me. The man hadn't noticed me yet, or at least, didn't appear to have. He wasn't drinking anything, nor was he eating a pastry. It appeared as if he'd come in and had found a quiet corner table to sit with his head down, phone in hand. His hair wasn't long or curly as far as I could tell, but if he was the same man who'd followed Vicki and me, he could have cut his hair, or tucked it beneath the cap this time.

I hurried down the stairs to join Beth.

"That's him," she whispered. "That's the guy who'd watched you talk to the murder victim."

The man couldn't have heard her, nor seen her, since his eyes were riveted to his phone, but he abruptly stood and made for the door, with his head down to hide his face.

There was no way I was going to let him get away that easily.

"Hey!" I called, but he kept walking. "Hey, you in the 49ers hat!"

He didn't stop.

"I've got this," Beth said when I glanced at her. "Go."

So, I did.

The man turned down the street and was walking away in that quick, brisk walk people did when they wanted to hurry, but didn't want anyone to notice them at the same time. I wasn't worried about people seeing me, so I started running, much to my body's annoyance. My knees immediately started complaining, but I didn't let that stop me. I caught up with the man after only a few moments, and stepped in front of him to halt his escape.

"Who are you?" I demanded, holding out a hand so he wouldn't walk into me. "Why are you watching me?"

The man froze, and I finally got a good look at his face. He was bronzed, with a smattering of freckles across a nose that appeared to have been worked on at some point in his past. He looked frightened, and nothing like a killer.

"I . . ." His gaze flickered past me. "I have somewhere to be."

"Not until you explain yourself." I put my hands on my hips for emphasis—*not* because I was winded after my short jog. Honest.

He licked his lips, and then removed his 49ers cap to wipe his brow with the back of his arm. While the shorter hair around his temples and the back of his head was light brown, the top of his head was a mop of bleach-blond hair. He smoothed it back and replaced the cap on his head.

"I'm not trying to hurt anyone," he said. "I was just watching."

"Watching because?"

"Because . . ." Another look past me, and then, with uncertainty, "Research?"

"Are you sure about that?" I asked. "Because you don't sound too sure of yourself. What kind of research?"

He cleared his throat. "It's not for me." He removed the hat, smoothed back his hair again, and replaced it. "Please. I wasn't supposed to get caught. She'll be mad."

"She who?" I looked him up and down. He didn't look like the guy who'd followed Vicki and me, but then again, I never did get a good look at him. He could have worn a wig, changed his posture and clothes. And while it looked natural, that tan *could* have come from a can. "Why did you follow me the other night?"

"Follow you?" He shook his head. "I never followed you. I'm here for the bookstore café."

What is going on here? My heart rate had slowed by now, and my certainty that this man was the source of all my troubles was waning. "Who sent you?" I demanded. If this was some sort of revenge tactic perpetrated by Judith Banyon, who likely still thought I'd busted the window of the Banyon Tree, she and I were going to have words.

Instead of answering, the man raised a hand. It took me a moment to realize he was beckoning someone over.

I hazarded a look over my shoulder, fully expecting it to be a ploy so he could turn and run the other way, but I was wrong. Stepping out of a car parked down the street was a long-legged beauty with hair spritzed and teased like it was still the eighties.

"*Valerie?*" Her name tumbled from my lips and splatted at my feet.

Valerie Kemp. The woman who'd bullied me when we were kids. Popular, arrogant, and completely unaware how awful she'd made my life growing up. She strode toward me in heels that made her long legs seem even longer. Her skirt, which was just this side of decent, clung to her body in a way that turned more than a couple of heads.

"You weren't supposed to let her see you, Hugh."

"I'm sorry, Val. She followed me out."

Hugh moved to stand next to Valerie. He put a hand on her back, which seemed to annoy her briefly, before she accepted his touch. *Dating?* I wondered.

"What are you doing here?" I asked. I hadn't seen Valerie since JavaCon, and even then, that had been a brief chat, for which I was grateful. Before that chance meeting, it had been years since we'd seen one another. I'd hoped it would be a few decades more before our next meeting.

Yet here she was, in Pine Hills, standing with some guy who'd been creeping around my store.

Valerie tapped a toe on the sidewalk. There appeared to be some sort of debate going on in her head, which, knowing her, could take a while. She looked me up and down, and then, oddly, raised her phone and snapped a photo.

"Remind me to find something more . . . fashionable," she told Hugh, who quickly started typing into his phone.

"What is going on here?" I was beyond confused. Had Valerie come all the way from California just to insult me? Or was she in on the plan to ruin my life? I had no idea how she would have known all the details about the murder investigations I'd been involved in over the years. Yet, if anyone fit the bill as being someone who would leap at the chance to harass me, it would be Valerie.

But how did she know Hamish Lauder? I refused to believe his murder was random—or done just to make me look bad.

"I suppose I might as well tell you, now that you're on to us," Valerie said with a sharp look at Hugh, who appeared suitably abashed.

"Tell me what?" I braced myself.

"I'm opening a bookstore café."

I blinked at her. "What?"

"You know, like you have there?" She nodded toward Death by Coffee. "I wanted to see what one was like, and decided to come here and investigate. I plan on making my place the go-to coffee shop and bookstore in all of California. Maybe the entire continent."

"You came all the way to Ohio just to scout my place of business?"

"Why not?" She shrugged as if the plane ticket and hotel and time away from home meant nothing. "I know you and Vicki and thought I might as well see what you two managed to do on your own. It's . . . quaint." She made it sound like an insult, which, I supposed, it was.

"I . . ." Was flabbergasted. Stunned. All of the words that meant I was so shocked, I had no words.

"I knew you'd act like this, which is why I didn't want you to see me." She heaved a put-upon sigh. Hugh massaged her back. "I recruited my boyfriend to get video of the inside, but he totally messed that up the first time, which was why I had to send him back."

"I'm used to an iPhone," he said, holding up his Samsung. It was one of the fancy new ones with about a half dozen cameras on the back. "I thought I *was* taking video."

I couldn't wrap my mind around it. "You were following me." It was the only thing I could think of to say.

"Following you?" Valerie rolled her eyes. "We were here for recon only. I took photos of your place, and that's it."

"Photos?"

"Here, look." Valerie stepped toward me, which caused me to take an abrupt step back. Another eye roll, and then she moved to stand beside me. She brought up her photo gallery and began flipping through the photos she'd taken.

Sure enough, there were images of Death by Coffee from every angle you could imagine, including some through the windows that gave a good look inside. Most of the photos, however, were taken from what appeared to be across the street, as in, from the front seat of a car.

Just like what Trisha had seen.

"Wait," I said, as she flipped through the series. "Go back."

Valerie hesitated, and then went back one photo. The image was sharp, without a hint of blur. "I took a few images of the area, to get a feel for the place," she explained. "Placement is important to the success of a business, you know?"

"When did you take this exactly?" I asked, heart hammering.

Valerie tapped the screen and the data popped up.

The photo had been taken five days ago.

"Those two had just come out of that building there," Valerie said, pointing. "I was in my car, catching the *feel* of the area, and thought it would be a good idea to get some photos of the sort of people who live here, not just the buildings. I'm trying to create a full-bodied experience with my place, you see, and—"

I wasn't listening. I snatched the phone from Valerie's hand and zoomed in to be sure I was seeing what I thought I was.

The man in the photo was wearing a Reds baseball cap. Long, curly hair flowed out from beneath it. He'd turned his head away from the camera when Valerie had shot the photo, so I couldn't make out his face.

But I didn't need to. It was the same man who'd followed Vicki and me from Scream for Ice Cream; I was sure of it. He was walking with the woman who'd found the cockroaches in her drink, talking to her like he knew her.

And the building they'd just exited?

It was Lawyer's Insurance.

22

"Thank you, come again." I handed over a caramel latte. My smile was forced, and my eyes kept drifting toward the window, and the building across the street.

I desperately wanted to confront Raymond Lawyer, but with Beth being the only other person working at Death by Coffee at the moment, I couldn't just waltz over. I refused to abandon her like that, even if Raymond might currently be sitting behind his desk, plotting my downfall.

He wouldn't do that.

Plotting, yes, but murder?

I was missing something; I had to be. Just because the guy who'd stalked Vicki and me was seen with the woman who'd found the cockroaches, and they'd both come out of Lawyer's Insurance, didn't mean they were connected to one another. Maybe they'd just happened to be shopping for insurance at the same time.

And maybe I was a fit supermodel who kept her nose out of other people's business.

Death by Coffee was hopping, despite it being early for our lunch rush. It wasn't like a weather change had prompted it either. It was more likely that people were stopping in to show support after abandoning us during the bug scandal. I was happy to see them back, but boy, did I wish they'd have waited a day or two more, at least until this murder thing was behind me.

I continued to work the counter, while Beth was running all over the place. One moment, she'd be upstairs, helping someone with the books, then she'd be cleaning tables in the dining area before rushing to the back to restock cups. Mason was due any time now, and I prayed that he'd show before Beth and I collapsed.

"Hi, Todd," I said, sweat beading my brow as he approached the counter. "What can I get you?"

The masked Todd Melville ordered, eyes wandering the store to make sure Trouble was nowhere to be found. His allergies only seemed to get worse as the years wore on, and I feared he'd eventually be too overcome by them to shop with us anymore. His eyes were watering, and he kept sniffing from behind his mask, but he refused to let his allergies keep him from his coffee.

As I filled his order, my mind started to wander. I knew the regulars. Even some of the people who only stopped in once or twice a week were familiar to me. If I didn't know their names, I knew their faces.

But the woman who'd found the cockroaches? I was pretty sure I'd never seen her in Death by Coffee before. The same goes for the curly-haired man. It was entirely possible they usually came in when I wasn't working, or that their visits were so infrequent I'd forgotten their faces over time, but I wasn't so sure that was it.

I handed over the coffee and mechanically took the next order. Why would strangers go to all this trouble to hurt me and my image?

Because someone paid them to do it.

My stomach was in knots by the time business slowed and I could take a breath. I really didn't want to believe Raymond Lawyer had anything to do with Hamish's death, let alone my harassment. It would cause far too much tension among my friends, which, I was afraid, very well might be the point.

When Mason came through the door a few minutes later, the knots turned into a vicelike fist. He was smiling and whistling under his breath, much like I had been doing when I'd started the day. Those few hours of bliss felt like they'd happened eons ago.

"I'm here," he announced, taking a quick look around the dining area, which was a bit of a mess. "And it appears I've arrived in the nick of time."

"We've been slammed all day," Beth said, coming down the stairs. She looked as ragged as I felt. "But we managed."

"Of course, you did. You're our superstars." He winked, and then turned to me. "I hope you don't mind, but Vicki is going to be pretty busy over the next few days and won't be able to work as much as usual. They're going to move forward with the play, stinky curtains and all. They're trying to make up for lost time, which means she has to be at the theatre twice as often as before."

"That's great." I tried to sound enthused, but it came out sounding miserable.

Mason's smile faded. He looked to Beth, who shrugged and returned upstairs, before he turned his full attention to me. He gave me a good looking over, before he put an arm around my shoulder and led me back behind the counter, away from the customers who remained.

"What happened?" he asked, keeping his voice low. "Please tell me there wasn't another bug incident."

"No, nothing like that." I debated on how to broach the subject of his dad with him, and couldn't come up with anything that didn't sound accusatory. How do you tell someone that their father might be an accessory to murder?

"Did you know a woman named Abigail Abele?" I asked instead.

Mason thought about it a moment before shaking his head. "The name doesn't ring a bell."

"Are you sure? This would have been years ago, back when you were in your teens maybe."

"No, I don't think I know her." He frowned. "Wait. You asked if I *knew* her. As in past tense. Is she . . . ?"

I nodded. "It was an accident." I paused, and then, with nothing else I could do, I pressed on with it. "I found an article about her death. Your dad is quoted in it."

"Hold up." Mason paced away, lightly scratching at his cheek in thought. "You said Abele?"

"Yeah. Abigail."

"I don't know the first name, but I believe I've heard Dad mention a Cal Abele. Any relation?"

"He's her father."

Mason snapped his fingers. "One of Dad's friends. The unsavory sort, if I recall." Mason perked up at having remembered the name. "I never met many of Dad's friends because they are far too much like him for my tastes. I was out of the house the moment I could afford a place of my own, and I never looked back."

"So, you'd never met Cal's daughter?"

"Not that I'm aware," Mason said. "I suppose it's possible that we met and I just don't recall. Brendon . . ." He cleared his throat and winced at his late brother's name. "He would have been the one to ask since he was part of that world." Understanding came into his eye then. "This is about the murder, isn't it?"

I took a deep breath and debated on how to bring up his dad without making it sound like I was accusing him of something.

"Abigail knew Hamish." I spoke slowly, choosing my words carefully. "They were friends."

"The murdered man?"

"The one and the same."

"That seems a rather harsh coincidence. Are you sure her death was an accident?"

"I've seen no evidence that it wasn't." Though I did see his point. If Hamish had murdered Abigail, could Cal Abele have sought revenge? He could have gone through Raymond, who then went to the two people who'd been skulking around me and my place of business.

But how did I play into any of this? I still couldn't figure out why I'd been chosen as a scapegoat, or why I'd been framed for other crimes—the vandalism, the hateful posts. It seemed like overkill.

"And Dad?" Mason braced himself as if waiting for a gut punch.

"There was that article I mentioned where your dad was quoted about Abigail's death," I said. "I want to talk to him about it, see if maybe there *was* a connection between Hamish's murder and Abigail's accident. They might have happened years apart but . . ."

"Sometimes revenge takes time," Mason said, nodding as he thought it through. "I could always ask Dad about—" His brow furrowed as he caught my expression. "What?"

"That's not all, Mason." I swallowed a fist-sized lump that had risen in my throat. "I have a witness who saw two"—I debated on what term to use and settled on—"suspects come out of Lawyer's Insurance together."

"Suspects in the murder?"

"Among other things. Vicki told you about the guy who followed us out of Scream for Ice Cream?"

"Yeah. She was more angry than scared."

"Well, that guy was seen with the woman who'd found the cockroach in her drink. He also matches the description of the man who asked for a piece of stationery from Jeff, which makes him the main suspect in the destruction of the theatre and planting the note demanding Vicki be given the lead role."

Mason's face didn't just grow troubled. He looked

as if I'd just told him his entire life was about to be flipped upside down and shaken about.

Honestly, if his dad is connected to any of this, I might have.

"It doesn't make sense," Mason said. "Why would Dad be involved with these people? You're saying the woman who was here, in this store, the one who'd freaked out because she'd found roaches in her drink, might be working with a killer?"

"I honestly have no idea," I admitted. "It could be a coincidence."

"But with everything that's been happening lately, it's unlikely." Mason closed his eyes and dug his palms into them.

"Yeah."

A customer entered and I took his order, which gave Mason time to digest what I'd told him. I was still holding out hope that something would spring to mind and he'd have a perfectly rational explanation for all of this.

But when I turned around, Mason looked green.

"You'll need to talk to him," he said.

"Talk to Raymond?"

He nodded. "I . . . I can't. If he admitted . . ." He snapped his teeth closed, unwilling to voice whatever thought had crossed his mind. It wasn't too hard to guess what it might be.

"I'm sure there's a reasonable explanation for all of this." But man, I was struggling to come up with one.

"Dad can be forceful," Mason said. "He often does things without considering the repercussions of his actions. And even if he does, he often doesn't care about consequences, as long as he gets what he wants."

"But what could he possibly want that would account for all of this?" I asked. "I get that he doesn't like me. But why go to all this trouble to ruin my name? And murder?" As much as I didn't care for Raymond Lawyer, I couldn't imagine him as a killer.

"There's got to be something we're missing," Mason insisted. "Dad wouldn't sign off on killing someone. Verbal abuse? Sure. But not murder."

I agreed. So, if Raymond was indeed working with these people, did that mean his accomplices had taken things a step further without his knowledge? Or could they have come out of his building, not because they were in cahoots, but because they were blackmailing him?

I clung to that thought. What if Abigail's death wasn't an accident? What if Raymond knew who killed her and had kept it a secret for all of these years? Hamish might not have had too many friends, but Mark had made it clear that someone had been with him hours before his murder. Could those two people have known him and killed him over Abigail's death?

And what about the similarity between Abigail and Abby? There might not be anything to it—lots of people have similar names to one another—but it was suspect.

There was only one way I was going to get to the bottom of this, and standing around Death by Coffee wasn't going to be it.

The dining area was mostly empty by now. It needed to be cleaned, but Mason and Beth could handle that.

"I should talk to Raymond now and get this over with," I said, dreading it even as I said it. "If you've got this covered . . . ?"

"Yeah, go." Mason waved me off. "Find out what he knows and then tell me before I drive myself crazy with worry." His fists clenched briefly and I saw the pure emotion in his face. His relationship with his father was already strained, and this was going to make it worse, no matter how it turned out.

"I will." I balled up my Death by Coffee apron and headed for the door.

Traffic was light as I stepped out onto the sunny sidewalk. Lawyer's Insurance loomed across the street, as imposing as the man inside. It was a stark building, void of life. Or maybe I was projecting. Either way, just the thought of entering the place made my palms start to sweat and sent my nerves jumping.

I paused at the street to look both ways, but before I could cross, fate stepped in and blocked my path.

Well, a car did, anyway.

"Get in."

My heart sank when I saw Detective John Buchannan's face. His expression was carefully controlled, though his eyes were hot.

"Where are we going?" I asked. I thought of those movies where the dirty cop offers a ride to the innocent woman and then takes her into the middle of nowhere so he could quietly end her meddling ways.

Of course, Buchannan wasn't a dirty cop, and in many eyes, I was far from innocent, but still . . .

"Please, Ms. Hancock," he said. No first name. That made me even more nervous. "Get in. We need to talk."

I took one more longing look at Lawyer's Insurance, and then, with no other option that wouldn't land me even further on the detective's bad side, I climbed into the car to let fate—and Buchannan—take me where it pleased.

23

Buchannan didn't take me deep into the forest, nor did he drive well beyond the hills where no one would ever find me. He didn't pull into an abandoned parking lot, or to a rundown factory where he could tie me to a chair and torture an admission of guilt out of me.

He, like the policeman he was, took me to the police station.

"Three times in a week?" I asked him as he led me down the hall, into the interrogation room. "Couldn't we have done this at Death by Coffee? I could have made us a couple of lattes and we could have had a pleasant chat by the window."

He merely grunted, deposited me into the room, and then he left to, as he put it, "make preparations." Whatever that meant. It was just as likely that he was sitting outside the door, snickering while he made me wait needlessly.

But I refused to be intimidated. Whatever this

was, I was innocent. I didn't care if he had more video proof of my wrongdoings, or a signed confession, forged by my harasser. I was confident I could talk my way out of whatever he had on me.

And since I had information on his murder case, I was pretty sure I could steer the conversation away from my possible guilt, on to someone more deserving.

You know, like the actual killer.

The minutes ticked by. I rose from my wobbly chair and paced the room. It smelled of sweat and stale coffee. A pillow lay on one corner of the couch. It was smashed, and likely should have been retired sometime last decade. A ratty blanket was balled up next to it.

Was someone sleeping here?

The petty part of me wanted it to be Buchannan, but found it unlikely. I felt like an intruder, as if I'd just walked into someone's bedroom while they were still snoozing. I turned my back to the makeshift bed, and instead chose to study the coffeemaker. It was just a basic model, and the carafe had a thin layer of what used to be coffee sitting inside it. It looked more like oil now.

The door opened and Buchannan entered alone. He motioned toward the wobbly chair as he sat himself down. He had another manilla folder with him. As I sat, I wondered if it was the same folder he'd carried before, or if this were a new one. He placed it in front of me, still closed, and then crossed his arms.

I mirrored his movements. I wasn't going to speak first. He'd dragged me down here when we could have had this conversation elsewhere. If

Buchannan wanted something from me, he was going to have to ask for it.

After a long couple of seconds, he reached out, flipped open the folder, and spun it around toward me.

"Can you tell me what this is, Ms. Hancock?"

I leaned forward to look. There were a handful of pages stacked in the folder. A photograph was pinned to the top sheet.

It was a picture of money.

I said as much.

"Keep looking," Buchannan said, motioning toward the folder.

Beneath the photo was a printed note.

I'm sorry for your troubles. Krissy is innocent.

"What is this?" I asked. I flipped the note over, but the opposite side was blank. Beneath it was another photograph of a stack of cash pinned to yet another note proclaiming my innocence.

"That's what I asked you."

"I have no idea. How much cash is there?" I squinted at the stack. It was a twenty at the top, so it wasn't piles of hundreds or anything. But it wasn't a small stack either.

Buchannan's eyes narrowed. "You don't know?"

"No, I don't."

He sighed and picked up the top page. "This was found at the Banyon Tree." The next. "And this one was discovered on the stage at the theatre." He set that one aside and picked up the next. "And this, at the local library."

"I had nothing to do with this," I said. If this was another attempt at ruining my name, it was a rather odd one. "Why would someone do this?"

Buchannan closed the folder and rested a hand atop it. "A bribe, maybe?"

"A bribe? For what purpose?"

"To clear your name? It's come up in some rather questionable situations as of late."

"I didn't do anything! This must be—" My teeth closed with a snap. *Oh, no.* Rita.

Buchannan leaned forward. "You thought of something."

I shook my head. *This* was what Rita had been doing when she'd left Johan at my place. I get that she was trying to help, but she had to have seen that leaving money and a note like this everywhere where I'd been accused of causing trouble had to look suspicious.

"Look, Ms. Hancock." He paused, frowned. "Krissy. I get it. You don't want to get anyone into trouble. And honestly, I don't have a problem with you, or one of your friends, donating money to these places. Some of them need it." He tapped the page that had been sent to the library. "But you have to see how it looks?"

"I do," I said. "And, honestly, I had nothing to do with this."

"Just like you didn't send that email to my wife?"

"I didn't!" I took a calming breath. He was asking questions, as he should as a detective. "Someone has been setting me up. You know me, John." I used his first name in the hopes that it would earn me some sympathy. It felt strange coming out of my mouth, but it did seem to have the right effect.

He sighed and sat back. "I know."

"You know?"

"That you haven't done any of the things you've been accused of."

I blinked at him. *He* knows? "Then why am I here?"

"You might not have done those things, but you *do* know something about them. I don't know if you've worked out who's responsible, or if you merely have theories, but I want to know what you've come up with before someone else gets hurt."

Was he asking for my help? I tried really hard not to show my pleasure. Okay, I kind of tried.

All right, fine. I grinned like an idiot.

Buchannan scowled. "Don't make me regret telling you that."

I managed to tone the grin down to a self-satisfied smile. For once, it appeared as if Buchannan was going to take me seriously, without throwing wild accusations my way. I mean, he's treated me okay before, but there was always a hint of distrust behind it. He seemed to genuinely want my help here. And if I wanted that to continue, I needed to tell him what I knew.

I went through everything I'd learned, leaving out the bits about Shannon, Raymond Lawyer, and Rita. There was no sense in bringing up the two women since neither of them had anything to do with the murder, let alone the vandalism or threatening emails. And Raymond . . .

I felt bad about not bringing him up, but I really wanted to talk to him first, to get his side of the story, before I dropped him in Buchannan's lap. Maybe if he weren't Mason's dad, I might have done it. It wasn't like I had any love for Raymond

Lawyer, but since he *was* my best friend's father-in-law, I refused to get him into trouble without proof.

"I did get a photo of the guy who followed Vicki and me," I said, fishing out my phone. "It's not great, but maybe you'll see something that will help you find the guy. I'm pretty sure he's involved in this." I found the picture I'd snapped and handed my phone over.

Buchannan took one look at it and scowled. "I see a shoulder."

"He's the guy past that."

He zoomed in on the image. "Are you sure? I can't make out anything."

"That's the best I've got. I know someone who took a picture of both the man *and* the woman together, but I don't have it myself."

"The woman who'd found the bugs in her drink?"

I nodded. "I think she planted them in my store. I believe the two of them—the stalker and bug planter—are working together."

"And someone has a photo of this?"

"Of them together," I clarified. "Talking. I'm not sure there's much evidence in the photo that they're actually plotting my downfall, but I'd say it's a close thing. I'll see if I can get the photo for you." If I could find Valerie, that was. For all I knew, she was already on a plane back to California.

"Give me this friend's name and I'll take care of it." Buchannan pulled a pen and a pad of paper from his pocket.

I almost told him that Valerie was in no way a

friend, but decided that wasn't important. I gave him her name, but warned him that she was from out of town. "I don't know where she's staying, and I don't know her number to call her. Sorry."

"I'll find her." He tucked the pad of paper away. "Is there anything else you've left out?" He narrowed his eyes at me. "Because if there is, I won't be happy."

I started to shake my head no, but caught myself. "Have you talked to Mark Cunningham? He was friends with Hamish Lauder."

Something flashed across Buchannan's face. Guilt? I thought so. "I'm working through a list of possible witnesses and I can confirm he's on that list."

That wasn't a definitive yes or no, but I took it as the latter. "He heard voices on the phone when he talked to Hamish on the night of the murder. A man and a woman." I gave him a meaningful look.

"I'll talk to him," he said. "But unless I can find someone who has a better description than," he checked his notes, " 'a curly-haired man who wears a baseball hat and a shortish woman with glasses,' I don't have much to go on."

"Jeff might have seen the guy," I said. "Jeff Braun. He works at Death by Coffee."

Buchannan nodded and made a "get on with it" gesture.

"If you can get ahold of Valerie's picture of the guy, Jeff might be able to verify that he's the same man who'd borrowed stationery from Death by Coffee." And then later, used it to frame me for vandalizing the stage.

"I'll be sure to talk to him." Buchannan rose,

clearly miffed I was trying to tell him how to do his job. "I think that's all I need from you for right now. If you have someone you can call to pick you up, you can wait for them outside."

I stood. "You're not going to drive me back?"

There was a glint in Buchannan's eye that told me he still hadn't forgiven me for the email I *hadn't* written. "I have a lot of work I need to do. Calls to make. I'm sure you understand."

I grumbled to myself as he led me out of the interrogation room, and to the front doors. There, he left me, but at least I wasn't alone.

"I see you can't stay away from this place." Chief Patricia Dalton was leaning against the wall, next to the doors, as if she'd been waiting for me. She probably had been.

"Detective Buchannan had some questions," I said, shooting said detective a dirty look he didn't see. "I helped out as best as I could, and then he abandoned me here."

Patricia grunted in what might have been an abbreviated laugh before she pushed away from the wall. "I have a little time. Come on. I'll take you wherever you need to go."

I followed her out of the police station and to her car. "I could always call someone to get me," I said. "I don't want to be any trouble."

"Nonsense. Get in."

I did as I was told. Chief Dalton wasn't a woman you defied. She might be on the smaller side, but she held herself like someone much bigger.

And considering I was dating her son, I wanted her to like me.

"Chief Dalton, I—"

She held up a hand, cutting me off. She didn't speak right away. She drove, eyes straight ahead. I sat back and waited. Her presence at the doors to the station wasn't just a coincidence, or an act of pity; she had something to say.

"This whole hubbub has been hard on Paul," she said after what felt like an eternity. "He's stood by you wholeheartedly, and that's something we all respect, and that includes Detective Buchannan."

She paused. I wasn't sure if she expected me to say something, or if she wanted me to sit there and listen. I chose the latter since it seemed safer.

"I get that you aren't responsible for other people's actions. I understand that you also feel the need to put yourself in situations that others might deem as reckless and unnecessary. Those people don't always see the results of your recklessness. I do."

I couldn't tell if that was a good thing or a bad thing and was too scared to ask.

"Paul has plans." She sucked in her lower lip, bit briefly, and then went on. "You're involved in those plans. I don't want something to happen to you which will end up throwing those plans awry. So, while I understand your need, and I can appreciate the help you've done for our local brand of justice, I can't condone such behavior from you."

She finally glanced at me, a hard look that said she would brook no argument.

"I understand." The words came out sounding like I was a properly chastised child.

"Good." She nodded once, and the tension in the car bled away. "Detective Buchannan will get to the bottom of these crimes that are being tied to you by someone who doesn't realize what kind of mess they're getting themselves into by going after our own local celebrity. Until then, I expect you to be good and steer clear of anything that might interfere with him, or put you in a situation none of us wants you to be in."

"I will." I mean, how could talking to Raymond Lawyer put me in any danger? I didn't like the guy, but I wasn't afraid he was going to murder me either. He might scowl a lot, and he would scream and yell at me, but that's as far as it would go.

Another glance, and another nod. Patricia, it appeared, was satisfied.

What does Paul have planned? I wondered in the silence that followed. There was a churning in my gut, an excitement and a fear, that had me squirming in my seat. I wanted to walk. Maybe even run. Could he be thinking of our future together? Or is it something smaller? Like a vacation? A trip to some exotic locale where we'd be alone and . . . and . . .

And Angela and Nina were standing outside the community theatre, arguing.

"Stop," I said, bracing a hand against the dash like I thought Chief Dalton would slam on the brakes at my word. "Let me out here."

"Here?" She slowed and then pulled to the side of the road, just past the theatre and arguing pair of women. "Death by Coffee isn't far."

"I know." I pushed open the car door. "Vicki's in the play this year and I want to stop by and say hi." I winced at the lie, but was looking back toward the theatre, so Patricia didn't see it on my face.

"If you say so." The doubt was thick in Patricia's

voice as I climbed out of the car. She leaned across the seat, finger pointed at me, just before I closed the door. "Stay out of trouble."

"I'll do my best." I slammed the door closed, and gave her the most innocent smile I could manage.

Patricia's eyes narrowed, then she shook her head, put the car in gear, and drove off.

I waited until she was out of sight before I turned to head to the theatre, and to put myself in the middle of where Chief Dalton didn't want me to be.

24

"I don't care! You wanted this role."

"I can't work under these conditions!" Nina jammed her hands onto her hips with such force, she actually winced. "You don't understand what I'm going through."

"Oh?" Angela mirrored her gesture, albeit with a little more care. "How about you enlighten me?"

Nina opened her mouth to respond, but snapped it closed when she saw me approaching. Her eyes narrowed, and she spoke through gritted teeth. "Can I help you?"

Angela turned to see who Nina was addressing. Her angry glare didn't soften when she saw me. If anything, it only grew in intensity.

"I'm sorry to intrude," I said, hands raised before me. "I was walking by and couldn't help but overhear."

"You can keep walking," Nina said. "We're discussing theatre business."

"I understand." But I didn't walk away. "I heard the play will go on as planned. I'm glad. Vicki was really upset when she thought it might get cancelled."

"We're managing," Angela said. "As best we can under the circumstances, anyway." She shot a look toward Nina, who was staring at me like I'd grown a second head.

"You know Vicki?" she asked, taking a step back from me, as if she thought that knowing Vicki was as contagious as a plague.

"She's my best friend. I want the play to succeed, and when I saw you two arguing out here, I grew concerned."

"There's nothing to be concerned about," Angela said. "It's nothing more than typical preshow tensions."

"There's nothing typical about it. I wish I'd never—" Nina cut off, eyes flashing toward me in panic.

"Never what?"

Angela and Nina shared a look. Something was going on between them, and I had a sinking feeling there was more to it than just Nina's less-than-stellar portrayal of the lead.

"I'll find out," I said, crossing my arms in a way that I hoped proved my determination. Stubbornness might as well be my middle name at this point. "You know I will."

Angela tensed, and for a moment, she looked as if she were about to tell me where I could shove my stubborn nose, but then she sagged. "I suppose we might as well tell her. It'll come out anyway."

"What will?"

Nina bit her lower lip, and then took an abrupt step forward. We were now standing in a close circle that would look suspicious to anyone watching us from the outside.

"It wasn't my idea," she said, voice pitched at a harsh, pleading whisper. "Really, it wasn't."

I looked from her to Angela and back again. "What wasn't?"

"You can't tell Vicki," Nina said. "Promise me you won't tell."

I hated making promises without knowing exactly what I was promising. Vicki was my friend, and if whatever Nina was hiding affected her, how could I *not* tell her about it?

But if I wanted to find out what was going on, I needed to give Nina what she wanted. "I promise I won't tell Vicki. What happened?"

Nina pulled a tissue from her handbag and dabbed at her eyes. "You see, I met this guy a few months ago. Cute, I guess. He was interested in me and the play, and well, he was just so charming, I couldn't tell him no when he asked me out."

"Despite the fact you were already seeing someone." From Angela's tone, I wondered if she was close to this other someone. It would explain the resentment.

And why Nina got a role she clearly wasn't ready for.

"Yes, well, I said I wish it wouldn't have happened." Nina dabbed at her eyes again, though they were dry as could be. "We went out and he was asking me all about the play and the theatre, like where we kept the props and what time we left and things like that. I thought he planned on sneaking in and meeting me after practice, you know? We'd duck into a utility closet or something, test out some of the supports. But he never showed."

"He ditched you?" I asked.

Nina's eyes narrowed at the insinuation that anyone could reject her for any reason. "It never had anything to do with me."

"I'm not judging," I said. "The guy must have been a jerk to leave you hanging like that."

That seemed to mollify her, because she nodded once before going on. "He knew I wanted the lead role in the play, and was sympathetic toward my cause. This was back when we were auditioning for our parts, before I'd landed the gig. I swear to you I didn't ask him for help; he just offered it up right then and there."

"On your first and only date," Angela said.

"I wasn't thinking clearly." Nina sniffed. More eye dabs. "It wasn't until later that I realized he was pumping me for information, that he planned to do, well, *that*." She gestured toward the theatre. "I also didn't realize that the information he gave me would cause so much trouble."

They know who vandalized the theatre! I wondered if Buchannan knew, but that wasn't the most important question right then. "What information?" I asked. I was already convinced the man she was talking about was my curly-haired stalker. It was too much of a coincidence for it not to be.

Nina looked to Angela, who was worrying at her lower lip with her teeth. A silent conversation went on between them, one that Angela eventually won.

"He told me things," Nina said. "About Angela.

About her personal life. You know, things she wanted to keep secret? And I did keep them secret!"

A metaphorical lightbulb clicked on above my head. "You blackmailed her."

"I wouldn't call it that . . ."

By Angela's expression, she most definitely considered it blackmail.

"I simply brought what I knew to Angela and said I'd keep quiet if I got the lead role. It was stupid of me, but I was desperate. I knew Vicki was going to land the lead if I didn't do *something*. So . . ." More eye dabs. More dainty sniffs. "This was my chance. I had no intention of ever telling anyone what he told me. I'm not a gossip."

One look at Angela's expression and I knew why they'd been arguing. "But it got out anyway."

Nina nodded. "I don't know how! I never told a soul. And now, with the stage all messed up, and the smell, I just don't know if I can go on."

"After everything you've done, you have no choice!"

I didn't want to lose hold of the conversation, so I cut in. "What did this guy look like? What was his name?"

Nina continued with her contrite, miserable show, even though her tissue was dry as a bone. If she regretted anything, it was getting caught in the trap, not blackmailing the director and stealing a role meant for someone else. "He said his name was Billy, but I think that was a lie," she said. "As for his looks, he had brown eyes that matched his long, curly hair . . ."

* * *

I walked the rest of the way back to Death by Coffee, mind racing as I tried to put the pieces together. Whoever this curly-haired man was, he was responsible for everything that had happened to me in the last few weeks, if not months. He was also my best suspect when it came to who killed Hamish Lauder. The more I learned about him, the more I heard about what he'd done, the more I felt I was getting closer to finally figuring out who he was.

Or was I?

I had little to go on. No name, other than the one Nina had given me, one that we were both sure was a fake. I had a general description of a man with curly hair who often wears a baseball cap. As far as I knew, he wore a wig to hide his real hairstyle. He might be bald for all I knew.

But, if all these stray pieces *did* connect to one another, then I knew one man who might be able to fill in the holes.

I paused outside Death by Coffee and peered inside. There were a few customers at the tables, and someone was browsing the books upstairs, but otherwise, it wasn't busy. Beth was chatting with Mason at the counter, and Jeff had come in since I'd left for my interrogation with Buchannan. He was upstairs, watching the man in the books weave up and down the aisles, waiting for the moment when he'd be needed.

They had everything under control.

It was time I talked to Raymond Lawyer.

But despite my determination to get to the bottom of how he was involved, each step grew heavier as I approached Lawyer's Insurance. I so didn't want to do this. Raymond and I didn't get along, even when we were being civil toward one another. Our personalities simply didn't mesh, and that's okay. Not everyone can be friends, let alone cordial. It happens.

No cops pulled up to stop me this time as I stepped up to the doors. I took a deep, bracing breath, and then entered Lawyer's Insurance. Despite not having been inside for years, I found it to not have changed much at all. The front desk was occupied by a woman who could have been Beth's twin sister, if Beth hadn't moved beyond the press-on nails and bottled-blond looks, complete with a bubblegum snapping personality. A nameplate on the desk told me her name was Hallie. She looked up at me, and then immediately dismissed me, as if realizing right away I wasn't there to apply for insurance.

"I'm here to speak to Mr. Lawyer," I said, glancing toward his office. The door was closed, but I could *feel* his looming presence through the wood.

The secretary snapped her gum, and then tapped something on her keyboard. She didn't tell me to sit, or that he was busy, or anything at all. I was guessing she already knew who I was and had orders to pretend as if I didn't exist.

As if that would stop me.

I paced away from the desk and found myself looking at Brendon Lawyer's old office. The nameplate was still there, the door closed, even though Brendon had been dead and gone for years now. I wondered if Raymond had left everything else in place, or if he'd moved all of Brendon's things out, leaving it an empty space that would never again be filled.

Raymond's office door opened. He stared at me in silence, and then turned and walked back to his desk, leaving the door hanging open. It was likely the closest thing to an invitation I'd get.

I entered his office and closed the door behind me. He was already seated, hands folded in front of him. He'd aged over the last few months. The already harsh lines of his face were deeper. His mouth was pulled down in a perpetual frown that wasn't entirely affected.

"Raymond," I said.

"Ms. Hancock." He took a deep breath, much like I'd done as I'd entered his place of business, before he motioned toward the chair across from him.

I sat. "I won't keep you."

He didn't react with anything more than a mild nod.

There was nothing else to do but press forward. "How did you know Abigail Abele?"

The name hit Raymond like a fist to the face. He rocked back in his seat, and for the first time since I knew him, he looked shocked, hurt even.

"Abigail?" he asked. Gone was the cynicism, the constant anger. He sounded human for once. "How do you know that name?"

"You know about what happened to Hamish Lauder?" Raymond nodded. "I was looking into some stuff about him and came across an article where you talked about Abigail after she'd passed."

"I remember that," he said. His hands trembled as he rested them on his desk. "It was a shame."

"So, you knew her well?"

"She was the daughter of one of my closest friends. She was a lovely girl. I considered matching her up with Brendon, but then she died . . ." He trailed off, eyes hazing as he remembered.

"The article said it was an accident? Is that true?"

Raymond's nod was slow, almost dreamy. "She fell. It was kids being kids. You know how teenagers can be? No one was truly to blame."

I caught something in his tone. "But someone *was* blamed?"

Another nod. "The Lauder kid; Hamish. He wasn't being held accountable by the police or anyone like that. And Cal, Abigail's father, didn't blame him. Even her mother, Karen, would have forgiven him, if she'd been alive. But Abigail's boyfriend . . ." He shook his head. "He didn't think Hamish to be so innocent."

I paused. A part of me assumed Hamish and Abigail were a couple, that he'd failed to protect her, which was why his friends had turned against him. Apparently, my assumption had been incorrect.

"Abigail had a boyfriend?" I asked.

"She did. She was a very pretty girl. She could have had just about anyone she pleased." He scowled. "And honestly, she deserved better. Brendon would have treated her right. Samuel was too quick to anger, too petty."

I decided not to bring up how Brendon had treated women before his death, which wasn't kindly. To say the son took after the father was an understatement. It was a wonder Mason hadn't turned out the same way.

I was considering how to bring up the man and woman who'd been seen leaving his place of business, when Raymond did it for me.

"Samuel has cropped back up again recently." Raymond's fists bunched and the anger I'd come to know and love so well was back. "He was here just this week, even though I'd told him time and time again to steer clear of me and my family."

"He has curly hair, right?" I asked. When Raymond gave me a curious look, I explained with a white lie. "I saw him come out of Lawyer's Insurance with another woman a few days ago."

Raymond grunted. "I warned him. He still believes Hamish was responsible for Abigail's death, and swore that he would make sure he got what was coming to him." If he was concerned that Samuel might have murdered Hamish, Raymond didn't show it. "I tried to tell him that an accident is an accident, but he refused to listen to a word that didn't support his belief. Eventually, I'd had enough. I didn't want to see him ever again, so I told him to leave Heidi alone or else I'd find a way to keep him out of her life myself."

I blinked. *What?* "Abigail's former boyfriend knows Heidi?"

Raymond's scowl just about seared my eyebrows, it was so fierce. "Of course, he does. It's why I'm so annoyed with the both of them. Samuel Cox and Heidi are dating."

25

The phone rang. No one answered, so I clicked off and tried another number. Same result.

"Why doesn't anyone ever answer their phone when I need them?" I grouched, tossing my own phone into the passenger seat. It bounced once, and then fell to the floor.

Just great. If someone called now, I'd be the one unable to answer. But since I was on the move, there wasn't anything I could do about it.

Thankfully, no one tried to call me back during my short drive. I pulled to a stop outside of Too Le Fit to Quit, mind already on what I was going to say. After my chat with Raymond, I'd popped in at Death by Coffee to see if I was needed, and since I wasn't, I decided to find Heidi Lawyer to ask her about her new boyfriend.

You know, the one who might be a murderer?

I climbed out of my Escape, nearly tripping over

my own two feet as I hurried into the store. One look around, and my heart sank. Heidi wasn't there.

Maybe she's on break. I found an employee crouched behind the counter. For a second, I thought he was hiding from me, but when he stood, he was holding a box cutter and nudged a freshly opened box of weights out of the way with his foot.

"I'm sorry to bother you," I said, eyeing the box cutter. My nerves had me imagining all sorts of horrible things. "But I'm looking for Heidi. She works here."

The guy didn't roll his eyes or come back with a snotty remark. Of course, he knew Heidi worked there. "Heidi?" he said, wiping his brow with the back of his arm. "She won't be in today. Called off sick."

"She's sick?" And now I was feeling a bit queasy myself.

"Yeah. She said it came on sudden like. It's shipment day and I almost told her to come in anyway, but she sounded pretty bad on the phone. Bet she's got the flu or something."

"You're probably right," I agreed, though I doubted it. Samuel likely knew I was closing in, and . . .

And what? Decided to take his girlfriend hostage? It didn't make much sense, but if he was angry that Raymond refused to believe him about Hamish and Abigail, then perhaps hurting his daughter-in-law was his way of getting revenge on the elder Lawyer.

"Thanks," I said. "I'll check in on her and make sure she's okay."

"Cool. Hey, do you need a supplement or something? I could ring you up a sale. Give you a discount even." He looked me up and down, and I could see the words, *you look like you need it,* all over his face.

"No. I'm fine." I hurried out of the store before he could try to force dumbbells on me, though if I'd thought about it, they might have served as a convenient weapon if I did bump into Samuel.

If I could lift them, that was. And if Samuel *was* indeed holding Heidi hostage.

I pulled away from the curb, mind racing as I tried to fit all of the pieces together. I knew I was likely overreacting, that Heidi was fine, but it was hard not to imagine the worst. Someone was already dead. My life was being shredded one setup at a time. If Samuel Cox *was* involved, then Heidi might be an unwitting part of it, a cog in his master plan. There was even a chance the cockroach woman had been used without her knowledge, all in an effort to put me in a bad light.

I still didn't know *why* I'd been chosen as the scapegoat. I didn't really know Hamish, never knew Abigail. If Samuel wanted to blame someone for Hamish's murder, why not someone with closer ties to the accident? Someone like Raymond Lawyer?

My phone rang, startling me out of my thoughts. Like a dingbat, I hadn't grabbed it from the floor when I'd run into Too Le Fit. I tried to reach for it, but with me driving, it was just too far away. I could see Paul's name on the screen and cursed myself for being too distracted to snatch it from where it had fallen. *And too lazy to pair the darn thing with my car.* The Escape had Bluetooth. It would have taken seconds to set up, but I'd put it off, thinking I'd get around to it eventually.

Well, I hadn't, and now I was paying for it.

The screen faded to black. A minute after that, a notification popped up, telling me I had a voice message.

I turned my attention back to the road. There was nothing I could do about the call until I stopped. I was already almost to Heidi's, so there was no sense in pulling over now. Downtown was behind me, and I was now within the shadow of the hills of Pine Hills. A few turns later, and the house came into view.

Heidi's home looked much the same as when I'd last seen it. It was clean, white, and well tended. The paved driveway led right up to a two-car garage, which was currently open, revealing a single car inside.

Another vehicle was parked crookedly out front.

Dread worked through me. Heidi lived alone. She didn't need two cars, so I doubted the brown Chevy belonged to her. And it most definitely wasn't her mother's car, since Regina had more expensive tastes.

I parked beside the Chevy and snatched up my phone as I climbed out of my car. A quick peek inside the strange car told me nothing about its owner. If I wanted to know who her visitor was, I'd have to go inside and ask.

Stuffing my phone into my back pocket, I approached the front door. A ceramic frog held a

"Welcome" sign outside it. He looked lonely sitting out there all by himself. He was faded from the sun, and a faint crack ran down the left side of his face where he must have toppled over at some point.

Poor guy, I thought as I pressed the doorbell. Once all of this was over, maybe I'd buy Heidi another frog so he could have a friend.

Focus. I stepped back and forced my mind to behave.

Seconds passed and no one answered. I considered calling Paul to tell him to get to Heidi's house, that something bad might have happened to her, but as I reached for my phone, the door opened, and there she was, alive and well.

Well, maybe not well. But not sick either.

Heidi looked like she'd aged a dozen years since I'd seen her the other day. She wasn't wearing makeup, so the lines that time and hardship had worn into her face were stark and bare. Her mom, Regina, had a lot to do with that, as did Raymond. But a majority of it had to do with what happened to her murdered husband all those years ago. It was no wonder Mason wanted to protect her.

Heidi's eyes were sunken and red, as if she'd been crying. When she saw me standing on her stoop, she gave a little snort of a laugh. I guess my arrival was expected.

"Heidi," I said, glancing past her, but I couldn't see anyone lurking in the background. "Are you all right?"

Her smile was bitter. She blinked rapidly and

looked up, over my head, as if seeking guidance somewhere behind me. Finally, she answered with a simple, "No," and then she turned and walked deeper into her house, leaving the door hanging open. I took it the same way as I had when Raymond had done the same thing; as an invitation.

I entered, closing the door behind me as I did. I followed Heidi the short distance into the living room. She was already seated on the couch, head in her hands, not quite crying again, but close to it.

And standing next to the wall, looking as guilty as all get out, was the cockroach woman.

"You!" I said, pointing at her. Not exactly a grand declaration, but she knew what I meant.

The woman flinched and then looked down at her hands. "I'm sorry." The words came out at a whisper.

The word "for?" was on the tip of my tongue. I glanced at Heidi, who'd sat back and was watching us. So, instead of aiming my questions at a woman who had already lied to me about the bugs, I focused on her, "Why's she here?"

Heidi picked at the arm of her shirt where a thread had worked its way loose. "To warn me."

"Warn you?"

"About Samuel." This from the woman.

I turned to face her. "Who are you?" And because I couldn't help myself, "Why did you plant cockroaches at Death by Coffee?"

The woman took a breath and let it out in a huff. She sagged, a woman defeated. When she looked at me, there was an odd smile on her lips. It wasn't sinister or amused, but was self-deprecating.

"My name is Natalie. You probably know me better as Abby."

I goggled at her. "*You* wrote those articles?" It was a relief to know Caitlin had nothing to do with them, but at the same time, I was angry to finally be standing in front of the person who'd been trashing my name.

"I wrote the first ones." She leaned against the wall, her head thumping lightly against it. "And I suppose a few of the recent ones as well. I used my mother's maiden name, Kohn, and Abigail's name because, well, it was fitting." She sighed. "You've done so much to this town, hurt it so deeply, I felt I had to let the world know what kind of person you really are."

"I didn't do anything!" I all but yelled it. "I've helped *solve* crimes. I've never committed any of them." Well, none that were anywhere close to murder. Maybe a little breaking and entering here or there, and I suppose I'd interfered with a crime scene or two. But I'd always done so in an effort to aid the police, not hinder them.

Natalie closed her eyes and frowned. "I was so angry with you for what you've done to this town. Without you, there'd be so many more people alive today."

"That's not fair, Nat," Heidi said from her seat on the couch.

"Maybe. Maybe not." Natalie shrugged. "At this point, it doesn't matter. What started as my attempt to tell others the truth, got out of hand so quickly, I lost control of it."

"You broke the Banyon Tree window," I guessed.

She was the right height and build. Throw on a wig, and she'd be the spitting image of the woman in the video.

Natalie's nod was jerky. "I figured if I ruined your name, ruined your store, you'd decide to go back from wherever you'd come from. Or maybe people would chase you away. Either way, you'd be gone, and Pine Hills would be saved. I spent so much time researching you, every case you'd ever interfered with, and knew I had all the ammunition I needed to end your meddling."

"I—" I snapped my mouth closed. If I kept trying to defend myself, I'd only make her angry. Some people, you just couldn't reason with. "How do you know Samuel Cox?"

On the couch, Heidi stiffened, but remained silent. Natalie coughed into her hand, shot Heidi a look, before she answered.

"He's my brother."

I took it like a slap to the side of the head. It made sense. Natalie didn't like me, blamed me for every bad thing that happened in Pine Hills since my arrival. She'd written articles about me, and then, when that didn't work, she went out and attempted to sabotage my name.

Samuel, on the other hand, was dating Heidi. He blamed Hamish Lauder for Abigail Abele's death, had never forgotten or forgiven him. He'd been told to stay away from Heidi by her father, Raymond, who was friends with Abigail's parents. He followed Vicki and me, likely on orders, because of his sister.

It was a woman's voice that Mark Cunningham

had heard when he'd talked to Hamish on the day he was murdered. But he'd said someone else had answered her, someone that wasn't Hamish.

"You were both with Hamish," I said, pieces of the puzzle clicking into place at a rapid pace. "Before he died."

Natalie pushed away from the wall and paced toward the kitchen. For a moment, I thought she might make a run for it, or go for a knife. Instead, she came to a stop and turned to face us, hands open and empty before her.

"It's why I'm here," she said. "I wanted to warn Heidi, to tell her she can't trust Samuel. I've tried so hard to rein him in, but after he took over . . ."

Took over? And then I got it. "You said you wrote only *some* of the articles. Samuel wrote the rest?"

She nodded. "He did. He claimed I wasn't going far enough, that I was letting you off too easily. He cares for me." Her tone was pleading, as if she thought I might be able to forgive him for what he'd done if she asked me hard enough. "He wanted to fix things, not just for me, but for Abigail as well."

"He killed Hamish, didn't he?"

Natalie looked to Heidi, who was sitting on the couch, hand covering her mouth as if trying to push back a scream.

"I'm so sorry," Natalie said. "Sam ran into Hamish outside of Death by Coffee before I'd planted the cockroaches, and got to talking to him. We were all friends once, but after Abigail . . ." She wiped away a tear. Unlike Nina's at the theatre, hers were real. "We spent the day together, but I knew Samuel had plans. I told him to let Hamish go, that what happened to Abigail was in the past, but he was determined. We argued about it, and I thought I'd gotten through to him. We agreed that after I got back from the Banyon Tree, we could talk about it some more, that he'd wait to do anything."

"But he didn't."

Natalia's shoulders slumped. "No, he didn't."

"That can't be true." Heidi was shaking her head like she couldn't stop herself. "You told me he'd done something bad, that it might hurt me. But . . ." She looked to me like I might have the answer. "You think he might have killed me?"

"No!" Natalie looked like she wanted to go over to comfort Heidi, but thought better of it. "He wouldn't do that. He cares about you, Heidi. But he's controlling. You've seen it. I know you have."

Heidi didn't say anything, but I could see the knowledge in her eyes.

"What happened, Natalie?" I asked. "How did you go from leaving cockroaches in my store to killing someone?"

"I didn't kill Hamish," she said, firm. "You have to believe me. I might have written letters, posted angry articles, taken a few photographs, and broken a few windows, but I'd never kill anyone."

"But you were there."

Natalie nodded, lower lip trembling. "I was. I called Samuel after the Banyon Tree. He sounded so proud of himself, so happy, that I knew he'd done something horrible. He told me to meet him at Hamish's house, and when I got there . . ." She sank down onto her haunches. "It was too late. He'd already done it, and he told me he was going to blame it on you, that we'd both get our revenge."

"You went along with this?" Heidi asked. "Why didn't you go to the police?"

"He's my *brother*," Natalie said, looking from Heidi to me, once again pleading for understanding. "I couldn't turn in my own brother. He made a mistake. The years since Abigail's death ate at him, turned him into what he is today."

"That's no excuse," I said.

"No, it's not." Natalie removed her glasses, let them hang from her fingertips. "And now, I'm afraid he's going to do it again."

My blood chilled, and I looked behind me, as if I expected Samuel to be sneaking up on me while we talked. "He's going to kill someone else?" I asked.

Natalie took a trembling breath. "I'd like to say no, but honestly, I'm not sure I know him anymore. He thinks he's doing it for me. Even though it's not what I want, he insists that it is."

"Who, Natalie?" I asked, taking a step toward her. I thought of Vicki and Mason, of Rita, of Jeff and Beth and everyone I'd ever known in Pine Hills. Any one of them could be a target, and this time, it *would* be my fault. "Who is he going after?"

"I don't know." When I took another step forward, she raised both her voice and her hands. "Really, I don't! All he said was that he saw you with her, you and your cop boyfriend. He said you were at that restaurant downtown together, and it looked like you were all getting along despite what we'd done." She stared into my eyes, and I saw the fear there, the misery over what her brother had done, what he was going to do. "He's going to kill her," she said. "And he's going to blame it all on you!"

26

Shannon. He was going after Shannon.

The first thing I did on my way out the door was to look up her address. The second was to call Paul, praying that, this time, he would answer.

My head was ringing and the world had a surreal edge to it as I climbed into my Escape and started the engine. Shannon hadn't done anything but know me, and barely at that. Why would Samuel go after her? Because he'd failed at ruining my life the first time? I couldn't believe someone would go as far as murder, just because their sister didn't like me.

"Krissy, I called—"

"Paul!" I cut him off as I swerved around a car parked a little too far into the street. "I know who killed Hamish Lauder."

"What? How did—"

"I'll explain later. He's going after Shannon."

"Wait. Slow down." From his tone, I could tell

he was already on the move. "Tell me what's happening."

A light turned yellow. I gunned the gas and shot through the intersection just before it turned red. Shannon didn't live too terribly far from Heidi, but I had to cut through a section of town rife with excessive traffic lights. If I had known my way through the hilly backroads better, I could have weaved through residential areas without all the lights.

But I didn't. And, even if I did, I'd have needed to be careful of kids playing, and of dangerous turns. Maybe this was indeed the best route, though neither felt quick enough.

"It's Heidi's boyfriend," I said. "His sister doesn't like me, so Samuel, the brother, decided to kill Hamish Lauder, who he blamed for killing his girlfriend. Not Heidi. An older girlfriend. Someone named Abigail Abele. Raymond told me about it. Well, I read about her, and then talked to Raymond, who filled me in."

A stretch of silence followed. I knew I'd rambled, and hoped Paul would be able to piece everything together. He'd known me long enough by now to be able to sort through my panicked recital of the facts.

"Let me call you back."

"Paul—" But he was already gone.

Another light. This one was red. There was no traffic, but I slowed to a near crawl, just in case, as I ran the light. I half expected Buchannan to pop out of nowhere and pull me over, but I made it through without anyone stopping me—or darting in front of me.

I would have felt guilty for breaking the law, but Shannon's life was on the line. I promised myself I'd do something to make up for the traffic violations as I pushed my car past the speed limit. My eyes darted from side to side, checking every side street, every spot where someone might step out into the road, but thankfully, there wasn't much foot traffic, let alone car traffic.

Proof that a divine being was looking out for me? That I was exactly where I was supposed to be?

Maybe. If I got the chance, I'd have to point it out to Natalie. Perhaps then she could write about me in a kinder light.

My phone rang and I answered without looking at the screen. I already knew who it would be.

"She's not answering her phone," Paul said. I could hear a siren coming through the line, telling me he was on the way. Unfortunately, I couldn't hear it elsewhere, which meant he was still too far away, meaning I might be Shannon's only chance to get out of this alive.

"I'm almost to her house," I said.

"Krissy, you shouldn't—"

"This is all my fault." But not in the way Natalie believed. Yes, Shannon was in danger because of me, but it was someone else who was the real culprit here. "These people are mad at me and are taking it out on those around me. I can't just sit around and do *nothing*."

"I'm on the way," Paul said. "So is John. We'll be there in a few minutes."

A street name flashed by. It was the one I was looking for. "I'm there now."

Before Paul could lecture me about not putting

myself in harm's way, or tell me to sit tight and wait for him, I clicked off. My phone immediately started ringing again, but this time, I ignored it. I'd apologize to Paul later. *After* I'd made sure Shannon was okay.

She's pregnant. The thought pounded in my head, screamed at me to hurry. I doubted Samuel would kill her if he knew. He was obviously disturbed, but that didn't mean he was heartless. Killing a grown woman was one thing. Killing an unborn child . . . I didn't think he'd go that far just to hurt me.

At least, I hoped he wouldn't.

"I just have to buy Paul enough time to get here," I muttered as I spotted Shannon's house. It was a rental, and looked the part, complete with siding that could use a cleaning—or, better, a repair—and a roof with a few tiles flapping in the breeze. It wasn't a dump, but it was clear that Shannon was just barely getting by on her Banyon Tree salary. I vaguely wondered how she was going to manage with a child, and then dismissed the thought as I pulled to a stop behind a car sitting in the driveway.

I could worry about how she would pay for a kid on a waitress's salary later. Now, I had to focus on making sure she *could* show up to that waitressing job.

There were only the two cars in the driveway—mine and the well-used Nissan I'd parked behind. Was that Shannon's car? There was no driveway, so I kind of hoped it was. There was no sign that anyone else was there. No cars parked down the street, no doors hanging open.

Please, let me be in time.

I jumped out of my car, leaving my phone behind. I didn't want Paul calling at the worst time and having the sudden sound cause Samuel to react violently. I'd seen enough movies where a popping toaster or ringing phone ended up with someone shot.

I considered calling out, but what if Samuel *was* indeed there? What if he'd shown up to kill Shannon, but she was currently at the Banyon tree, working? He could be hiding inside, lying in wait for her. Work would explain why she hadn't answered her phone.

I crept up to the door. The curtains were thick enough I couldn't make out much through the windows as I passed. The vague outline of a couch. A chair. Something that might have been an antique set of drawers like the one my mom used to own. There was no movement, no hint that anyone was inside.

To knock or not to knock?

I opted for the latter.

I twisted the knob and found the door to be unlocked. I moved it slowly, as not to make a sound, and then gently pushed the door inward. Thankfully, it didn't groan or squeak.

A splash of red caught my eye. It was on the doorframe, and wasn't much more than a single splotch splashed across the wood. It was fresh, and was quite obviously blood.

Oh, no. I was too late.

A bag rested on the floor just inside the door. A

patch on the side claimed it was from the electric company, though I seriously doubted it. It was more likely Samuel's bag, a ruse to get through the door.

And it apparently had worked.

My jaw ached from keeping it clenched. I wanted to call out, to ask Shannon if she was okay, but if Samuel had her, doing so might make him act.

I didn't have a weapon, so I quickly scoured the immediate area, hoping to find something that would work in a pinch. The shape I'd seen through the window was indeed an antique, but nothing but a doily and small glass candle holder sat atop it. A coatrack with a bucket sat to my right. Inside was an umbrella. It wasn't much of a weapon, but at least it was *something*.

I pulled the umbrella free and held it at the ready as I moved farther into the house.

Another splotch of red led me toward the hallway. Something thumped past the kitchen, like the banging of a loose door in the breeze. I started to follow the sound, but saw another, bigger stain on the wall down the hall. It was in the shape of a handprint.

My hands were shaking on the umbrella as I followed the bloodstains. Sweat made the wood slick and I had to adjust my grip to keep it from slipping from my palms. In the distance, sirens could *finally* be heard. The cops were almost there, but, like me, were likely already too late.

I passed a small bathroom. No one was inside. Down the hall, a door was partially closed, and another handprint was smack dab in the middle of it, as if whoever had made it had slapped the door in frustration.

Maybe Shannon wasn't here and Samuel cut himself on something. I could be alone in the house. No bodies, no living souls. My worry might be for nothing.

Or I could be among the dead.

I was about to find out.

Using my foot, I pushed the door open, umbrella cocked back and ready to swing.

A roar, followed by the downswing of a baseball bat followed. My umbrella, and surprisingly quick reflexes, kept it from denting my head. The umbrella snapped under the impact, however, and my palms stung from the vibration caused by the two meeting. I scrambled back with a yelp, my weapon gone, and nowhere to hide.

"Get out!"

That voice. I knew that voice!

"Shannon? Wait! It's me!"

She was reared back, hair untamed and wild, ready to swing the bat again. I noted there was a stain on the bat, telling me I wasn't the first person she'd swung it at recently.

"Krissy?" Her eyes were wild, and I wasn't so sure, despite saying my name, she really recognized me.

"Yes, Krissy." I held up a hand to ward off another blow, but if she were to swing, it would do little to protect me. "Paul is on the way."

"Paul?" Her eyes left mine to look down the hall, like she expected him to be standing there.

She was clearly in shock, but she was also clearly alive. I'd take shock over the alternative any day.

"Hear that?" I asked as the sirens grew loud enough that I knew he was seconds from bursting through the door. "That's Paul." Or Buchannan, but Paul was a name she could latch onto.

"That man . . ." Her hands tightened on her bat. "He was in here. In my house."

"He's gone?" I asked.

Her nod was jerky. "He said he needed to check the meter. I told him it was outside, but he said there was one inside. I didn't believe him and refused to get out of the way, so he forced his way in past me. I had a bat."

"I see that." I cleared my throat. "Could you maybe put it down?"

Shannon looked at the bat, and then dropped it to the floor. It bounced and then rolled over to bump up against the toe of my shoe.

"He came in and chased me. I hit him and he ran. I . . . I think I broke his nose."

Good, I thought, none too kindly. It would make him easier to spot. "You're safe now." A car screeched to a stop outside. Footsteps pounded on the pavement, and moments later, Paul was inside.

"Shannon?" He found us in the hall and immediately went to her. He wrapped her in a hug, which she accepted without hesitation.

"He was here," I said, relieved. I wasn't sure what I would have done if Samuel had returned before the police arrived. I might not have needed to do anything, since Shannon appeared to be quite proficient with a bat. "She chased him off."

"I tried to call the police," Shannon said. "But the line was dead. And my phone . . ." She took a shuddering breath. She wasn't crying, but I had a feeling that it was coming. "He broke my cell-phone. All my pictures were on it."

"We'll get you a new one." Paul released her and touched my arm. "Are you all right?" he asked me, eyes raking over me.

"I'm fine." And then, because it was true. "She needs you."

Outside, more sirens neared. A few moments later, Detective Buchannan entered the house. He took one look around, eyes briefly hesitating on me, before he turned his full attention to Shannon, where it belonged.

I knew Paul would have questions for me, but right then, I wasn't important. I eased toward the door as Shannon began to tell her story about how Samuel had tricked her to get inside, how he'd smashed her phone after she'd smashed his nose. She kept trying to say she'd been weak, but from the sounds of it, she'd been anything but.

She was safe. And knowing Paul was there for her, I knew that nothing would happen to her.

As other cops arrived, Buchannan sent them searching the area, just in case Samuel was still lurking about. I was only in the way, so I decided to make my exit.

Paul saw me as I left. He nodded once, both a thanks and a promise. I smiled at him, and slipped outside. He'd make sure Shannon was safe, and the thought made my feelings for him that much stronger.

I wasn't afraid I'd lose him to Shannon any longer.

But Samuel Cox needed to be afraid.

As his sister had tried to warn him, it appeared he'd finally taken things a step too far, and now, he was going to pay.

27

A loud screech came from next door. It was followed by a riff that seemed inhumanly fast. Caitlin was at her game again, and I wondered if this was going to be my life now. I crossed the room and closed the window, cutting off most of the music, though it could still be heard as a faint throb that vibrated the walls.

"Maybe I can get a set of drums and Caitlin and I can start a band," I said to Misfit, who was sitting in the middle of the living room, tail swishing back and forth. Whether it was the music that annoyed him, or the fact that I had been pacing, I couldn't tell. He was ready for lap-time, but if I sat down now, I'd probably go insane.

It was already dark, and I had yet to hear from Paul, outside a quick, "we're on it" text. It was only a matter of time until they caught up with Samuel Cox. I wondered if Buchannan had taken Natalie in for questioning, or if she was busy packing her bags. She might not have killed Hamish, but I was pretty sure she was in some deep trouble for keeping the murder a secret.

Not to mention breaking the Banyon Tree window, and making my life miserable.

I brought up a browser on my phone and checked *The Eyes of the Hills*. I was met with a page much different than before. Now, instead of articles detailing my evil escapades through Pine Hills, a single message was pinned to the otherwise blank page.

Due to personal issues that have interfered with unbiased reporting, The Eyes of the Hills *has been taken down indefinitely.*

Something told me it wouldn't be coming back ever again.

I closed the page with a sigh of relief. A weight had been lifted from my shoulders now that I didn't have to worry about the site any longer. Natalie *could* have retracted her previous posts with one that explained that I had nothing to do with the murders, that I never killed, or had anyone killed, in all my time in Pine Hills, but this would work too.

But would it be enough for everyone else?

I grabbed my phone and dialed. It was answered on the second ring.

"Hi, Rita," I said, before she could say anything. "I just wanted to let you know that I talked to Detective Buchannan. While I appreciate what you tried to do, I don't think giving money to those affected by the recent attacks was the right move. He took it as a bribe."

There was an unnatural stretch of silence, especially for Rita. I glanced at the screen to make sure the call hadn't been dropped, and that I'd called her cell, and not someone else. As I put the phone back to my ear, I received an answer.

"I will let her know."

My chest tightened at the sound of the man's voice. For an instant, my brain tried to twist it into Samuel Cox's voice, which I assumed was the man who'd called Death by Coffee to breathe at me. But it wasn't him.

I swallowed back my worry, and replied with a quick, "Thanks, Johan," before I clicked off. Why was he answering Rita's cellphone? It seemed like an invasion of privacy to me, though I supposed she could have been indisposed and he'd answered as a courtesy to the both of us.

Still, like everything else about the man, I found it creepy.

The music died away next door. I tensed, waiting for the noise to start up again, but it remained blissfully quiet. Apparently, Caitlin was done for the night.

I paced to the window, thinking I might open it again, but changed my mind. It wasn't exactly *warm* out there, but I liked the fresh air, as did Misfit, who would spend hours chilling in the windowsill whenever given the chance. But after hearing Johan's voice when I'd expected Rita's, I was feeling a smidge jumpy and didn't like the idea of an open window anywhere.

So, instead, I sent Paul a text.

Any updates? Could use some company. I followed it

up with a winky face, and then I tossed my phone onto the island counter. A watched phone never rings, or something like that.

I crossed the room, but found myself gazing back toward my phone, already antsy to check it even though I hadn't heard it buzz. If I picked it up now, I'd send another text, and then another, right up until Paul got ahold of me in annoyance, or flat-out blocked me.

I was anxious to be doing *something*. I hated sitting around, waiting for the police. What if Samuel escaped? What if his sister had lied to me and she was more dangerous than she'd let on? Had I made a mistake in leaving Heidi with her?

Calm down, Krissy. I took deep, calming breaths. *You're safe. Heidi is safe. Everything is going to be all right.*

Misfit's head jerked up, eyes going completely black, ears perking up like antenna. Normally, that meant someone was coming to the door. I peeked outside, but the driveway was empty of everything but my Escape.

And his head hadn't turned toward the door.

He'd looked toward the bedroom.

I went completely still as Misfit rose. His back wasn't arched, and he didn't growl or hiss, but I could tell something had caught his attention, something he didn't like. He used to ignore most sounds, but after a couple of unwanted visitors, he'd grown cautious of most strange noises.

"Did you hear something?" I whispered to him. He shot a kitty glare my way that I translated as *Shut up, I'm listening.*

So, I did the same.

And heard absolutely nothing.

Still, I was unsettled now. I slipped into the kitchen and grabbed a knife from the block. I gave a few experimental jabs with it and, satisfied I could poke an intruder without stabbing myself, I headed for the hall.

In the time it had taken for me to grab the knife, Misfit had vanished. Since the sound that had spooked him had come from the direction of the bedroom, my best guess was he was hiding behind the couch. I hoped he'd stay there, and wouldn't get underfoot, just in case something— or some*one*—was indeed there.

The urge to ask, "Hello?" was so strong, I was making an "h" sound under my breath. I forced myself to stop as I entered the hallway. I still hadn't heard a sound, and knew that it was entirely possible a squirrel had jumped from the roof or a bat had zipped by, catching Misfit's attention.

I checked the bedroom, flipping on the light with my free hand. The windows were closed and no one was lurking beside the bed. I moved on to the spare room, as well as the laundry room and bathroom, and found them all to be likewise empty of predators.

I sagged against the doorframe. "Misfit, you're going to give me a heart attack!" I called to him.

A click sent all the hairs on my body shooting straight up. It was followed by a long creak.

The front door!

I'd left it unlocked when I'd come home, thinking Paul would soon arrive and we could spend the rest of the night relaxing after such an exciting day. It wasn't like I was used to locking it before

bedtime—the neighborhood was normally safe—
though now I was regretting the decision.

I patted my back pocket, looking for my phone,
before I realized I'd left it on the counter in the
kitchen.

There was another click. The door closing?
Locking? I couldn't tell.

I gripped my knife even tighter and then did
the only thing I could do that didn't involve cower-
ing in my bathroom.

I went down the hall to see who was there.

"Hello, Ms. Hancock."

I screamed and very nearly dropped the knife.
Samuel Cox was standing just inside the front
door, which was indeed closed behind him. His
face looked exactly like you'd expect a face to look
like when it was struck by a baseball bat. Both eyes
were swollen and would soon become the world's
biggest pair of black eyes. His nose was crooked
and red and the size of a baseball. He still had
caked blood on his upper lip.

He smiled at me. He was missing his left upper
front tooth. From the bloody stains on his teeth, I
assumed he'd lost it when his face met Heidi's bat.

"You've proven hard to break," Samuel said, the
words coming out slightly slurred. He didn't have
a weapon in hand, but his entire body was coiled,
ready to spring. "It's rather irritating."

"Samuel," I said, eyes flickering toward my
phone. He was much closer to it than I was, but I
did have the knife. "The police know you killed
Hamish. Natalie confessed."

"Did she now?" He sighed. "I always told her she
wasn't strong enough for this sort of work." He

clucked his tongue, which must have hurt since he winced afterward. "She started all of this, and yet she couldn't finish the job. But that's what she has me for."

"You didn't have to kill Hamish," I said.

"Oh, but I did." He took a step forward and then stopped when I brandished the knife. "Knowing you, you've likely done your research. He *killed* Abigail. He might not have done it with his own two hands, but his actions, his mere *presence* caused her death. He got away with it for far too long."

I swallowed. A fervent gleam had come into his eye. "Okay, maybe he deserved it." Perhaps appeasement would work. "But I had nothing to do with Abigail's death. I've only met Hamish the once. There's no reason to come after me, or Shannon, or any of my friends."

"Isn't there?" Another step. I held my ground, clutching the knife like my life depended on it, which, it very well might. "My sister would disagree."

"Your sister took down her website."

Surprise flashed across his face, and then was gone. "As I said, she isn't strong enough. She knows what she wants, knows what's right, but she can never take that final step to victory."

And with that, he lunged.

I'd expected it, yet, at the same time, I hadn't. The sudden movement caused me to yelp and hop back a step, while, at the same time, I struck out with the knife.

I missed. Badly.

Samuel caught my wrist as I tried to pull my arm back. He jerked my arm sideways and twisted, causing my fingers to go briefly numb. The knife fell to the floor with a thump and bounced away. I opened my mouth to scream, but he covered it with his hand.

"Shh," he said. "We don't want to wake the neighbors."

I bit him.

It tasted like dirt and sweat and copper. He cried out and jerked his hand back, though his grip on my wrist held firm.

So, I kicked him in the shin.

He cursed, fingers slipping from my arm as he reached for his injured leg. Since he was between me and the front door, I spun and headed for the bedroom. If I could get inside, if I could get the door closed and locked, I'd be safe. I could slip out the window, run to Jules and Lance for help.

"Get back here!" Samuel shouted, apparently not heeding his own warning about the neighbors. He actually *growled* as he gave chase.

I bounced off the wall, hitting it with my shoulder so hard, it dented the drywall. Something in my shoulder screamed at me that the drywall wasn't the only thing that had been damaged. It wasn't broken, but I'd definitely jammed something. I careened off the wall, staggered forward, and all but fell into my bedroom, completely off-balance like the out-of-shape hater-of-exercise that I was.

I caught myself on the bed with both hands, which caused my shoulder to buckle. I regained my balance and then spun around to slam the door.

But I was already too late.

I took all of Samuel's weight as he leapt at me. My shoulder shrieked once more as he landed atop me, half on, half off the bed. Both of his eyes were watering and were half-slitted like he had a pounding headache that was approaching a migraine. With the state of his face, it was no wonder. Up close, he looked like a bad caricature of a person, with all his features disproportionate to the rest of him.

You know, like big, hard-to-miss targets?

I had one hand free, so I reared back and punched him square in his broken nose.

It made a sound like when you crush a bunch of peanut shells in your fist. Samuel screamed and fell back toward the door. Blood dripped from between his fingers, onto hands that were already stained red from when his nose was broken the first time.

I tried to right myself before he could recover, but he was too quick, too angry. His eyes were gushing tears now, and he said something that was likely a curse, but I couldn't quite tell since it came out sounding so mushy, it was hardly words. He caught both my wrists as I swung at him again, and he used his thigh to block my next kick.

"Thath enouth of thath."

"You bet your ass it is."

A loud *clonk*, followed by a discordant *twang*, echoed in the bedroom. Wood and plastic rained down atop me as Samuel's eyes rolled into the back of his head. He fell over sideways, hitting the floor with a thump that shook the entire house.

Standing in my bedroom doorway, guitar neck

in hand, was Caitlin Blevins. Strings hung from the broken neck, and chunks of the body dangled from that. She watched Samuel to make sure he was going to stay down, and then, with a grin that made her entire face light up, she looked at me and said, "Looks like I'm a hit after all."

And then she held out the broken remains of her guitar and dropped them onto Samuel's unconscious form.

28

"You really have to stop catching killers with your face."

I pouted out my lower lip, which was already sticking out a tad farther than usual. "It wasn't my fault!" My eye was black, and no amount of make-up could hide it. I didn't even remember getting hit in the face, but when Samuel and I were tangled, he must have struck me with an elbow or shoulder.

Paul chuckled as he patted Misfit atop the head. My orange cat accepted his attention for about three seconds before he swished his tail and sauntered toward the bedroom for his evening nap.

Days had passed since Samuel Cox had been arrested, and I was still jumping at every strange sound. I guess that sort of thing happens when you're not just assaulted, but when it seems like the entire world is out to get you. Thankfully, since Samuel's arrest, and since the story of Natalie's deception had gone public, my life had calmed considerably.

Paul gently touched my cheek. It stung—another reminder of my close encounter with a killer—but I leaned into it nonetheless.

"I'm glad you're okay."

"Me too." I smiled at him. "Though you could have shown up a few minutes earlier and saved me a beating."

"Or I just won't ever leave your side again."

That sounded good. Really good. "Then maybe *you* can be the next person who gets to knock someone out on my behalf."

"It *is* becoming a habit."

"It fit the theme." Paul gave me a questioning look, so I explained. "The espresso beans, the teapot. Samuel and Natalie kept using old murder cases against me. Is it any wonder that this one should end like one of them?" Though a guitar being the instrument of my rescue was new.

Paul thought about it a moment, and then laughed. "No, I guess not."

The sound of his mirth shot through me in a way that made me really not want to leave the house for the next few hours. Maybe days. "You know, we could—"

A knock at the door interrupted me, which was probably a good thing. Vicki would never forgive me if I missed the play, no matter the reason.

I tried not to show my trepidation as I crossed the room and answered. A movie played in the back of my mind, one where I would open the door and Samuel would be standing there, a mad grin on his face. He'd leap at me, and I'd learn that Paul was in on the murder and attacks on my character the entire time.

But when I opened the door, it wasn't Samuel Cox, or his sister Natalie, waiting for me.

"Caitlin," I said, just barely suppressing my sigh of relief. "I'm glad you came."

"Hey." She looked embarrassed as she looked past me to Paul. "I should have waited until later, but your message said you wanted to see me?"

"Come in." I stepped aside. Caitlin hesitated and then entered, only to stand awkwardly by the door. Even though she'd saved my skin, she acted like she was afraid I might throw her out at any moment. "Give me one sec."

I patted Paul on the arm as I hurried past him, to the spare room. My heart was pounding in time with phantom music. Fast, loud music. I was afraid I'd made a mistake, that I'd misremembered, but wouldn't know until I went through with it.

I removed the oblong case from the spare room and hefted it into the dining room, where I set it atop the table. I stepped back and waited to see Caitlin's reaction.

She just stood there, eyes slightly too wide. She looked from me, to the case, and then back again. "What is that?"

"It's yours," I said. "A gift for saving me."

She took a step forward, then stopped. "You shouldn't have."

"I should, and I did."

She bit her lower lip, which was quivering ever so slightly. With a tentative hand, she reached out

314

and popped the three clasps keeping the case closed. Then, with a reverence often reserved for prayer, she lifted the lid.

Her entire face bunched up as her hands went to her mouth.

"I know it's not the same—"

"No." She cut me off with a hard shake of her head. "No, it's perfect."

I didn't know much about guitars, but knew the name Les Paul. The Gibson had cost me a pretty penny, but I thought every cent was worth it. I mean, Caitlin *had* saved my life, and in doing so, lost her own instrument. This was the least I could do.

Slowly, she reached into the case and removed the guitar. For the next few minutes, I think both Paul and I were forgotten as she inspected every inch of it. She checked down the neck, and then strummed a few chords, which showed it was slightly out of tune, before she returned it to its case.

"This is too much," she said.

"You deserve it," I said. "I don't know how you knew to come over and save me, but I'm glad you did."

Her face reddened. We hadn't had much of a chance to talk about my rescue since it had happened. The police—both Paul and Buchannan—had arrived minutes after she'd knocked out Samuel, and afterward, my life had been a whirlwind of making things right with everyone else in town.

"It was my cameras," she said, shooting a glance toward Paul, as if she thought having cameras for security purposes was somehow a crime. "One of them went off. When I checked, I saw the guy sneaking around my house, toward your place. It didn't look right, so I came over to make sure you were okay."

"With your guitar?" Paul asked. Not in an accusing way, but more out of curiosity.

"He looked creepy, and I didn't have anything else on hand." She shrugged. "When I got to your house, I heard the noise, and knew something bad was happening, so I came in. I know I shouldn't have walked in without knocking first—"

"We're both glad you did," Paul said, putting an arm around me.

Caitlin looked away, still embarrassed, despite our assurances. "I saw him attacking Krissy, and I didn't think. I didn't expect the guitar to break like that either. It wasn't an expensive one, not like the Gibson there." Her eyes drifted to her new guitar, and she finally gave in and let a couple of tears fall.

We spent the next few minutes laughing and bonding over the guitar, before Caitlin packed up her gift, and went home to give it a try. Paul and I stood outside and waited until the first notes echoed across the neighborhood.

"I'm not sure your neighbors will forgive you," he said, grinning ear to ear as the song picked up speed.

"They'll get over it." I closed my eyes and just listened. Despite the blistering pace, despite the muffled screams, I found the song to be the perfect coda for my day.

Almost. There was one more thing I needed to do before I could call it a night.

Well, maybe more than one.

"Shall we?" I asked, holding out my arm for Paul to take.

He looked at it with an amused glint in his eye before slipping his arm through my own. "Let's."

Vicki's play was tonight and nothing was going to keep me from watching it.

And then afterward?

Perhaps Paul and I would put a fitting end to the night, and make frenetic music of our own.